I0682357

DREW
TYPE 2
COMING OF AGE

RODNEY BLANC

CreatvSeed Branding | Texas

ISBN-10: 0578950189

ISBN-13: 978-0578950181

Cover design by: Rodney Blanc

Printed in the United States of America

DEDICATION

To my family, friends, and students. I dedicate this work to you all.
Thank you, and may you be inspired. Enjoy.

CONTENTS

"Without a struggle, there can be no progress."
- Frederick Douglass

CHAPTER ONE

SCHOOL DAYS

He runs.

As his heart races and breathing deepens with every stride, he continues to sprint into a dark void of nothingness. If not for the faint voices he hears from afar, he would drift away in this infinite space that seems to have no beginning or ending. He's been here before. But this time seems a bit different.

"I hear the voices. It's not like the usual ones I hear... It sounds like... chanting..." he thinks.

But where are they?

He continues to run with persistence and conviction as he listens carefully to the chanting getting louder.

The chants possess the air, filling his ears with words from a language that is unfamiliar to him...

The beating of drums begins to match the rhythm of his pulse. "B-boom..b-boom…b-boom…"

The way they are both in sync is undeniable, and so are the chants as they grow louder and louder. Despite the expanse of darkness, he knows he is headed in the right direction.

Unexpectedly, the chanting ceases. It's as if these invisible strangers are suddenly aware of their visitor's arrival. Drew stops running and bends over, reclaiming his breath.

"Why are you here?" A loud hollowed voice demands as it echoes throughout the vacuum. The rasping undertone of the voice seems eerily similar to that of an elderly lady.

"I-I don't know why I'm here." he responds. "I think I'm lost. Wh… Who are you?"

"Lost, you say? Hahahaha…more like, a wild seed with no soil, hahahaha," the mysterious woman responds as her laughter fades into the void.

There he stands, puzzled about what has just happened and unsure of what to do next.

Then, familiar voices begin speaking. These he knows. He's heard them many times before. They begin speaking almost in concert with each other.

"You can't separate peace from freedom because no one can be at peace unless he has his…"

Another voice chimes in, as the former voices continue speaking … "Any real change implies the breakup of the world as one has always…"

Then another voice comes… "Nothing is easy to the unwilling…"

And finally… "Drew…Drew…my love…"

These voices are all recurrences to him, but they always seem to be coming from a great distance: voices of civil rights leaders from the past. He admires them all. But why are they constantly in his dreams? More importantly—

"…that last voice…" He wonders.

Suddenly, a very familiar voice cuts through the din like a hot knife through butter.

"Drew! Hurry up, son. You're gonna miss your ride to school. Or are you planning to do some exercise and walk all the way?"

Drew blinked and woke fully, his dad's voice rousing him from sleep. Rays of sunlight streamed through the windows and he realized it was already late in the morning. He cursed softly. He knew his phone's battery must have run down again, or else he would have been awakened by its pre-set alarm.

"Walk? Nah, pops. I can't miss my ride anyway. You are my ride," Drew replied.

"You think I enjoy being your personal chauffeur?" His dad snorted. "Keep this up and you'll have to start taking the school bus like everyone else."

It was another day of school for Drew Tatum. A normal Tuesday, which meant he had no real motivation to *"make the day count and not have the days count for you,"* as his father liked to say. Since he was much younger, his father had been reciting that mantra. However, it was not nearly as frequent as it had been since they moved to New Easton Hill, a city known for its downtown historic art and jazz district, diverse communities, and affluent schools—things Blake desired for his son.

Drew didn't really feel like complying with the saying today. He was preoccupied and if anyone could see his face at that moment, they would have described the look on his warm sepia-touched face as distant and thoughtful. Actually, he was thinking about the strange dreams he had been having for a while. The dreams always left him feeling confused. In many of them, he kept seeing the faces of historic people, long dead. At first, he had thought it was because of all the time he spent watching TV, but how did that explain the weird dreams? How did it explain the voices he heard in his sleep? Especially that feminine voice, the one that always called him by his name. Drew did not know the answers to these questions yet, but he was sure he would find them.

"Come on, Drew! I've got things to do," his father called, jolting him out of his thoughts.

"Coming!" He yelled back, bending to tie his shoelaces. He was fairly tall for his age and with a moderate wiry build like a track athlete.

"Also, don't forget to take—"

"My prescriptions, yeah," Drew mocked. He could hear the front door shutting as his father left the house to go start the car.

Drew took one of the pills in one hand while the other held a glass of water. As he did every morning, he wondered what the hell the pills were made of while attempting to retwist one of his locks with his finger.

Darned things are so big, I can barely swallow them. They taste horrible too, he thought as he downed the pills with the glass of water and picked up his school bag.

Outside, the car was idling, and his dad sat at the steering wheel. He seemed to be lost in thought, staring off into space. Drew noticed that the car radio was tuned to a station that was blaring more white noise than actual music.

Drew was not too surprised. His father was always doing this, zoning out at random moments.

"Err...Dad? You ready?" He asked.

"Oh, hey. Yeah, let's head out." His father nodded, blinking rapidly. "Do you need the car charger?"

"You know I do, pops," Drew retorted, getting in the passenger seat and rubbing his eyes. His night had been far from peaceful due to his disturbing dreams, and he was hoping he could catch some shuteye on the ride to school.

"I might have to start charging you to charge, you get it?" His dad smirked, winking.

"Please, don't start with the dad jokes," Drew groaned.

As his father eased out of his parking spot and onto the street, Drew lowered his seat back and covered his head with his hoodie. Drew's father headed through a backroad to save time. Both of them kept to themselves for the quiet ride. Like father, like son. Drew simply closed his eyes to his thoughts. Car ride conversations with his father were very infrequent, with the occasional one-line reminders and wisecracks. To mask the lull, Drew's father relied on his favorite radio stations as Drew would pretend to sleep.

"Hope you didn't forget your—"

"My prescriptions, yeah. Already used 'em. Oh, and I've actually been meaning to tell you this, but I think there's something wrong with them."

His dad almost hit a car that had been driving beside them in his sudden panic, but he got the steering wheel under control again and turned to his son.

"What's wrong with the pills, son?" He asked nervously.

"Whoa, calm down, pops. I was just saying they're too big and bitter. Maybe they should make a sweet syrupy form or something," Drew replied.

His father heaved a sigh of relief. "Don't you think you're too old for that?" He asked.

"Pops, I think everyone would want medication that tastes good. These are just awful!" Drew responded.

"Point taken." His father chuckled. "I will see what I can do about that, but you have to give me time. Just don't stop taking it! I mean it!"

"Yea, yea, I hear you Pops."

As Drew's father decided to search for his usual jazz station on the radio, Drew believed it was time to let his dad know about his dreams, though he hesitated because of how ridiculous it seemed.

Well, here goes nothing, he thought.

"Hey…Pops, I've been meaning to ask you something. It's about my—."

"There it is! Yes, right on time! Some good ole *Trane!*" Blake interrupted, while snapping his fingers to the unmatched saxophone riffs of the late, great John Coltrane. "I remember playing this for you as a child with your—" Drew's father abruptly fell silent. His face saddened and his eyes glazed, realizing where the conversation would lead if he continued. He still hadn't healed from *it* yet. It was then that he realized his son was actually trying to tell him something.

"I'm sorry Drew, you were saying?"

Drew didn't answer. Drew knew his father was about to mention *that* situation again. He could see the school's gates already.

Worth a try, he supposed.

The car stopped and Drew jumped out, closing the door behind him.

"Hey, Drew! I might not be around when you get back. Got some installations to do, you know," his father announced. Drew's father owned a solar engineering business, but he also worked part-time on his own personal projects.

"No probs, I'll just shoot some hoops at the court before coming home."

"Alright, son. Have a great day. And don't forget, make the day count—

"…and not have the days count for you. Yeah, right. Bye Pops."

Drew watched his dad drive away. He couldn't help but notice that his father's eyes had become distant again.

One day soon, we'll have a good talk about that, he thought as he turned towards the school.

"Yo! What's up, man? We're gonna be late. Bell's about to ring."

Drew turned towards the familiar voice. It was Levi Makosso, one of Drew's closest friends. They met a couple of years back playing a few pick-up ball games in the park. He was always the funny guy with a large personality and a talent for mechanical engineering in school. He was also one of the biggest trash-talkers on the court that Drew knew. This was why Drew's fitting nickname for him was—

"Motor! How's it going?"

"I'm good, man. So why are you late this time? Let me guess, you forgot to charge your phone again." Levi snickered as they entered the school.

"Actually, there was a bit of traffic," Drew countered.

Levi snorted in disbelief.

"Traffic. Pfftt. Save the weak excuse bro. Your pops know all the shortcuts. He's always using back roads."

Drew grinned. Levi knew him too well.

They entered the school, Douglass College Preparatory, just as they did every other day. Douglass was relatively new and was not at all cliché, which meant there were no popular snobbish girls or petty drama and romances. Everyone at Douglass was college-bound and it was reflected in the seriousness of their subjects and the studious atmosphere. They did subjects like Introduction to Engineering, Biochemistry, Applied Mathematics and so on. A third of the students at Douglass were international students like Levi, who was originally from Congo, or their friend Sumi Aoki, who once lived in San Francisco but was actually from Japan. Sumi wasn't fully Japanese. Her father was a Jamaican American Naval Lieutenant, but she lived with her mother ever since her parent's separation.

Drew knew he was fortunate to be here. Douglass accepted only the brightest, and his previous grades made the transfer easier.

This didn't mean that all of the students were friendly, however, as the subtle presence of prejudice lingered in the halls everywhere he stepped since he first arrived. But his friends were different. Levi was also very smart, though he knew people tended not to have that impression at first, maybe because he was over six feet tall with a husky build like a football player or a pro wrestler. He always liked to act all goofy and unserious, with his larger-than-life smile flattering his rich and dark tawny exterior. Levi always had a thing for carrying his handy brush for his "waves", showing them off whenever he could. But he was one of the smartest people Drew knew, alongside his other friend, Sumi.

"Hey, what's up twitches!" Sumi greeted them. She always found an unusual way to insult them, especially Levi. This time, she'd decided to combine the word "two" with another word. Both Levi and Drew shook their heads playfully in disapproval.

Sumi was a genius. If anyone told the guys that she was the smartest of the trio, they wouldn't argue. She met Levi back in middle school, years ago. She didn't open up much at the time since she'd lost a close childhood friend some time back. But Levi's personality cracked her social shell open in no time. A couple of years back she met Drew through Levi. They immediately clicked. Sumi wasn't just book-smart either. The boys knew it. By day, she was an A-plus student, breezing through the most complex subjects in class but by night, in the privacy of her room, she assumed the role of an amateur hacker named *REBL*. She made nightly excursions into the deep web, and often used the boys as pilot testers for the dozens of random, and often disruptive, phone apps she created, like the infamous one called "Spark." This notorious app allowed users to enable notifications to ring every time a secret admirer was nearby. Needless to say, this had caused so much unnecessary drama, that the school banned its use. Sumi sorta had dark humor when it came to trends and popularity, always looking to create a bit of social disorder with her tech. She was also quite opinionated and never skipped blogging about new tech companies and growing corruption of personal data use, or the wealth gap in the country.

"Hey, Sums," Levi greeted.

Drew just nodded, his mind already far away, thinking about the ride to school, which seemed to piss Sumi off, but he didn't notice.

"Actually, if you're done being distant, I was wondering if you've decided on where we would do our science project," she snapped, finally getting Drew to blink and focus on her.

"Oh, hey my bad, Sumi!" Drew apologized. "I was just lost in thought. So, can we use your place?"

"I don't know," Sumi doubted. "You know how my mom is. She wants to control everything. She might not allow..." She trailed off but the boys nodded to show that they understood.

The bell rang for the first period and the trio headed to class together, Levi and Sumi began discussing their afterschool plans, while Drew walked silently beside them, hands in his hoodie pockets.

"To calculate the electromotive force, we have to..."

Drew stopped listening to the teacher. He had not really been listening since the class started. Sometimes, he wondered why he even bothered with school, really. He picked things up faster than other kids and was a natural genius with anything that had to do with calculations and science. He didn't even make an effort to try to understand what the teacher was saying. He was staring off into space, still thinking about his weird dreams.

What the hell? Do other people have strange dreams like this?

He knew the answer to these thoughts, of course. The answer

was no. Other boys his age dreamed about girls, cars, and other normal stuff.

Normal kids don't dream about MLK or Malcolm X. Nah. There's something wrong somewhere. It's like I ate some kinda magic mushroom.

He sighed and reached into a pocket, bringing out a wireless earbud which he discreetly plugged into his ear. Gentle music wafted from the earbud, and he felt laziness creep up on him. He was as distant as he could get from the class, his mind disconnected from his body.

He was aware that somehow, he must be daydreaming. It felt good. He felt a need to do something with his hands because the other students were writing stuff down. So he dragged his notebook closer and started moving his pen over its surface.

At first, he had no idea what he was drawing but he soon realized what it was. A face. An angry face. He kept drawing until he had fully defined the face. It was not the face of someone he knew in real life. It was *Kazuka*, a character from one of his favorite mangas. He was shading the Jitsu warrior's purple eyes when he felt someone tap him.

Drew blinked and looked to his right. Sumi was leaning towards him with a frown on her face. She was whispering something. He removed the earbud so he could hear her better.

"...the hell are you doing, Drew?"

"Look, I-"

"You need to focus, okay? Pay attention! We need most of what's being taught right now for our project to be a success. You realize that, right?"

"Sumi, look, I don't..." Drew tried to describe how he felt lately and explain why he seemed distracted or distant, but words failed him.

Sumi looked at him intently for a couple of minutes, her expression softening. Her perceptiveness kicked into place then. She looked at him, recalling how much more distant he had been lately, even in the company of his closest friends.

She reached across the space between their seats and placed a hand on his arm.

"Is it because of your dreams?" Sumi asked in a gentler tone than the one she had used earlier.

Drew didn't speak. He just nodded 'yes'. Sumi was one of the only people he had told anything about his strange dreams. He figured that if he told people, they would think he was crazy or something. But as demanding as she could be sometimes, Sumi was the most compassionate person he knew. She wasn't like other people.

"Are you still having them every night?" She asked. Drew nodded again.

"Ok, so what do you feel it means? Like, what does your gut feeling tell you about these dreams?"

Drew thought about her question. The teacher droned on about electromagnetic induction. Both of them ignored her.

"Well, maybe I daydream too much. Or maybe I ate something weird, you know, like those strange mushrooms? What are they called, halogens?"

"Hallucinogens," Sumi corrected, but her expression was skeptical. Drew made some more assumptions.

"Okay, I don't think I ate anything strange. Oh, I know. Damn. It must be the late-night documentaries." Sumi frowned, obviously uninterested.

"Yeah, it has to be. My dad and I, we watch these old documentaries every other night, you know? On the history channels. Footage of old parades and riots and stuff like that. They even do replays of interviews with the activists and revolution leaders. We've been doing that for as long as I can remember. That has to be causing the dreams, right?"

But before Sumi could reply, Levi leaned forward from his seat behind Drew and whispered, "Whatchu guys talking about?"

"The... err, the project," Sumi stammered, giving Drew a pointed look.

"Yeah. Yeah, that's right," Drew added, changing the topic as well.

"So, have you gotten any ideas for your project? Who's your partner by the way?" Sumi asked Levi.

"Oh, lots of ideas. You know that car engine I built?"

"The one that won you all those state competitions?" Drew asked.

"Yeah, that one. We're thinking of making an upgrade to the design. But Max is good, he can handle it," Levi assured.

"Max is your partner? Good luck getting anything done," Sumi sassed.

Levi just shrugged and straightened. The other two followed suit.

"Err, Miss Sanders?" Levi asked.

Drew glanced back to see his friend with his hand raised as if he had a question to ask the teacher. But he also saw that look in Levi's eye that meant he was about to do or say something mischievous.

"Yes, Levi?" Ms. Sanders paused, after rattling off the values of constants.

"May I ask a question?" Levi interrupted.

"Of course."

"Err, the question is not related to your class, ma'am. I can still ask it, right?" Levi smirked.

Ms. Sanders thought for a beat, confused. A couple of the students chuckled.

"What is your question?" Ms. Sanders sneered, recognizing her class clown was up to something.

"I'm really feeling a sudden surge of uhh...*electromotive force* near my rectum and I'm fearful of what will happen to the uhh... *stasis* of the class if I have a spontaneous discharge."

"You're serious right now Levi?" Miss Sanders questioned.

"Affirmative. Oh no, I feel it coming now!"

"Levi hurry up and step out of class." Ms. Sanders responded, clearly annoyed.

There was a burst of laughter. Drew joined in, holding his ribs because he was laughing so hard. Even Sumi chuckled and shook her head.

Classic Motor, Drew thought.

He watched his friend stumble out of the class, almost colliding with the wall on his way out. The other students clapped and cheered him on. Levi's head was bent to hide his wide grin and Drew couldn't even repress the large smile forming on his face.

Levi had just single handedly eased the boredom in the class and even though he didn't know it, he had also eased the tension in Drew's mind. As the day dragged on, he replayed the incident in his mind and chuckled every time he did, thinking about Levi's question and the way Ms. Sanders had been confused.

It was enough, for the moment, to keep his worries at the back of his mind.

Drew's father, Blake, was in the backyard shed, where his actual project was ongoing. It wasn't really going well. He resisted the urge to kick the complicated piece of machinery in front of him. There were just a couple of things left to do and once he did, he would have to find an investor to help fund his remaining work. He sighed and glanced at his wristwatch while rubbing his coarse beard. He needed some rest.

He had been working on the project for months. Ever since he moved with his son out of state, he had needed something to occupy his time. It started with an idea he'd originally had when he first arrived, and he had warmed up to it quickly. Soon, after he started laying out the blueprint, he knew exactly what he was building. It was a satellite communication module. But not just any type of module. Unlike most of the devices like this one already in existence, Blake's invention did not use solar energy or batteries, or electrical energy. In fact, it didn't use any source of energy that the average person could readily understand. The alternative source Blake had been able to find was similar to antimatter, considered by most people to be pure fiction.

Maybe that was why all the communication companies he had tried had turned him down. He had been trying to pitch his module for a while and the constant rejections were beginning to discourage him. Then he'd heard about this fast-rising communication company and thought about giving it a shot. He figured that the big companies were too calculating, not wanting to take a risk that might backfire, mainly because they didn't understand the module's source of energy. But a rising company would surely be willing to invest in something like this. For them, there was more to gain than lose.

Blake rubbed his eyes and dropped the screwdriver he had been holding. He was making some small adjustments on the module before taking it out for his presentation, but he was too tired to do anything else. He wanted to do nothing more than crawl into bed and sleep, but he couldn't afford to do that.

He got to his feet, walked out, and locked up before walking to his car. He opened the door and slid into the driver's seat. Then he started the car and put on the radio. As always, there was nothing but white noise. He glanced down to make sure he was tuned to the right frequency. Then he listened.

Five minutes. Ten. Fifteen minutes. Twenty.

Nothing but white noise.

He closed his eyes and an image of his wife appeared. Of course, she wasn't really there. He was just imagining her exactly as she used to be: beautiful, strong-willed, compassionate, and clever. He was reminded how her thick coil-ly hair would gently rest on her shoulders, complimenting her rich umber skin and radiant smile. Him and Drew were her whole world, and she'd do anything to protect her family. She was also one of the few people he could think of who was actually smarter than he was. He remembered how she used to beat him at chess while their favorite jazz records played on vinyl.

Out of nowhere, he relived *that incident.* The accident that had changed everything. He could see everything in his mind's eye. The way he and his family had screamed came back to him and he shivered.

Blake thought about his wife, who never made it out of the accident, and of his son, who had gotten Traumatic Brain Injury in the crash. Drew had lost most of his memory after the incident. Most of the important parts of his memory were gone and at the time, Blake had been filled with despair. It was not until time passed that he realized that the incident was an opportunity for Drew to grow up as a normal kid. Blake couldn't afford to lose his son like he had lost his wife and he knew his wife would want him to protect Drew no matter what.

Whenever he was depressed, he only had to think about his wife, and he would be alright. He recalled her last words to him before she left him. There had been a firmness in her voice. Tears sparkled in her eyes, but she didn't cry.

"Don't lose yourself, darling. Protect our son. I... I will always love you guys." She assured, holding his hands tight.

Even at the end, she was strong and focused. These recollections brought tears to his eyes, but he blinked them away furiously.

She wouldn't want to see you cry, Blake. Snap out of it. Remember her last words.

The radio still didn't produce any distinctive sound.

It has never worked before. What the hell was I expecting?

He sighed and got ready to drive away. Then he caught it. Barely above a whisper. A voice, speaking underneath all the distracting white noise. He bent and listened harder, trying to hear what it was saying, and then he heard the word clearly. A greeting.

"*...hello...*"

CHAPTER TWO

A BEAUTIFUL MIND

"Nothing is easy to the unwilling..."
"Drew...Drew...my love..."
"Strange fruit, hanging..."
"Drew! Come to me—"

The voices that usually came, were now accompanied by images. Drew could see the people who were talking. He knew some of them too. They were historical figures, politicians, artists, and even musicians. Many of them were dead and had lived long before Drew's time. This was what confused him. His dreams were feeling too real to be dreams. They seemed more like memories to Drew. But he knew they had to be dreams. There was no other logical explanation. He couldn't possibly have occupied the same space as those people. They had existed decades before him. When he woke up from sleep, he didn't get up immediately. He just laid there and thought for a while. He thought about what he had told Sumi was probably the reason for the strange dreams. All those darned documentaries he would watch with his father late at night.

But what about the one voice that calls my name?... The only voice in my dreams that has no face attached to it? He thought.

He knew that part was certainly not influenced by the documentaries. He still didn't understand it, not fully. But there was something about that voice that made him feel a flurry of emotions whenever he heard it. He didn't know what the voice was, but he was sure he would find out.

Drew sat at the edge of his bed, fully dressed and ready for school. He had gone through his usual routine: wake, brush, bathe, dress and now he was about to go downstairs to join his dad. He had woken up to the sound of his phone's alarm, so he was pretty sure he wasn't late. There was just one thing left for him to do before leaving the house.

Prescriptions.

Drew looked at the big pill in his palm and tried to come to a decision. He didn't really know what the prescriptions were for, to be honest. The pills had no markings he could see, and the drug manufacturer's name was nowhere to be found.

Man, I don't even know what these pills do, Drew thought to himself. His dad had never been direct with his answers whenever Drew asked him about the purpose of the pills.

Ain't ever seen them on the internet or at the pharmacy either.

He had searched the internet and even Googled the pills even though there was no name on its case. He'd found nothing at all.

I mean, why the hell should I use this shit? I don't know what it is or what it does, but I'm always told to use it every day. Really? Nah, it doesn't make sense to me, man.

Maybe these things are expired or something, he thought. Or maybe they weren't. But Drew had made his decision. Instead of getting water from the kitchen to take his drugs, he went to the bathroom instead and tossed the big pill into the toilet. He flushed and watched the brown pill swirl a little before getting sucked under.

My pops is gonna be so mad if he finds out. But I guess what he doesn't know can't hurt him. I'm done taking these weird pills.

He turned and walked out, taking his phone out of his pocket. He sent a short text to his dad.

I'm taking the bus today, pops.

He hit the *Send* button and adjusted the school bag strapped to his back, walking to the bus stop, his mind already on the day's school activities.

As it turned out, he didn't get to enjoy those activities very much.

After meeting up with Levi and Sumi, they all headed to the first class of the day. It was a calculus class, and the teacher was droning about differentials and whatnot. Then, suddenly, Drew felt a dull pain in his head. His first thought was: *a headache in the middle of the day?*

But this was no ordinary headache. In fact, it didn't last long. The pain faded quickly, leaving Drew wondering if he had imagined the whole thing. He blinked and focused on the whiteboard, or tried to.

The board and the teacher, Mr. Walker, seemed to move in and out of focus. Actually, everything in the classroom looked blurry one second then crystal clear the next. Drew had no idea what was happening to him. He rubbed his eyes, wondering if this whole thing was because he never got enough sleep.

Just when he was about to raise his hand so he could be excused from the class and maybe go to the school clinic, the bell rang twice to signify the end of the period. Students scrambled all around him, picking up bags and getting up but Drew was first out of the door.

His eyes kept acting up as he walked aimlessly, torn between going to the clinic and trying to figure this out on his own. Eventually, he decided to try to work it out by himself. Drew hated being a burden to anyone. He already felt that way at home.

"Hey, man!"

It was Levi, walking quickly to catch up with him. Drew slowed down as his friend got closer and they shook hands.

"Yo, err... sorry I didn't wait for you after Calculus. I've got some eye trouble," Drew mentioned.

Levi's face was immediately filled with concern.

"What do you mean? You wanna go home or to the clinic?" He asked.

Drew didn't reply. He grabbed his head suddenly. The headache was back and this time it was accompanied by more strange things. He blinked and looked down the hall. He could see the red fire safety tips posted on the far wall from where he stood. But not only could he see it. He could read the words, even though that shouldn't have been possible, even for someone with glasses.

"Oh, man," Drew worried. In his mind, he was really freaking out, but he smiled to reassure Levi and tried to assure him that he was fine. Levi inspected his face for a while and shrugged, satisfied.

It was different with Sumi. Drew was having his lunch at the school cafeteria when she plopped her tray down on the table. Actually, he had heard her come through the doors, even though there were people all around murmuring. That was another weird thing he'd noticed since math class. His sense of hearing seemed somewhat enhanced, along with his sense of smell.

It was really disconcerting. He sat with his food in front of him, the sandwiches blurring out of focus every time he blinked. Somewhere in the huge cafeteria, two people were arguing if it was right to cheat in their upcoming Introduction to Engineering pop quiz. He heard a group of girls fawning over Chet, one of the guys on the basketball team. He heard scraps of other conversations, some of them passing through his ears too quickly for him to make any sense of them.

"Hey."

Drew's eyes had been shut but when he heard her voice, he glanced up at Sumi and immediately wished he hadn't. At once, he saw the pores on her light brown skin, the finest strands of her dark hair, and the smallest thread at the hem of her shirt. It was as if his eyes somehow had magnifying glasses planted into them. Then, without warning his vision became blurred again. He sighed and dropped his head.

"What's up, Sumi?" He slurred.

"I'm fine. But you don't look so well. What's up?"

He waved her question away as if she'd asked something ridiculous.

"I'm fine," he responded but still, he didn't look up. Voices buzzed into his ear from all around him. He had become some kind of magnet and all the conversations in the cafeteria were iron filings.

"No. You're definitely not fine," Sumi alleged. Drew wasn't looking at her. He wasn't looking at anything as his eyes were closed tight but he could hear the frown in his friend's voice. She hated when he acted so distant, and he knew it.

But what could he say?

Like father, like son, Drew thought bitterly. He avoided Sumi's probing questions and for the rest of the day, he forced himself to ignore his heightened senses, which was very difficult. He heard a lot of things he would rather not have heard. He also had problems matching the images his eyes sent to his brain with what he knew to be true: stairs for instance, posed a big problem. Because of his improved eyesight, he could see miles ahead and this led to him tripping on his own feet as he couldn't see what was right in front of him.

When he got home, he met his dad at the door. He was obviously going somewhere in a hurry.

"Hey, Pops. Where are you headed?"

"Oh, hey. Welcome back, son. I'm headed out, and it might take a while before I return."

"Oh, okay."

"Yeah, I need to meet some investors, you know. It's just a few miles away."

Drew shrugged and dropped his bag. His strange, heightened senses seemed to have receded somewhat. For a split second, he thought about telling his dad what had happened in school, but a part of his mind warned him not to. He was sure his dad was going to flip and give him a verbal lashing. If there was one thing his dad was strict about, it was the prescriptions. He decided not to say anything, yet.

So, he remained quiet as he watched his dad drive away towards his meeting, his eyes still blurring slightly every time he blinked.

Drew turned and went back inside, heading to the bathroom as fast as he could. He pushed himself through the door and stumbled over to the toilet bowl. He bent over it and puked.

He rinsed his mouth with water from the sink and leaned his head against the wall for a moment.

OK, what the heck just happened, man?

He wasn't so sure of the answers to the silent question he had just asked himself. He was guessing it was another side effect of skipping his strange medication.

Or maybe it's because I'm so nervous about keeping stuff from Dad.

Drew had been alone with his dad for a while. Even though their communication wasn't perfect, they did everything together, and he had never lied to his father. Until now.

He sighed and returned to the sink to wash his face. He cupped his hands under the tap and brought the water to his face, looking up into the small mirror above the sink as he did so.

He froze. A stranger stared back at him from the mirror.

The stranger was in his clothes and looked like him but—

Man, that is definitely not me. I mean, look at me. I look like I'm eighty years old.

It was true. Drew's reflection showed him just how much the recent events had taken their toll on him. But he immediately noticed something else as well. The longer he looked, the more he could see. He saw past the tiredness and looked at the layout of his face itself. There were dark micro- spots scattered all over his face, most of them scars from faded acne. He could see the pores in his skin, the tiny hair follicles above the few wisps of hair that were the beginning of a mustache, the vertical crevices on his pursed full lips.

He moved closer to the mirror and saw his own eyes. His pupils were constricting and dilating rapidly, affecting how he perceived the lighting around him. One second, all was dark. The next, light. It kept alternating in this manner.

What's happening to me? Drew thought. He looked at his unfamiliar reflection in the mirror.

"Who are you?" He demanded his reflection. "You think you are some kind of superhero? You Miles Morales?"

He chuckled at his silly comment. He wouldn't be surprised if he could shoot webs. He guessed there was no harm in trying and feeling a little foolish, he put out his hands to see if they would produce webs.

Of course, nothing happened.

Talking to a mirror, thinking I'm Spider-Man. Damn it. I'm losing my mind.

Drew splashed water on his face, trying to ignore the mirror as much as he could, and walked out of the bathroom.

After the long day he'd had, Drew slept fitfully that night.

This time, he didn't just have dreams about voices or see unclear pictures. This time, he could see very clear events. Speeches, protests, even wars on an old turn-dial TV. He felt like he had been in those places in person. But that was impossible, he thought.

Then his dreams changed. *"Drew...Drew..."*

He heard the female voice again, the one that was familiar.

Then out of the mist, a hand was held out to him.

Come to me, Drew...

On the woman's forefinger, there was a ring. It was a gold band with indistinguishable markings. Drew felt a pull in his heart. He knew that ring. He was sure of it. Just as he was about to grasp the offered hand, he woke up.

There were tears in his eyes, but he didn't care. He finally knew who the woman was. It was someone who had long passed; someone he had wanted to meet for as long as he could remember.

It was his mother.

CHAPTER
THREE

FAMILY TIES

Blake drove as fast as he could without breaking the speed limit. He occasionally consulted the GPS to confirm he was headed in the right direction. His destination, a small ranch, was only a few miles away.

He had set up the meeting as quickly as he could, taking care not to attract undue attention to himself and keeping his moves from everyone, including his son. The boy was smart and capable, but Blake had his reasons. He wanted Drew to live a normal life for a little bit longer.

He made a turn and glanced at his rearview mirror. Perhaps it was just a coincidence but at that exact moment, he saw three motorcycles driven by men in black. They were hot on his tail. Filled with alarm, Blake wondered why he had only just spotted them.

He cursed and thought about what to do. Just to make sure the mysterious men were actually following him; he made a couple of tight and aimless turns. They followed, confirming his suspicions.

Of course, he couldn't see their faces because of the helmets they were wearing but it didn't really matter. What mattered was that he was being followed even though no one was supposed to know who he really was or what he'd been working on. That was what really bothered him.

The men in black were still following him so he knew he had to think fast. The solution came to him suddenly and he let a rare grin appear on his face. He turned into someone's back road, immediately slowing down because of the uneven surface. He was sacrificing his speed for concealment but that was OK. He knew these back roads better than anyone. Drew was always complaining about the bumpy ride on the way to school, but Blake ignored him. He was sure his mysterious pursuers wouldn't be able to catch up with him.

He drove for a couple of minutes before cutting back onto the road and heading straight for a parking lot with several vacant spaces. He parked and got out of the car, looking around as he did. He didn't spot the men in black or anyone suspicious, so he waited for the man he had come to see.

His first contact with the man had been on the radio. They had been unable to hold full conversations though, because of the perpetual and annoying white noise. But the man's voice had given him the directions so they could meet face-to-face and discuss the project.

"Good afternoon. You must be Blake." The man was of average height and build, with dark hair, brown eyes and a very forgettable face.

"Yes, I am," Blake confirmed, taking the guy's outstretched hand for a shake.

"So how are things going with the module? My boss, well, he seems familiar with your work, you know. He believes you can deliver," the man relayed.

Blake sighed and shrugged at the same time.

"It's going very well," He assured. "But there's still lots of work to be done."

"As long as you keep your end of the bargain and give him a majority stake in your business, he is prepared to make an... anonymous investment."

"Yes, the deal remains," Blake replied.

"Alright," the man conceded, glancing around nervously. "But please be careful. I think all of us are being followed. My boss has very powerful...competitors...which is why he remains anonymous."

As if on cue, both men heard a high-pitched whine and turned to see the men on their bikes approaching fast.

"Damn." The man shuddered. "You were followed?"

Blake just nodded. "I thought I lost them," he muttered.

"Well, apparently, you didn't." The man grumbled. "You have to leave."

Blake nodded. He didn't want to endanger the man. He ducked back into his car and started the engine. He looked in his rearview mirror. The bikes were almost upon him. The man he had come to meet had made his escape.

Blake took a deep breath and drove out of the parking lot.

The men in black followed.

Day three or four of not using his pills; Drew wasn't keeping count, but he was really seeing changes. After that first day and all the disorientation that came with it, he had adjusted rather well to his new abilities. He could control his senses now and could switch off the whole hyper-receptive thing when he liked. He also could see things from far distances and tune his ears to hear whispers from far away.

Of course, the emergence of these new abilities affected his performance on the basketball court. On his best day, Drew was an ok shooter and a solid passer. He scored at least 10pts per game, all mid jumpers. While he was better on the outside, Levi dominated in the paint.

But now, with his increased reflexes, strength and improved senses, he was scoring 25 points every game. He hadn't really been too popular among the other guys at the court but slowly he was gaining their attention and respect. He was becoming the talk of the entire park.

Now, whenever he and Levi got to the court, there were already several teams eager to play against them. All of them lost, of course. Nobody could match Drew's brilliance. Every day, people increased in number around the chain-link fence, waiting to see if Drew would do something as extraordinary as they had heard. He was single handedly making the court more popular than any of the other players.

Somehow, news of his newfound prowess quickly reached the ears of Coach Redding, the head coach of the high school's basketball team. The coach sent for Drew and told him he would like him to try out for the team when the season began. Drew declined as politely as he could. Many people didn't understand his decision, including Levi. He tried to convince Drew but didn't succeed. He didn't know that Drew hated the attention. He was not a fan of it at all. He was the sort of person who kept to himself. An introvert, basically. He was uncomfortable with all the people coming to watch him play and the way they murmured that he was potentially College Division I material. He didn't embrace this part of the game. Instead, he started to play badly on purpose. It was difficult because his abilities made him able to see things fractions slower than it played out and almost as if he could clearly anticipate his opponent's next moves, but he succeeded in downplaying his skills.

This way, all these people will see that I'm not special and they'll leave me alone. He thought.

Levi saw through him and tried to reason with him.

"Bro what's the deal? You know you are better than this now. All those hoop videos we were watching over the summer. All the pick-up games. It was bound to kick in! It's our time, man!" Levi exclaimed.

"Nah," Drew replied, "I'm too low-key for all this attention. All those eyes on me right now are making my stomach turn, bro. I can't stand it."

However, if there was anything Drew liked about his newfound form on the court, it was the way he and Levi put a beating to every duo they previously competed against. He especially savored the looks on their faces, as if they couldn't believe he was the same person they dominated a week ago. Most of all, he enjoyed the surprised looks on the faces of Frank and Tony, Juniors from a near-by high school who were rarely seen outside the park. They were notorious for bullying their wins against any opponent they were matched up against. Their tall and slender builds easily towered over both Drew and Levi by 3-4 inches. Frank was a great ball handler, known for trying to embarrass his opponents with his quick speed and ankle-breaking moves. He also didn't take too kindly to kids from Douglass like Drew and Levi. He felt they were privileged and looked down on every other school, but this wasn't the case with most of the kids from Douglass, especially Drew and Levi. Frank often made them the butt of his jokes on the court, saying nerds like them could never be good enough to hoop like him. Tony usually followed Frank's lead in the insults with little to offer on his own, except his extremely brutal defense on the court. Opponents called him "Tony the Chopper" because of his constant hacking. Despite their egos, they were both formidable players and starters on their varsity team.

Frank yelled out. "I hear all this talk of a new king on the court. So, what up! Let's see it!" As Tony stood at his side, Frank challenged Drew and Levi with a 2 on 2 game.

"Bet!" Levi immediately agreed, much to Drew's annoyance.

Frank and Tony laughed, believing that this would be an easy win for them. Then as soon as Drew stepped on the court, Frank and Tony recognized his newfound tremendous presence. The confidence Drew carried with him seemed to have this outer glow of sorts. Frank and Tony were noticeably uneasy but tried to play it cool.

The game begins:

Frank receives the ball immediately, breaking past Levi with ease, but Drew is there. Frank spins past him going for an uncontested 3 pointer, or so he thought. In what seems like a blink of an eye, Drew catches up to him and blocks the shot. Frank is surprised and stumbles, but he can't react quickly enough to block Drew's fast break lay-up. People begin gathering around the fence in awe of what just happened. Frank realizes that this isn't the same kid he's been harassing all this time.

As the game continues, Tony gets the ball on offense when Levi comes to block him. Levi jumps and realizes this is a pump-fake when Tony slips by him and shoots a quick fade-away shot. Except once again, Drew comes swiftly, and whacks the ball out of bounds. Drew secretly knows this was thanks to his slight time-delay vision. Levi laughs as both Tony and Frank look at each other in confusion.

"You guys must be new to this, let me introduce you to your

teacher, my boy Drew. Say Drew, why don't you show them that new math!" Levi taunts.

Levi's comment only fuels their anger, while Drew's gameplay confirms their fears from the beginning. The game intensifies with the fence surrounding the courts now packed shoulder to shoulder with spectators giving their own "ooh's" and "ahh's" while recording with their smartphones. Drew and Frank have both electrified the growing crowd with their dazzling speed and handles. Levi even manages to receive a few ally-hoops and dunks.

The boys are accidentally putting on a great show for everyone, as roars and shouts are carried through the entire park. Nonetheless, it's down to the wire with both teams tied for game-point. Drew now has possession of the ball. Frank, clearly exhausted, looks Drew fiercely in the eye. With both talents drenched in sweat, creating small puddles on the floor, Frank begins to taunt Drew on his last shot.

"You think you're some kinda big shot now huh, well let's see how clutch you are." Frank says.

Ok, I didn't want to do this, but it's time to shut you up for good.

Drew uses his amazing dribbling and agility to avoid Frank, who is blocking him. He then takes a spin move with a quick dribble and gets past Frank with incredible speed. Just as he is about to make a game winning lay-up, Tony comes flying through the air like a thunder god and ferociously swipes down at the shot attempt, slamming his hand on Drew's face with a loud whack.

"Oooooohhhhhhhh!!!" The crowd erupted, instantly recognizing the hard foul.

The slap sent Drew on his back as the loose ball was picked up by Frank, who put an end to the game with a mid-range shot. Tony looked back with a menacing grin, acknowledging what he had done. Levi immediately sprinted over to check on Drew, visibly concerned.

"Bro you alright?" Levi worried.

"Yea Motor I think so, just can't feel my damn face right now," Drew retorts, "It feels red even though I'm black!" Drew tried to laugh it off.

As much as he was one for jokes and giggles, Levi was not having any of it this time. He rose up like a bear ready to attack and immediately headed in the direction of Tony with his fist balled up tight enough to bust a blood vessel. Drew, recognizing what was about to happen, immediately got up and restrained Levi, as he and Tony were now having a shouting match with each other. Drew managed to calm him down as they walked off the court, with the crowd still shouting and cheering them on in a strange twist of events. Frank and Tony were left only to sounds of booing for their foul play. Despite this, they still reveled in their win.

After such an energetic and brutal game, Drew eventually made it home with a lot to recover from. The exhilaration and intensity that buzzed through his body on the court, reminded Drew that these enhanced skills were not normal and had come to him by surprise. This last game finally brought him back to the reality that all of this was a mistake. This was something that he had to deal with somehow before everything fell apart.

I know Dad never explains anything to me. He probably would be more upset about me not taking my medication. I will have to find out what I can by myself, he thought.

A couple more days after he stopped taking his prescriptions, Drew discovered yet another strange ability. He had taken his bike for a spin around the neighborhood and was listening to music on his earbuds.

Drew didn't hear the horn until it was too late. He reacted too slowly, still shocked, as a car approached him at top speed. He could see the driver through the windscreen, trying to stop the car before he hit Drew. The man applied the brakes but before the car could come to a complete stop.

Skkrrrrrtttttt!!!

The car hit Drew and sent him flying off his bike to crash roughly on the asphalt.

"I'm so sorry. Oh, my God. Are you okay, young man?"

The driver jumped out of his expensive car. He was dressed in a grey suit and was returning home after a long day at work. He ran towards Drew, apologizing profusely. Drew took a few seconds to gather himself and took a couple of deep breaths. Then he looked up at the driver as he stood up.

"Yeah, I'm good," he asserted, wincing a little. He dusted himself off and walked over to his bike, inspecting it for any damages and nodding to himself when he found none.

He looked at the driver again.

"Yo, just be more careful next time, huh? You might kill someone, driving like that," he hollered, wheeling his bike away and leaving the petrified driver standing in the middle of the road.

Drew had walked home in pain and made sure he didn't let his dad see him in that state. He didn't want to answer any questions that may trigger his father to think about *that incident*. A few minutes later, he sat in his room and inspected his body. All his bruises had disappeared. He felt good, as if the accident had never happened. He prodded his left leg, which had supported his weight as he fell. There were no cracks or breaks that he could feel.

Can my body...heal itself? Does this mean—

He decided to test this new ability. A part of his mind was telling him that he was crazy and was only going to hurt himself, but he shut it down. He went to the bathroom, a razor in hand. Then he stood in front of the mirror and placed the edge of the razor against his palm.

He hesitated for a moment, debating what he was about to do.

Maybe I wasn't hurt when I fell from the bike. Maybe I just thought I was hurt. Maybe...

He shook his head to displace the doubts and looked down at the razor. The blue steel felt cold on his deeply brown skin. Drew took a deep breath and broke skin. He winced as the blade of the razor parted skin and blood flowed from the cut. He dropped the razor in the sink and looked at the bleeding wound.

Damn. What was I thinking? I must be going crazy.

Then he gasped, because something that defied logic was happening right before his disbelieving eyes. The blood stopped flowing and the cut on his hand slowly sealed itself. He watched, stupefied, as his skin healed. When it was all done, there was no scar or mark to show that he had even wounded himself in the first place. Drew was suddenly both afraid and amazed.

"What the hell is happening to me?" He shouted. But there was no one to answer him. He could not fathom what he was witnessing. In no time, the pain he felt was no longer throbbing through his palm.

I have to tell someone. But what would they think? What would Motor and Sums think...What would Pops think…

He made a silent note to at least tell Levi and Sumi the next day, but he never did.

"So where do we start?" The voice was Sumi's.

Drew looked at Sumi who was seated on the floor with all the equipment they needed for their project strewn in front of her. Levi lounged on a nearby couch, typing away on his phone's screen. Drew's partner for the project was Sumi and Levi had his own partner, but he had bailed so he could be with his friends at Drew's house.

"I don't know, where do you think we should start? The blueprints, maybe?" Drew asked.

Sumi shrugged and started assembling pieces deftly.

"Levi, you shouldn't have bailed on Max, you know?" Sumi disapproved without looking up.

Levi just rolled his eyes and retorted, "He's so lame, guys. Plus, I'm sure he can handle it. By the way, D, where's your dad? I haven't seen him since we got here."

That was all Drew needed. He started talking before he even realized what he was saying.

"Oh, I don't know. Off to meet some people who obviously have no names or something. He never tells me anything so how am I supposed to know? Ugh. It pisses me off sometimes and when I try to communicate with him, he gets this faraway look in his eyes. I just don't know, man." Drew's eyes began to glaze as he paused for a moment of reflection. "Sometimes, I feel like I'm around a shell of a person that I used to know."

For the next two minutes, the room was paralyzed in silence after Drew's outburst. It wasn't often that Drew aired out his emotions so recklessly. Drew was a much more thoughtful person, always thinking before he spoke up and rarely confrontational. It was obvious that something had changed about him. Finally, Sumi spoke up.

"If it helps, my mom is like the exact opposite, which can be very stifling. She doesn't give me any breathing space. Like, I love computer science and coding. But she wants me to be a neurosurgeon or a physicist or whatever other ridiculous careers she thinks of that are respected and paid a lot. It has to be her way and nothing else. She tells me how to live every aspect of my life and I'm sick of it."

"Hey, man. Me too, for real," Levi related. "I mean, the way I'm built you'd think they'd give me some peace or at least respect my decisions huh? Nah, bro. It's really crazy. Nobody listens to me or anything. And even though I have all these accomplishments for engineering, they still want me to use my size to play football. I mean I love sports, but I'm more than my size. Every family function, I feel like I get a physical examination. Not to mention a dozen questions about sports and my future. The only one that really knows me well in my family is my big brother."

"Right! I mean, last year my mom practically forced me to travel to Kyoto with her to see some relatives. I didn't want to go. I mean, it was summer break. There were so many fun things to do! But she took me to Japan. Ugh," Sumi added.

"I mean, Japan is a pretty dope place. The art, history, and culture. I would love to pick up a few mangas from there," Drew countered.

"Yeah, why didn't you enjoy the trip to Japan?" Levi asked.

Sumi gave both of them a look, while making some corrections on the instruction manual they had created for their project.

"Because… that was the first time I was ever called *Zasshu*, which means *mutt*," she replied quietly, eyes on the floor. Once again, the stillness in the room was enough to cut through as she continued, "It's a terrible thing to call someone, especially when you know what it means. It's like, they can never forgive my mom for marrying a Jamaican American man and having me. They make me feel like a mistake or a freak. We went to this family communal ceremony when we were there in Japan, but I wasn't allowed to enter until way later on purpose. It's crazy."

Levi leaned down and put a big hand on Sumi's shoulder. "It's okay, Sums," he spoke. "I understand. I've been attacked because of how I look too. For one, Douglass isn't exactly perfect. I hear the remarks most of the international students say under their breath about Drew and myself. There aren't too many of 'us' there so they think we have some kind of athletic scholarship, because we couldn't possibly be smart enough to be there. I hear their comments in the halls and cafeteria all the time. I try to smile it away, but the truth is we constantly have to prove that we belong. I took a walk with my big brother once and this police car kept following us. Later, they pulled right up beside us and got down. Questioned us, then searched us. When they found nothing, they barely gave an apology and explained that we matched a description of two drug dealers on the run. You see how messed up that is?"

"Wow, I didn't know that was happening at the school. And the police... just like our parents, when will they try to understand us before making assumptions?" Sumi scolded, shaking her head.

"It's ok, we know you can be too heavy in your books sometimes to see what's happening in the halls. Besides, you are 1/3 of the Drew Crew!" Levi retorted.

"Drew Crew?" both Sumi and Drew exclaimed.

They all laughed in relief, dispelling the tension that had gathered in the room from sharing their stories and frustrations.

"You see, Drew?" Sumi assured, reaching up to place a slim hand on Levi's. "We both understand exactly how you feel. We are here for you, okay?"

"Right! And if you feel like you want to talk to your dad more, maybe you should really take the first step. Don't take no for an answer!" Levi added.

Drew looked at both of them and smiled. He knew they were trying to make him feel better by sharing their stories. He didn't say anything though. He didn't have to. They were his friends and friends do not always need to hear you talk to understand you.

As long as they were with him, he was happy.

CHAPTER FOUR

TRUE LIES

"Hey, dad."

Blake looked up from the files he'd been reading to see his son standing before him. At once, he saw that Drew was upset about something.

"Hey, son. You don't look so happy. You okay?" He asked.

"No," Drew replied shortly.

"You know you can talk to me, Drew. What's going on?"

"A lot. I've got some questions," Drew responded.

After the conversation with Sumi and Levi from the previous day, Drew finally felt like he had the confidence to confront his father about everything.

"First of all, what do those pills really do? What's wrong with them?" Drew asked.

Blake frowned, suddenly feeling very uncomfortable.

"The pills? What could be wrong with them? Drew, the pills are fine okay, I thought we'd been through this already." Blake dismissed. "I'll try to see if I can get the flavor changed."

Drew was shaking his head before his dad had finished speaking.

"No. No, Dad. The time for giving vague answers is over, okay? For your information, I stopped taking the prescription."

Blake immediately stopped shuffling through his files. "You did what?" Blake blurted in shock, his eyes widening in apprehension. Drew knew he was treading on thin ice, but he couldn't stop now.

"Yeah, I stopped. And you know the interesting thing? Ever since I stopped, strange stuff has been happening to me."

Blake grew visibly alarmed and got to his feet.

"What happened?" He asked, his face filled with concern as he reached over and raised his son's arm before checking his neck and ears for anything abnormal.

Drew pushed him away.

"Look, that's not the point, okay? I just want you to be here! I don't want to keep feeling unwanted. I need you with me. Half the time, you're lost in your head when I really need you. The other half, you are barely here, or you are working on your projects. It's frustrating, okay?"

"Drew—"

"No, Dad. You have to listen!... I know losing Mom must have hurt you a lot, but I've been trying to be here for you, and you just lock yourself away. I wish I could remember it all. You know what? Maybe it's all my fault. Maybe—"

"No," Blake interrupted, raising a hand to stop him from continuing. "Son, don't blame yourself. None of this is your fault... Listen, I understand how you feel, I do. But everything will be explained soon. In time, you'll come to understand too."

Drew was visibly upset; the heat of his frustration was starting to burn deeply inside of him. He realized that after expressing himself, his father took him right back to square one.

"Nah. That's not good enough," Drew protested, shaking his head as he walked out on Blake, slamming the door.

Blake was paralyzed with shock as he watched him go. He sat down slowly with his head in his hands.

"This wouldn't be happening if you were here, darling," Blake muttered somberly. In his mind, he pictured his wife, Alice. He imagined that she was seated at the table with him, listening to him rant.

Then, he remembered *that fateful day*, the day that had marked a new beginning for his son. That was when everything started falling into place once more...

Beep...Beep

It was a few days after the accident. The big one. The one that had taken everything from Blake. He was devastated and demoralized. He spent his days beside Drew's hospital bed, praying he'd open his eyes, all of the cords and tubing communicating his vitals as the steady beeping of his heart echoed through the room. Blake didn't know what he would do if his son never snapped out of his coma. If Drew's life was also taken like his mother...

Blake forced himself not to think about the fact that he had lost Alice. A part of his mind was refusing to believe it. He hoped she wasn't gone, even though all available evidence pointed to it. Blake fell on his knees as tears rolled down his chestnut-hued cheek to his strong jawline, soaking the sheets with his sobs.

Drew, please wake up. Please, son. I can't lose you too—

"D-Dad?"

Blake snapped his head up to Drew's face. His son's eyes were open and focused on him. Blake's own eyes were filled with sudden tears of joy.

"Oh my... son, you're awake. Oh, God. Yes, it's me, son. It's daddy." Blake shouted, relief flooding his body. "How are you feeling?"

"I-I don't know. What happened, Dad?... Why am I here?" Drew whimpered.

"You were in a bad accident. But you are OK now. You just need to get your energy up by resting. I'm so glad you're back, my son. Everything will be alright," Blake promised, clasping one of Drew's hands in his own.

Blake went on to give Drew the most careful bear hug he could. He knew Drew couldn't begin to process everything that had just transpired. He knew Drew just needed him at that moment.

The moment ended with Blake realizing what he needed to do next.

"Son, listen to me. This is going to be very hard for you to hear." He explained, trying his best to hold down the build-up of remorse and hurt in his throat.

"I'm sorry to say this to you, but your mom... is…is gone."

A long silence fell in the room. Even the beeping of the heart monitor seemed to have quieted down in respect for the moment about to take place. Everything became still as if time stopped. As Drew struggled to fix his mouth to respond, Blake was bracing himself for the worst. In his mind, he was prepared for anything. Unfortunately, he was not prepared for this.

"What mom?"

That moment replayed in Blake's mind from time to time. After all they had been through together, he believed that Drew deserved more.

"Drew's a good kid. Always has been, even through all that has happened. He should know what's going on, right?"

Of course, there was no answer. He wasn't expecting any.

He sighed and got to his feet.

"By this hour, he can only be going to Levi's place. I should be able to catch up with him if I take the car." He muttered to himself. "I'm going to tell him everything. He can even help me with my project once he knows all the details. It's gonna be really difficult for him to understand. I don't know if I can do it, but I have to try."

"I wish you were here," he prayed to the silence and sighed.

Blake took the car, figuring he could catch up with Drew faster that way since Drew would be on his bike. He looked left and right all the way to Levi's house but didn't spot his son till he got right near the driveway.

He saw Drew getting off his bike and pressed the horn to get his attention. When he saw that Drew was looking back at him, he waved at him to stop.

He got out of the car and walked towards his son, thinking about how he should start his explanations.

"Dad? What are you doing here?" Drew asked, confused.

"Something I should have done long ago," Blake replied.

"Son, I'm here to apologize."

Drew's frown deepened but before he could speak, his dad continued.

"There are so many things I want to explain to you, and I don't even know how to begin but I want to start with an apology. I'm sorry if I've made you feel neglected. Your mother was—"

"Dad, look out!" Drew yelled.

Blake was interrupted by the squeal of tires as a large white van pulled up behind him. Just as he turned around to look, two men in black jumped down from the van. One was holding a cudgel. Blake didn't have time to think or react. The cudgel made contact with the back of his head and made a dull thud sound. He collapsed and fell into the waiting arms of the second guy who carried him easily, pushing his limp body into the back of the van. Then the guy with the cudgel got inside and the van sped off.

Drew stood rooted to the spot, stunned in disbelief. The cold efficiency with which the men in black had operated scared him. Also, he was struggling to process what had just happened so quickly in front of him because he was trying really hard to even believe it.

His dad had just been abducted.

CHAPTER FIVE

---⟨◊⟩---

VOICES OF MYSTERY

Blake was dreaming. He knew it was a dream because he could see Drew. He saw his son standing in front of him with an anguished expression, begging him to be present. He saw his son rolling his eyes at another one of his dad jokes. He saw his son hugging him tightly, as if he would never let go. He saw lots of memories of him and Drew together. In some of them, Drew was happy and laughing. In others, he was moody and sad. But the third type of memories were the ones where he was alone even though his dad was right there. Those were the ones that saddened Blake the most. In his subconscious state, he regretted spending so much time and effort on other things and forgetting to reach out to his son.

Wake up, Blake... wake up...

The woman's voice interrupted his dreams and musings and startled him awake like a bucketful of cold water to the face. He opened his eyes, or tried to.

For a horrifying moment, he thought he was blind. Then he felt the cloth tightening around his eyes and realized that he was blindfolded.

"He's awake. Make the call." The gruff voice must belong to one of the men in black, he thought. He listened as someone dialed a number. All the while, he was wondering about the identity of the woman that had woken him up, while trying to ignore the pain from the back of his head where he had been struck.

"Hello. I hope my men didn't hurt you too much, my friend?"

The voice spoke from a telephone held to Blake's ear. At once, he realized there was something familiar about the voice, but he couldn't place it.

"Who the hell are you?" He growled. There was a grim chuckle from the phone.

"You'll know. Maybe you already do. I wish things were the same as before. I really do. But time has a way of showing you the bigger picture," the voice quipped.

"Look, I don't understand what you are going on about, but whatever it is, this is not the way," Blake contested, attempting to mediate the situation.

"We know that you have been secretly working with a... colleague of mine. Don't worry, we've already dealt with him. He is in full compliance with my...takeover," the voice responded.

"I know you are the people that were following me before. Listen, I'm not involved in any criminal activity. The guy I was working with was a simple investor. I was just looking for funding to complete my project. Please...let me go...I'm just an engineer," Blake pleaded, trying to make the mysterious caller see reason but the voice was filled with nothing but scornful amusement.

"You can fool my colleague, but you can never fool me. Your problem is you do not see the full picture yet," the voice continued. "But your work will help the world in the long run."

"How?" Blake questioned. "Where are you taking me?"

"Oh, you have a very important role to play. We will use you to find the others. Goodbye, Blake," the voice concluded.

"The others? Who? Hey—"

But the voice was gone. The connection had been terminated and Blake was plunged into a sudden stream of thought.

Others...Who is this guy? How does he know about my project?

Drew ran as fast as he could, but it was no use. He ran till his feet hurt but the van was faster. Finally, he had to stop, panting, with his hands on his knees.

Dammit...why couldn't I have just move when it all went down?

He blamed himself. He had reacted too slowly. The van had peeled away from the curb, and he just stood there watching dumbly for a couple of seconds before he thought to move. In hindsight, he knew he should have taken his bike because it would have been faster, and he might have had a better chance of catching up with the van. But panic leaves no room for rational thought.

There had been moments, as he ran, when he was so close, he could touch the van's back doors. During one of those moments, he had brought out his phone and taken a picture of the van, hoping it would help identify the vehicle later.

Now that he had clearly lost the van, he took out his phone and looked at the picture, zooming in to see if there were any details about it. He got his answer at once. The van had no license plates. Drew cursed aloud, attracting glances from passers-by. He didn't care. He turned back towards Levi's house, thinking furiously.

This is the second time. First with the accident, now this? What's wrong with me now? I just knew those abilities would disappear when I needed them the most.

His next thought was the police.

This was an abduction. It should be within their scope of work, right?

The police station was just a couple of blocks away from Levi's place, but he was already having second thoughts. If he showed up at the police station, he was sure he wouldn't make it past the front desk. The reason was simple. He was a minor and would be dismissed almost at once as a prankster or held back for further questioning. By the time he managed to convince someone, his dad might be seriously hurt. Or worse.

He shook his head to get rid of the dark thoughts and tried to think along another path. He decided to head home, hoping in a smaller part of his mind that he would find his dad there, unhurt.

He walked to his fallen bike and found his dad's car keys on the ground. They had probably fallen from his hand when the men grabbed him. He picked up the keys and walked to the car, scanning the insides. He spotted his dad's phone on the driver's seat and picked it up. Then he locked the car and went to pick up his bike.

Drew pedaled fast in the direction of home, his mind a jumble of unrelated thoughts.

Levi was playing an online game, still waiting for Drew to come over like he had texted when he heard the car screeching. At first, he had put it down to the usual neighborhood noise from passing cars and the little children who played outside but there was something different about this disturbance. Just to be on the safe side, he decided to check it out. He paused his game with a sigh.

"Yo, fellas, hold on a minute. I'm hearing a lot of tire screeching and noise outside; I'll be right back," he announced, speaking to the other gamers.

He had just been about to snipe his opponent for a 15-kill streak too. It was not until he heard a familiar voice cursing right outside his house, noisily upset, that he quickly got to his feet and ponderously moved to the window. But by the time he made it there, most of the noise had quieted down.

He peeked out and was surprised by what he saw. He could make out someone pedaling furiously away from his house. He didn't need to see the person's face to know that it was his best friend.

"Yo D!" Levi called out his window. No response.

"H-Hey where you are going, you could come inside. Aye, did you hear that noise too?" Levi asked.

Drew gave no response. He didn't even turn back. "What's wrong with him?" Levi muttered to himself. "He should be coming here, not riding away."

They had planned to meet up that evening. They would play games and maybe even head over to the basketball court together, where they could get in a couple of quick sets. But now his pal was on his bike, obviously headed back home.

Levi left the window and walked to where his phone was charging, unplugging it and dialing Drew's number. He listened to the phone ring and ring, but his friend didn't pick up. He walked back to the window and looked outside, checking to see if there was something he had missed earlier.

"What the—"

There was a car parked at the curb. A big black pick-up truck. It was a vehicle he knew; one he saw every morning on weekdays. There was no doubt about it. The truck belonged to Drew's dad. Getting more puzzled with every passing second, Levi sat down to think.

It was undeniable, something strange was going on and somehow his friend was caught up in whatever it was. It took only a few minutes for him to make his decision. He picked up his phone and dialed a different number.

"Hey. I need your help," he demanded.

CHAPTER SIX

LOST BOY

Drew sat on the sofa, staring at the blank TV screen. If anybody had asked him, he would have answered that he was thinking but what he was actually doing was closer to freaking out.

The house was quiet. He had gotten home to find the place deserted, with his faint hopes of meeting his dad at home crushed. Without his dad in the house, he felt truly worried, and lonely. He missed his father's voice, the smell of his aftershave, his shouts that Drew should take his prescriptions. He missed his dad's silent presence, even though he was distracted most of the time.

He closed his eyes and swallowed. His heart pounded rapidly against his chest and his skin was clammy with sweat. He found it difficult to breathe. Dimly, he realized he was having a panic attack.

His thoughts were scrambled. He didn't know what to do. He had never been so scared and alone before in his life.

Then there was a knock at the door, and someone came in. Drew remembered in his panic; he didn't shut the door all the way. He immediately picked up the nearest object he could find to use as a weapon. Drew stood in absolute silence like a wooden totem pole attempting to read the footsteps of the strange visitor.

They are probably here to get me as well. I won't go down without a fight, Drew thought.

Two shadows emerged from the lighting of the hall as the intruders made their way into the living room. Drew hid behind the wall next to a family portrait, waiting for a moment to strike.

"Hey Drew...it's me. Are you ok? Your door was open."

They turned the corner and found him trembling, tears leaking from his eyes.

The person was Levi. His strong but gentle hands grabbed Drew by the shoulders and shook him while he whispered under his breath.

"Stay with me, man. Come on," he pleaded over and over.

Sumi moved into sight from behind Levi's large frame. She also placed a slim hand on Drew's arm. After a few minutes, the presence of his friends helped Drew return to a state of calm. He looked up at them and tried to convey his loneliness and guilt without words. They understood him. He didn't need to say anything.

"I heard some of it," Levi responded gently.

Drew nodded and closed his eyes. Then he started telling them exactly what had happened. To his ears, his voice sounded hollow, as if it belonged to someone else. When he finished talking, there was a hush in the room. Then he heard Levi and Sumi whispering to each other. He opened his eyes to see Sumi standing in front of him.

"I was already coming here for the project. But now...I think it's better if we stay," she resolved.

"No," Drew rebutted. "You guys...I'm fine... Don't stress yourselves."

"Drew, look. I know you don't like people to worry about you, but you are not gonna sideline us on this. We're your friends. We're staying," Sumi insisted in a voice that brooked no argument. She had that stubborn look in her eyes. It was a look Drew knew well. She had made up her mind. She could also tell that she lightened his mood.

"Good! Since we all agree, I'll have to come up with a reason for staying over," Levi replied. He thought for a moment, then he picked his phone and dialed a number.

"Hey, big bro. Yeah, thanks for the ride... Err look, something's come up and I need to stay with D tonight... Yeah. Can you tell Mom and Dad that I'm with you? Come on, man... Alright, I'll pay you... Okay."

Levi grinned as he slid the phone back into his pocket. His brother was none other than Jacob Makosso, but most people called him "Jake" or "Jay Mod." He used to be a well-known linebacker in high school but suffered a leg injury that hurt his chances to play in college. After high school, he became a celebrated street racer, driving some of the highest performing, custom engines that he modified himself. He taught Levi everything he knew, even helping him in many of his projects.

"How's Jay been these days?" Drew asked.

"Man, when he's not charging me for everything, he's fine," Levi snarled. "He's one of those ride-sharing drivers now. You know that's a huge step down from how he used to handle cars. But he's paying for college classes, which is why he taxes me for everything."

Meanwhile, Sumi had moved to the other side of the room and

was having a conversation with her mother.

"Yes, mom. We're studying through the night. No. I've told you, I'm at Anne's place. *Hai. Sayonara.*"

She turned to face the boys as she put the phone away. "Well, that's one problem solved," she sighed. "Now, we should probably search for clues or something."

"Wow guys... listen... I really appreciate what you're doing here," Drew commended, overwhelmed by the support.

"Yeah, we know, we're the best and all that!" Levi retorted. "So, where do we start?"

They started at the backyard shed, where Drew expected to find his father's invention, but it wasn't there. He had concluded sometime during his brooding that the men in black were after his dad's invention. Why else would they abduct him? His dad wasn't exactly an interesting man, as far as Drew knew. He wasn't a spy or something. Just a guy who built stuff and worked with solar panels.

As he looked around, Drew's train of thought carried him to the first time he could remember his dad creating a special toy for him. It had been some kind of miniature robot that could move on its own. Drew didn't remember when or where his dad had given him the toy, but he knew he had loved it, even though he'd never understood the robot's source of power. There were no batteries or solar panels to charge it, but it moved and spoke in a mechanical voice. When he asked his dad about the "*batteries*", the reply had been vague, and in time, Drew had stopped worrying about it.

"Hey, look! I found something," Levi shouted. Drew and Sumi ran over to see. In his big hands, Levi held a remote, but there was nothing in sight that it could control. They passed it from hand to hand, loudly wondering what it was. There were less than ten buttons on the remote; most were black but one of them was red while another was green.

"Probably tossed here by someone. Doesn't look useful," Levi noted, examining the remote with his best detective impression. It was back in his hand, and after a few more observations, his child-like urge had overtaken him. He pressed the red button.

"I don't think you should—"

Sumi's voice was cut off by a loud ringing noise in Drew's ears.

"AHHHHH! THAT SOUND! MY EARS! MAKE IT STOP! PLEASE!"

He clamped his hands over his ears instinctively and fell to his knees. He could hear his friends shouting. He could see Levi frantically jabbing the button with his finger without any results. Sumi dashed into the house, probably trying to get something to help. The ringing continued in Drew's ears and when he took away one of his hands, he saw that it was smeared with droplets of blood.

The ringing stopped as suddenly as it started. Drew held his head with both hands and exhaled. He could hear a very muffled sound of Levi asking him if he was okay. It was as if his ears were clogged. But oddly enough, he could also hear another voice in his mind clearly.

"Drew, you have to help me. Drew..."

He knew he was awake, so this wasn't like the other times when he had heard voices in his mind. He was pretty sure it wasn't his mother who was talking to him this time, but he knew the voice. It was a man's deep baritone. It was the voice that yelled at him every morning to take his prescription, the voice that delivered stale dad jokes, the voice he had last heard in front of Levi's house.

It was the voice of his father.

CHAPTER SEVEN

THE OPERATION

"Dad? Is that you? How is this happening? Am I just hearing things?"

Sumi returned with a roll of tissue and a bottle of peroxide from the bathroom med cabinet. Levi was on his knees, afraid to touch Drew after what he believed was his fault.

"Drew! Drew, are you ok? You have blood on your hand! Oh my god, please respond! Your eyes are open, but you haven't blinked! You are really scaring me right now!" Sumi cried out, hoping to squeeze a response out of him by gripping his shoulders tightly.

"Bro... please don't tell me I made you go deaf!" Levi lamented as his eyes welled up next to Drew, who was seemingly immobile.

"Drew, you have to find me...Please, I can feel myself drifting further away from you."

"But Dad...How is this happening? Can you actually hear me in my thoughts? Please tell me I'm not crazy! Is this really you?" Drew asked in his head.

"Son...yes it's me. I swear to you it is. I'm sorry about earlier...but we don't have much time, I promise to explain everything to you when this is over. But right now, please be calm and listen to my instructions. Only you can save me," Blake responded.

Levi managed to sit Drew on the ground with his back against the wall.

Sumi was touching wads of tissue paper to his ears. They had stopped bleeding within a few minutes. The tissues were red with his blood, and he was still wondering what exactly had happened. Sumi tended to Drew as she recommended Levi to bring the strange remote back indoors and lock it in a cabinet till they could think of what to do with it.

"My dad," Drew finally spoke.

Sumi quickly called Levi back as Drew continued.

"My dad...he's alive...he spoke to me...in my head," Drew whimpered as his gaze peered through both Sumi and Levi. It was like he was in a trance.

The crew, confused at his statement, remained silent as they listened intently.

"He wants us to follow his trail... Through my connection," Drew stammered, recognizing their bewilderment.

"I know the way. I can... feel him somehow."

"...Feel...my body. Wait, I think I get it now!" Drew thought. Instantly, he snapped out of his trance and grabbed Levi's shoulders with his now cleaned hand. This scared both Sumi and Levi momentarily.

"I'm not sure what you did bro. But thank you. Listen guys, we have to go now." Drew responded as he quickly got to his feet.

Sumi and Levi both stared at each other baffled by the sudden change in behavior. Sumi, still concerned and a bit irate, called him out.

"Wait a damn minute! First of all, don't scare us like that. We thought you lost your mind or went deaf. You blacked out on us Drew. Which brings me to my second point: are you even ok right now? Have you listened to yourself?"

The big guy scratched his head.

"She's right D. You are not yourself," he added.

"I'm sorry guys. I promise, I am fine now. I am not deaf, and I think my ear is good now for some reason. Look, I will explain everything. But we have to find a way to reach my father. Please help me out."

"Ok...I don't believe that you are fine.... But I'll help," Sumi conceded. "So, you mentioned you have a plan. Let's hear it."

"Right. So, I think there might be a way. But I'm not too sure about it," Drew spoke up. The other two looked at him, waiting for him to go on. Drew felt like he had finally made some connection with everything going on with his body.

Time to come clean.

Drew took a deep breath and told them everything that had happened to him since he had stopped taking the prescription. Well, he mentioned most of it and left some parts out. Many things were unclear to him, and he didn't want to pass across any of his doubts to his friends. They listened attentively. When he was done, Levi was the first to speak, as usual.

"Wait. So, you're saying you can hear your dad even though he's in an unknown location right now? And when we went hooping at the park...all of that was because of the pills you are not taking?" He asked.

Drew nodded.

"I'm just really confused about all of this. You are being serious right now?" Sumi questioned.

"Bro, that's some Star Wars level stuff!" Levi interjected. "Can you also move objects with your mind?"

I didn't think the reaction would be this crazy, Drew thought, while letting out a sigh.

"Uhh, let's get back on track, please. So, Drew, you heard him in the yard? After Levi pressed that button?" Sumi asked before Drew could answer Levi's questions.

Drew nodded again.

"Okay, Drew Crew. I think our first step is very clear." Levi declared, stretching his arms in preparation.

"And what would that first step be?" Sumi asked.

"Find Drew's dad of course!" Levi declared as if it was the most obvious thing in the world.

"Yeah, but how?"

"Oh, I know how," Drew answered. "We're gonna use these strange abilities I have. That's how. I'll guide us to his dad."

"And then?"

"Then we use D's super powers to rescue his dad." Levi remarked.

"It won't be that easy," Drew warned. "We don't know who the guys in black are. "We don't even know how many of them there are. Also, these so-called powers are still suspect. I'm not some kind of superhero. I think we need to plan this very carefully."

"Okay, let's just take this step by step," Sumi agreed.

"Fine! But let the record show, I believe in these new abilities of yours!" Levi proclaimed, pointing his finger to the air.

Then they put their heads together and started planning.

About forty-five minutes later, they had a framework of the plan they were going to work with and were finalizing the details.

"Okay, so we don't know what type of place Drew's dad is being held, right?" Levi asked. Sumi and Drew nodded. "It might be some isolated house, in some quiet neighborhood. In fact, that's what it's most likely to be."

You've been watching too many movies, Motor," Drew retorted.

Levi offered a grin as if he'd been exposed.

"No, man. Well, yes, I have. But I know these things, okay?"

"How do you know? Have you abducted someone before?" Sumi asked, faking a horrified expression.

Drew and Levi both chuckled.

"Look, I just know this. I lived in this terrible neighborhood once and kidnappings were rampant there. The guys involved always pressured me to join because of my physique but I always refused," Levi recalled.

"I hear you on that Motor, so what do we do when we get there?" Drew asked.

"Well," Levi explained. "One thing is constant, regardless of the nature of the place. Stealth is our greatest ally. Going by what D touched on, these guys in black are sizable and strong and there are probably a lot more of them. We can't rush in there and demand that they should release your dad. We take things step by step."

"Okay. How do we get there?" Drew asked, getting to his feet.

"I'll give my brother a call. In the meantime, you guys should get ready to leave," Levi replied.

CHAPTER EIGHT

MAN IN THE ARENA

They followed the directions Drew's dad gave his son through telepathy. Before they left the house, Levi had called his brother again and had managed to get him to come and drive them to their destination.

Jake was just as big as Levi was. He had dark skin and serious eyes that he rarely took off the road, simply nodding whenever he had to make a turn.

Levi and Sumi had to take the backseat because Drew had to be giving the instructions. He directed Jake from the front seat while he was being directed in turn by his father's voice. It was difficult, even with this telepathic conversation because Drew's dad had been tossed in the back of a van and blindfolded so he could not give actual directions. The method they used was that the connection between them grew stronger whenever Drew got close enough. They knew the van couldn't have gone too far so they had high hopes of finding its destination soon.

While Drew concentrated on his father's voice, Sumi and Levi were making further plans. They didn't know what they would find at their destination but they both steeled themselves to prepare for the worst.

"Look, you know they might have done something to Drew's dad, right?" Sumi asked Levi in a whisper.

"Yeah, so we've got to be expecting the worst but hope for the best, huh?" Levi replied, keeping his voice at the same low level.

"Exactly. Also, we need to know what to do when we get there. We can't just go in there and ask those guys to release Drew's dad."

"Hmm. I gotcha. We'll have to be invisible. In and out before anyone notices us."

"And how will we do that?" Sumi asked.

"I'll think of something," Levi responded as he closed his eyes to think.

Half of Drew's mind was focused on his dad's voice while the other half was lost in a daydream. He was remembering a summer day when he had gone on a fishing trip with his dad. He couldn't remember how old he had been or where exactly they had gone. He couldn't remember much about that day, but he was sure it had happened. He remembered the lake. It was wide, so wide that he struggled to see its end. He remembered how cloudless the sky had been, just a light blue canvas stretched above them. He remembered the feel of the fishing rod in his hand. He had been an inexperienced fisherman and he could still hear his dad laughing at him as he grappled with the rod when it buckled. His dad showed him how to reel in his catch and he followed his instructions.

His catch turned out to be a bass that was almost as long as his arm. He had removed the hook from its gaping mouth and held its wriggling body in his hand. The body of the bass glinted when it caught the light of the sun.

He remembered his dad squeezing his shoulder, a wide and proud smile on his face. He remembered how he had felt that afternoon: genuinely happy.

In the front seat of the car, Drew followed the link, driving away from his half-formed thoughts. He told Levi's brother to make a couple of left turns and felt the connection get even stronger. He knew then that they were very close.

"Get ready, guys," he called to his friends in the backseat.

"We're good to go, man," Levi replied.

Drew told Jake to turn right. He did as Drew instructed and straight ahead of them, Drew knew with certainty, was where his father was being held. When he saw what was waiting before them, his suspicion that his father had been abducted because of his mysterious invention was only reinforced.

"So much for your isolated house theory, Levi," Sumi muttered.

The place was a sort of convention center. The three friends got out of the car and stood on the sidewalk, looking around. The convention that was currently being held was a sci-fi con. There were lots of people selling stuff at booths: comics, miniature UFOs and robots, alien costumes, and so on. The place was very big.

Too big, Drew thought.

How could they find his father in this? There had to be hundreds of people here, milling around. It would be harder than searching for a needle in a haystack.

Drew felt a hand on his shoulder and looked up at Levi's face.

Levi had his game face on, the one he wore before demolishing opponents in all the sports he played.

"Are you ready to go get your dad, bro?" He asked.

"I am...but Motor, this place is crazy. This crowd... I don't know..."

"It doesn't matter if there are a thousand people between us and your dad. We are going to find him, okay?"

The confidence in Levi's voice strengthened Drew. He took a deep breath and nodded. He caught Sumi's eye and she also nodded in encouragement.

With his friends by his side, Drew prayed he was not too late and let the crowd swallow him. Thoughts of the memory he had briefly remembered in the car spurred him on. He felt his resolve hardening.

I'm coming, Dad.

CHAPTER NINE

FACE OFF

The Drew Crew were unlucky at first. They searched everywhere, with little results. They looked in closed stalls, the halls, and even unmonitored conference rooms but found nothing. All the while, there was a loud buzzing in Drew's mind. He couldn't make out a single word, but he understood what the buzzing meant anyway. His dad was here. He was sure about it.

The three of them might have made more progress and maybe even covered more distance if they had split up but they had decided that it was wiser to stick together.

"Let's check the back. Are you still hearing from your dad?" Levi asked Drew.

"Something like that," Drew replied.

They circled to the back of the convention center. As the theme song of *Starlite Battles* can be heard through the empty halls, there was a lone room set at the edge of the place. The buzzing in Drew's head increased in volume immediately when he saw the door. Drew was sure whoever had taken his father was in that room. His telepathic powers were suddenly stronger than ever.

Before they stormed in, Levi reminded them of the plan. In and out without being seen. Sumi didn't look too pleased with this summarized plan, but she just nodded.

The door was unlocked. The three of them entered the room, alert and ready to react to anything that might be thrown their way—

And came face to face with three men in black. The men in black were the only ones in the room. They were putting on ski masks and got to their feet immediately as the Crew burst through the door.

"Who the hell are you kids? What are you doing here?" One of the men asked. There was an unmistakable menace in his rough voice.

Drew stepped forward; his expression fierce.

"You've got my dad. I'm here to know why you captured him and take him home. Police should be here any minute," he declared.

"Your... dad?" The guy that had spoken sneered, apparently confused. They blatantly disregarded his mention of police.

"Yeah. You knocked him out with a stick and threw him in the back of a van. Where is he?" Drew demanded.

"So, you're Blake's son?" Another guy in black asked. He looked around at the other two.

"Didn't see that coming," one of the other masked men muttered in a low voice.

"What do you guys mean?" Drew protested. He was getting annoyed by then.

"We think you were adopted, kid. You didn't show up on our sensors. You're not one of them," the first guy dismissed, as they continued to hold their guard.

Drew did not understand. Why would they think he was adopted? What was this sensor they were talking about? And who was this 'them'?

Too many questions with no answers in sight. His confused expression must have been noticed by the men in black because one of them pressed a button on the wall and moments later the door opened. This time it was Drew's dad who was pushed into the room, followed by one man in black.

"Dad!" Drew exclaimed and ran to him. He saw at once that there were handcuffs on his dad's wrists, but they were not like the normal handcuffs that policemen used. These cuffs were big and had all sorts of symbols and buttons. It was obviously very complicated tech. Drew had seen cuffs like them only in movies where they had been used to limit the powers of mutants or stuff.

"So, is he your son?" The lead speaker of the men in black, the one who had been doing most of the talking, asked Blake.

There was a moment of silence, then— "No."

"What do you mean no?" The man questioned.

"He's adopted," Blake declared. "He's obviously not like the rest of us."

Drew felt numb. He blinked, wondering if this was a dream but it was real. Even though the sounds around him seem to fade away from the shock, he could hear Levi cursing loudly and Sumi was staring daggers at Blake. Levi moved forward and caught one of the men in black in the chin with a punch. The guy staggered under the force of the blow but before Levi or Sumi could do anything else, more men in black stormed into the room.

They overpowered Levi and tied his hands behind his back.

Sumi was also restrained even though she kicked and punched the mysterious men. But the men in black were experienced and ruthless and had numbers on their side. They got Drew's friends zip-tied up and shoved them to the floor.

Drew, meanwhile, just stood still. He was staring at the man he knew to be his father. Tears welled up in his eyes. He was confused and didn't even know what to say.

Drew, I am so sorry.

Drew blinked. It was his father's voice, echoing in his mind.

I am sorry for everything. You are my real son. I just told them that you're adopted so I can keep you safe. That's all I've ever wanted, son. I want you to be safe. But I have done it the wrong way and for that I am sorry. The time for lying is over. Go home and check my room for the box with the words "Type II". You may not understand everything you read or see at first, but it won't take too long since you've stopped using the pills. I don't want you to worry too much. These men won't kill me. They need me to find "them". Son, when you finally find out the truth, do not tell anyone who you are, no matter what.

The voice of his dad went quiet. Drew clutched his head in his hands. He had never held a telepathic conversation that lasted as long as this. He was having a severe headache. He tried to call for help but he couldn't even open his mouth. Before he knew what was happening, he fell to the ground and passed out from the exertion to his mind and body.

The leader of the men watched the boy collapse. "Take them away," he ordered. Just then he recieved an update in his ear-piece about Drew.

"Yes sir. 10-4."

He made a slight gesture, a secret code that his men understood perfectly. They were to silence the two other kids because they had seen too much and would jeopardize the mission. But they now needed Drew alive.

No, the kids! And how did they discover the truth about my son so quickly? Blake thought, as he struggled with the men also carrying him away.

Stay alive, my son. Save the others.

The men bound Drew's hands as they had bound his friends and carried all of them out to the back of the convention arena.

Drew didn't see any of this happening. He was in another one of his memory dreams. He realized at once that he was at a rally of some kind. The speaker was ferocious and had the undivided attention of the crowd. But Drew had eyes only for the people beside him. His parents. Both of them listened attentively to the man on the stage.

Drew also turned out of curiosity to see who it was that had everyone so interested in his every word. He gasped. A man he had only seen on TV and in history books was addressing them. A freedom fighter who had died several years ago. Drew couldn't believe his eyes, but the man was there.

Malcolm X.

CHAPTER TEN

LEVEL UP

"We declare our right on this earth to be a human being, to be respected as a human being, to be given the rights of a human being in this society, on this earth, in this day, which we intend to bring into existence by any means necessary."

The eternal words of Malcolm X echoed in Drew's head as he woke up. He knew he had heard those words before.

Maybe I read them in a history book or saw a documentary.

Then the incidents of the past few minutes dawned on him. His dad, his friends, the men in black. It all came back to him in a rush. He realized that he was blindfolded, and his arms were bound securely behind him. He was lying on his side on a hard surface. He could hear Levi somewhere beside him. He seemed to be giving the men in black lots of problems, and by the sound of it, they were struggling to keep him down.

Likewise, Drew could hear Sumi struggling with one man who seemed to be dragging her away. Levi called her name and tried to get to her, but he was overpowered by the other men.

Drew was filled with anger. He couldn't let them hurt his friends. They were here because of him.

No, I can't...I won't...I... I will not freeze up again. They are here because of me...my pops...all of this is because of me.

In desperation, he cried out for his abilities to return to him.

Please...let me have it... one...more...time!

He focused on his bonds and tried to free himself, the surge of strength taking him by surprise. His bonds broke as if they were made of paper, and he got to his feet. He didn't have time to take off his blindfold. One of the men, the fastest to react from the shock of seeing him free himself, approached him. Drew heard him coming and stepped aside, avoiding his first punch before coming up under his outstretched arm and knocking him senseless with a single blow to the chin.

Drew took off his blindfold. The whole thing had taken a couple of seconds. The men who had been holding Levi down, all three of them, rose and attacked him. Behind them, Levi freed himself at last and grabbed a 2x4 lying on the ground. He raised the plank of wood and used it to hit one of the men on the head, making him fall to the ground.

Meanwhile, Drew ran to an overflowing garbage dump and pushed with all of his newfound strength. The garbage dump struck two of the men in their chests and slammed them against a wall while Levi hit another one with the plank.

The boys looked at all the men on the floor, panting hard. "Bro, forget the pills, you must've been bitten by a radioactive spider or something!" Levi shouted, looking at Drew in amazement.

Drew just shrugged. He also didn't know where the sudden strength had come from.

"Maybe it's the adrenaline," he hesitated. "But we've got no time for that."

The both of them ran to the corner where the other guy had dragged Sumi.

Sumi was standing over him, a taser in her hand. "Oh. We thought—" Levi started.

"I carry it for protection," she quipped as she approached them.

"Woah. That's hardcore, Sumi. Remind me never to annoy you," Levi mused, taking a playful step backwards.

"You always annoy me, Levi," Sumi ridiculed as she returned the taser to her pocket.

"Wow, guys we really did it!" Drew blurted out, as his heart was still racing from his boost of strength. "I'm seriously glad you guys are not hurt." As the crew checked for any injuires, Drew continued. "Listen, we need to get out of here, guys. Let's go back to my place," he suggested, thinking about what his dad had told him. He knew they had to return to his house to begin their search. He still wasn't sure exactly what they would be looking for, but he knew they had to get moving.

"What about your dad?" Sumi asked.

Drew was quiet only for a couple of seconds.

"He... He'll be fine. He sorta told me stuff I have to do. I'll let you know when we get to the house. Motor?"

"Yeah. I'll call my brother," Levi relayed as he brought out his phone. He made the call and told Jake to come pick them up at the convenience store opposite the convention center. Then the three of them turned and left as fast as they could, leaving the men sprawled on the ground.

When they were gone, one of the men moved slowly, clearly in pain. He lifted a phone to his ear.

"The kids escaped," he reported, grunting in anguish. "They're going to Blake's place... Yes. Also, just to confirm sir, the boy is definitely one of them, just like you figured... Yeah."

He paused, waiting for the person on the other end to reply... "Find them. And bring the boy to me. I sense his potential."

CHAPTER ELEVEN

OUT OF TIME

They got to Drew's house in no time. Drew, Levi, and Sumi got out of the car. The boys stepped forward, eager to go in and begin the search but Sumi held them back.

"Not so fast," she demanded, "You guys made so much noise beating up those guys. Someone might have heard us and followed us here. We can't keep charging into places. We might be walking into a trap."

Drew and Levi thought about her words and nodded in agreement. Then Levi spoke up.

"You're right. We've got to be careful. I think we should go in through a side window."

The others agreed with him. They circled the house and found a window they could use. Drew went in first, followed by Sumi and then Levi. They were in a small room where Drew's dad worked sometimes. There were some machine parts littered around so they decided to start their search there. They didn't find the box, but they did find things they could use as weapons in case the men in black came after them. Sumi already had her taser, so she picked up a long screwdriver with a flat head. Levi picked up two thick metal poles and swung them to test their balance. Drew found a hammer and took it with him.

They walked into the hallway and quietly agreed they would cover more ground and complete the search faster if they split up.

"I'll take the garage," Levi called out, making his way to the port entrance.

"OK, I'll search the kitchen and storage room," Sumi added.

"Alright, I'll be in the attic. Yell if you need me," Drew directed. The others nodded and moved away, careful not to make any noise to alert people that might be lying in wait.

Drew quietly stepped into the attic. When he realized the area was safe, he started searching. There was a coat of dust on most of the boxes there and as he started moving them around, he unsettled the dust and coughed when the particles got into his nose. He moved several boxes aside, searching for something distinctive. He had a feeling he would know what he was looking for when he saw it.

He dragged a crate away from the wall and saw something gleam behind it. He reached forward and picked up the object: a stainless-steel time capsule box. He turned it over in his hands, inspecting it. On top of the box, he could see some strange markings that he couldn't make sense of, though he had a feeling that he should be able to. He blinked a couple of times and saw that the markings looked slightly different, as if they were in English but written in an untidy scribble that was difficult to decipher.

He blinked again. The markings—no, words—got even clearer until Drew could read them.

"Type II." He gasped in amazement. *I found it!*

Just as he completed his train of thoughts, there was a buzzing sound, and the box scanned his thumb.

Drew was awed.

He realized that there must be fingerprint scanners all over the time capsule. The box glowed bright blue and started to open up.

"What in the world?"

Dad...did...you make this?

When the box was completely opened, Drew started going through its contents. There wasn't much to see, not really. He found a journal that was bookmarked with clippings from old newspapers, yellowed with age. The newspaper clippings were distributed through all of the journal's entries. Underneath the journal, he found a strange necklace with a dark stone in the place of a pendant. The stone looked unfit to be attached to the chain. Drew touched it and found that it was cool to the touch but nothing special happened.

He started going through the journal and received his first shock on the very first page. The entry was dated: "**April 1, 1950.**"

Okay, what's going on here? Dad is definitely not that old. Nah. Could this be my grandparents or something? Nah. He never mentioned anything about my grandparents.

If the journal didn't belong to his dad, who did it belong to then? The handwriting wasn't really familiar. He turned the pages, looking through the journal and newspaper clippings, and was surprised by what he found. The clippings were the headlines of the assassinations of people involved in the Civil Rights movement, especially leaders like Martin Luther King and Malcolm X.

Wow, this may be priceless...but...dad is an inventor, not a historian.

I know he loves history documentaries, but why does he have this? Drew thought.

He shrugged and kept looking through the journal. He saw more clipped articles, but these had different contents. They contained reports on the Cold War and rumors of UFO sightings. Drew couldn't make any sense of it all.

It's like a damn madhouse in this journal. Nothing's making any sense.

He didn't bother checking the next page, instead he turned to the very last one. As he did, a couple of small pictures fell out of the journal to the floor. As Drew bent to pick them up, he saw that they were very old photos in black and white. He frowned and turned them over. There were five pictures in all and in every single one of them, even though something in Drew's head was screaming that it was impossible, his parents were captured attending one historic site or the other. In one of the pictures, he could see his father holding his mom.

"They visited the pyramids...wow, mom was so beautiful..." Drew wondered aloud, surprised. "He never told me about these trips."

He didn't really speak about these great moments at all...

Drew's face contorted in a frown. All these happy memories, why had his father kept them to himself? And why were the photos in black and white? His eyes were lost in the distance and his lips moved soundlessly as he tried to recall if his dad had even mentioned any of the events in these pictures.

At last, he sighed and looked back at the photos, focusing on his mom.

The picture was awkwardly angled as if someone small had taken it, but they were both smiling. Drew couldn't remember the last time he had seen his dad smile so brightly. He was standing behind his wife in the picture, his arms encircling her with his hands resting on her stomach.

"Okay, this is crazy," Drew gawked in disbelief, with his hand on his head, wiping the dews of sweat. *These pictures are damn old, man. Look at what they are wearing! They both have afros!*

He kept looking through the pictures till he got to the last one. It was another picture of his parents but this time they weren't visiting a landmark. They were participating in a civil rights march. There was no mistaking it. Drew blinked and stared at the picture.

But the Civil Rights movement was like fifty-something years ago, man! Pops isn't over 50!

How?

He didn't get any answer to his unspoken thoughts because at that moment, his eyes slid to the person who was beside his mom, holding her hand. He trembled and the picture fell from his suddenly nerveless fingers. He dropped to his knees, all the strength leaving his body in one breath.

The person holding his mother's hand was a brown kid with bright eyes. Drew couldn't believe his eyes, but he was looking at himself in a picture that was over fifty years old.

Over fifty years ago…

CHAPTER TWELVE

THE GLOW

"Yo, D! Where are you, man?"

"Yeah, Drew are you still up there?"

His friend's voices roused him. He moved quickly, remembering what his father had charged him about not letting anyone know. He didn't fully understand what he had found himself, but he decided to obey his dad's instructions. He grabbed a backpack and tossed the journal and photographs into it, before climbing down from the attic.

"Hey, guys! Over here. I found something," he called out, making sure the items he had taken out of the box were out of sight. He walked into his room and his two friends joined him there. Levi's jacket was covered in dust, and he was carrying a big magnet in one hand.

"Just something I found lying around," he joked, grinning. "Didn't want to look like I didn't find anything, so I just picked it up."

Drew grinned back. Motor never lost his sense of humor. Sumi, on the other hand, was not holding anything except her taser. She rolled her eyes with a smirk at Levi's comment. Crossing her arms, she stood to one side, waiting for Drew to reveal what he had found.

Drew took a deep breath. He hated lying to his friends, but he also knew that he had to obey his father's instructions. There were so many things that weren't clear to him about the whole situation, but he had decided to act on the little he knew, and one of the things he knew was that his father knew a lot. So, he was going to do as he instructed.

"Yo, so what did you find?" Levi asked.

"This," Drew responded and set the box down on a table so his friends could examine it.

"The only things inside are those old newspaper clippings and the necklace." He dismissed, not meeting their eyes. Sumi narrowed her eyes suspiciously, but she didn't press him. He knew she suspected that he was hiding something. He was pleased when Levi broke the silence again.

"What type of rock is this?" He questioned, turning the necklace over in his hand. "Looks like something a person with terrible fashion sense would hang on their neck, you know?"

Sumi took the necklace from him and also examined it. "There are some markings here," she pointed out, peering closely at the surface of the strange stone. The two boys moved closer to see. Sumi was right, something was scratched into the stone. Drew saw at once that it was the same thing on the cover of the box.

"Guys, check this out. It's the same thing written on the box.

Think this is what we're looking for?" He asked. His friends nodded in agreement.

"OK, we have the weird necklace. What now?" Sumi asked.

It was a good question. Drew didn't know what to do next. He was thinking of running back to free his dad or maybe trying to crack the whole crazy case on his own when Levi spoke beside him.

"Oh, man. D...y.. you seeing this?" He stammered.

Drew turned his eyes to Levi's hand. His friend was holding the necklace and the stone was glowing faintly. Drew took the stone from Levi, and it continued to glow. He turned it over a couple of times but saw nothing else that was distinctive, so he gave it back. Levi handed it over to Sumi and there was a collective gasp from all three of them as the stone glowed brighter than before.

"Did you see that!"

"It got brighter!"

"Err...you think it's radioactive or something?" Levi wondered.

"Maybe it reacts better to the feminine touch," Sumi responded.

Drew hushed them and held his head with his hands, trying to make sense of what was happening. He began to think out loud.

"Guys, Sumi is standing in the doorway. I'm here on my bed. Levi is between us. I think there's some sort of reference point somewhere outside. Sumi is the closest to that point because she's in the doorway. I'm thinking this is like the time when we learned about the characteristics of magnetism. Look, let me show you."

He held a hand out to Sumi and she passed the stone to Levi, who gave it to him. The three of them didn't take their eyes off the necklace so they didn't miss it when the glow dimmed as it went from hand to hand. They reversed the process and witnessed it get brighter as it approached Sumi's position.

"Wow. That's crazy," Levi emphasized in shock.

"But why now all of the sudden? What caused it to start up in the first place?" Sumi asked.

"Electromotive force!" Levi shouted. Sumi and Drew looked at Levi confused.

Levi continues. "Remember, a few days ago in class, Ms. Sanders explained that electromotive force is the electrical action produced by a non-electrical source...Hey I may have had gas in class that day, but the lesson was actually good!"

"So whatever kind of stone it is, somehow, we may have given it a kick start by touching it," Sumi added.

"Yup, and Drew had it first, so maybe he ignited it unknowingly," Levi concluded.

"And now it's attracted to a certain magnetic field. Something much stronger than whatever energy we are giving off... This has to be it! The thing we were supposed to be looking for the whole time was this stone!"

"But when did your father tell you this?" Sumi asked.

"Err...I will explain on the way. More importantly, all we need to do is go in whatever direction the glow is brightest, you know?" Drew stuttered. His friends nodded.

"But it won't be too accurate," Sumi noted after a moment.

"Well, if I call my brother again, we'll be in a car. So that will be faster, right? Eventually, if we continue on the right path, the accuracy should improve. Someone will just have to use the stone to guide my bro. Oh, and we should be okay. He is not the type to really ask questions," Levi explained.

Drew thought about it and nodded.

"How is it that he is always available for you?" Sumi asked.

"Let's just say, I bailed him out a few times...plus I'm gonna have to pay him. Listen guys, let's limit our adventure to just one more trip, my pockets are hurting," Levi entreated.

"Alright, Motor. Call Jay," Drew instructed.

Drew was seated in the front seat again, the stone on his palm. It was much brighter now than it had been when they were in the house.

"Thanks again Jake, for taking us around the city again. We appreciate you helping us with our project," Sumi expressed, rubbing the back of her neck with a nervous smirk, hiding their true intentions.

"Yea we appreciate it, Jay," Drew added, with more finesse than Sumi.

"No problem, as long as Levi's taking care of the finances, we're fine," Jake replied.

"Don't remind me," Levi retorted.

We must be getting closer already, Drew thought.

Just as Levi predicted Jake hadn't asked any questions like why Drew was holding a glowing rock attached to a necklace when he picked them up. He just followed the directions Drew gave.

Guiding a driver with the stone was not easy. Sometimes they had to turn around obstructions like roadblocks and the stone would get dimmer until they were back on track. It lacked the accuracy of a compass, but it worked as Drew cross-referenced it with his map app.

The stone suddenly glowed its brightest, momentarily blinding Drew, who had been staring at it intently. He blinked and heard Levi say something.

"What did you say, Motor? I didn't catch that," Drew asked.

"I was saying, I think we've reached our destination, man."

Drew looked up. There were still spots in his vision from where the full force of the silvery brightness had burned into his retinas, but he blinked rapidly to clear them and looked out the windscreen through blurry eyes.

There was a huge mansion directly in front of them. It was set in the middle of an enormous field and had a gate in front. The mansion looked old but not in the way old things were expected to look. It wasn't broken down or ugly or sporting a haunted house look, no. With its stoned-wall exterior, steeply slanted roof, two elaborate bricked chimneys, decorated narrow doorway, the mansion looked like something from the Tudor era of the documentaries Drew watched with his father. He could tell, somehow, that whoever lived there was not the average rich person and had been rich for many years. The giant property proclaimed vast wealth in a subtle way. Drew wondered who owned the place.

"Okay, who lives here? Bruce Wayne?" Sumi echoed his thoughts, her voice dripping with sarcasm.

"We can find that out easily enough. Let's get out of the car," Levi commanded.

"So, what do you guys need me to do? If I stsay around, time is money!" Jake barked.

"Uhh yeah, about that. You can go ahead and do your routes. We shouldn't be too long. Besides, I saw a little diner not too far away from here. If anything, we'll wait for you there."

"Cool. And I'll see if I can work out a discount for you, bro. Just call me when you are done with this project," Jake mused.

"I guess I have to go into my savings for this one, sheesh," Levi answered as the other two chuckled.

They all got out of the car and Levi's brother drove away.

Drew put the still glowing rock into his pocket and turned to face his friend.

"Okay we're here, now what's the plan?" He asked.

Levi didn't answer immediately. Sumi just whipped out her phone and started swiping and tapping the screen. Drew and Levi watched her in silence. She must have found something because she suddenly smiled.

"Found it!" She proclaimed at last. "Found what?" Levi asked.

"The guy who owns this house, of course."

"But how?" This time it was Drew who fired the question.

"Okay," Sumi went on. "I used an old mod-app I made. It's called GaiaMaps. I wanted to improve on the map apps on our phones since they were so lame—"

"Oh, I've heard of that app," Levi interrupted.

Drew and Sumi both looked at Levi, knowing he was lying. Levi tried to get under Sumi's skin with that comment as often as possible.

"Anyway, this mod has all the typical features. Street names, directions, and all that stuff. But the difference is that I created an algorithm to get more information on registered buildings and houses that show up through the app once you aim your phone at your target. So, I looked this place up. All you have to do is hold the camera up at the place after you input the address and you see all the info you need, including the owner."

"Wow. Nice one, Sumi. So, what did you find?" Drew asked.

Sumi replied by holding the phone out to them. They could clearly see where the name of the owner of the house was written. Drew read it out loud.

"The app describes the place as a mansion that's the property of Nox Comms."

"Nox Comms? Sounds familiar," Levi pondered out loud, hoping to recall anything with his eyes squinted and finger to his chin.

"Uhh...yeah!" Sumi chimed. "Guys, it's the name of this fast-rising communication company. This adds up, since their headquarters is downtown. I wrote an article about this company on my tech blog last week. I guess you guys didn't really subscribe when I told you to. Just wow."

"Well, I was gonna, but you see what had happened was…" Levi started trying to explain.

While Levi and Sumi were arguing, Drew realized after Sumi's comment about the company, that his deductions about the owner of the house being not-so-average had been right after all. He pulled out his phone to learn more about the history of the company but realized that his phone was already dead from using it during the car.

"Dead again, huh?" Levi pointed out with a smirk on his face.

"Seriously Drew, you need phone intervention," Sumi remarked.

He suddenly remembered something. He reached for his backpack and pulled it open, making sure his back was turned to his friends so they couldn't see the inside of the backpack. He still hadn't told them about the journal because of his dad's instructions. It would be awkward if they found out about the pictures without warning. It was really difficult to keep things from them, but he knew it was for the greater good. His dad's phone was at the bottom of the backpack. Drew couldn't remember the exact reason why he had thrown it in there but was suddenly glad that he had. He brought it out and unlocked it.

Drew turned to Sumi and Levi.

"My dad left this in the car. I'm glad I nabbed it when I did. Give me a sec guys, I'm gonna do a quick research."

He began reading the company's bio from the internet and saw that it was founded by Mr. Darian Nox, a former stock investor who cashed out big and decided to venture into communications and tech.

"So… what next?" Sumi asked.

"I don't know," Drew answered. They stood there, staring at the large steel-enforced security gate, undecided.

After a couple of minutes, Drew decided to simply contact the number listed in the app about the property. As he started to type the number on his father's phone the number immediately pulled up from the missed call log under the name "Investor".

What in the world...Dad, you know this guy?

Drew thought for a while, suddenly recalling his dad saying he was going to meet up with some investors.

"Guys... my dad... I think Dad was in contact with this Nox guy," Drew revealed. "Now, when I think about it, the other day, he mentioned something about meeting some investors. Maybe *he* was the investor."

"Wow, that would make sense. This is all starting to connect," Sumi emphasized.

"Yeah. This is really getting crazy," Drew responded.

"Ok. I got it. D, let me see your phone," Levi ordered, transforming back into detective mode.

Drew and Sumi turned to Levi as Drew handed over the phone that had helped them make this sudden breakthrough.

"Alright," Levi continued. "Real-talk guys, let's head on over to that diner we passed and grab something to eat. I'm starving."

The second Levi finished speaking, Drew became acutely aware of his hunger.

"Yeah. And instead of barging in like last time, we probably need to really plan this one out," Sumi added.

They all nodded in agreement and the three of them moved away from Mr. Nox's mansion, searching for a place to eat. They figured that until they could flesh out their plan, they might as well not do it on an empty stomach.

It was getting late, and the sky was painted with hues of orange and pink as it neared sunset. The group had a perfect view of the landscape as they walked up the street near a few restaurants. They found the diner Levi mentioned blocks away from the Mansion. It had a simple and forgettable name, Gabe's Kitchen, or something along those lines. The three friends trooped in and sat at a table in the corner. Not long after they settled down, a young waitress came to their table and asked what they would like.

"I'll have your smoked-bacon cheddar burger, with fries, and a coke," Levi requested.

"Same," Sumi added.

The waitress turned to Drew expectantly. He didn't have an appetite for anything, but he knew he had to eat something to keep his strength up.

"Same thing, but with root beer instead of coke," He responded. The waitress nodded and walked away.

The crew spent the entirety of their waiting time discussing everything that previously happened, hoping to puzzle everything together.

"So, this Nox guy. If he is really the investor and he knows my pops, do you think we can trust him?" Drew asked.

"We don't know for sure," Levi answered. "Can we check your dad's phone for any other information?"

Drew was about to say something but at that exact moment, the waitress returned with their food. He waited as she laid out the plates and drinks. Then, when she walked away for the second time, he looked at Levi.

"Dad didn't really like storing important info on his phone," he told his friend. "But sure, check."

Levi just shrugged and kept tapping with one hand while eating with the other. Drew forced himself to eat as well. The food was surprisingly good. He found himself devouring his burger and was on his fries when Levi's face lit up.

"You found something?" Drew asked, speaking for the first

time in minutes.

Levi nodded.

"I found some voice recordings titled '**Project Notes**'. I think we might be onto something here," he proclaimed. His excitement was infectious. The three of them bent forward to see the phone's screen. Levi placed it on the table and pressed the play button on the voice note.

"Alright. Let's hear what your dad has to say, D," Levi whispered.

The recording started to play, and Drew heard his dad speaking so clearly it was as if he was at the table with them.

"Alright. Day Forty-Six. Err... progress report. So, the tracker is almost complete. Three complete tests conducted so far. I've been able to modulate the signals and adjust the sensitivity of the tracker. As I have noted in previous reports, I've gained access to the satellite which will aid me in rerouting the signals. Hopefully, by the time I run final diagnostics, the tracker will be ready to run."

There was a click sound and the recording stopped. "Is that all?" Sumi asked.

Drew glanced down at the phone, seeing that the voice message they had just listened to contained a couple of subsequent recordings.

"There's more. But before we listen to them, I think we should talk about what we just heard," Drew noted, as the others nodded their assent.

"So, your dad's invention was a tracker?" Sumi asked, sipping the last of her drink.

"And it connects to a satellite. That's crazy," Levi added.

"Yes, but what is this tracker supposed to find?" Sumi wondered.

"I think we'll learn that in the next voice note," Drew answered and tapped the phone screen once. Once again, his dad's voice floated out of the phone's speakers.

"Day Fifty-One. Synchronization complete. The tracker has linked perfect-

ly with the satellite and is now fit to track the required radiation signatures. I have curated a list of persons of interest and will try to verify if they are among the people I need to find. Of course, I need a key of some sort. A reference to the radiation signature that triggers the tracker's sensors. For that purpose, I'll use the special stone pendant. I should probably have an earthlier scientific name for it, but I've never been good at naming things. If only Drew knew about this project, I'm sure he would have the perfect names for everything. Maybe I should call it the glowstone? It does glow when in contact with the radiation signature, making it the perfect reference key... but it all sounds so unoriginal. Hmm. Well, I'm logging off for this session. Hopefully, the investors will be pleased with the upgrades I've made."

The recording ended and the three friends looked at each other in stunned silence.

"Okay, that was a lot of information," Levi stressed.

"We finally know what this is for," Drew asserted, drawing the necklace out of his pocket. The stone was still glowing and felt warm in his hand.

"The key," Sumi pointed out, nodding. "But what's responsible for this radiation signature that the tracker is supposed to follow?"

"I don't know. There's still so much we don't know," Drew replied, frustrated.

"We know that the investors were deeply involved with the project," Levi concluded.

"Wait a minute, guys," Sumi paused with her arms in stop motion. "Why don't we call the investors with your dad's phone? We might be able to learn important things before they realize he's not the one on the line. It's worth a shot, right?"

"I don't know Sums, it's a very risky move." Drew replied scratching the back of his head. "But what choice do we really have at this point? Let's go for it."

Drew picked up his dad's phone and scrolled to the contacts.

He searched till he found the number saved simply as *Investor*, took a deep breath, and called the number.

They all waited patiently.

The phone was picked up on the second ring.

"Hello? Blake?" A masculine voice responded from the other side of the connection.

"Yeah. Um, yeah. This is Blake," Drew stuttered in a passable imitation of his dad's voice.

"You're not Blake," the voice snapped sharply.

The phone was on hands-free mode so Levi and Sumi could hear the whole conversation. They both frowned, unsure of what to do next. But Drew made a quick decision to be partially honest with this mysterious investor, hoping that would get them the answers they needed.

"Err, you're right. This isn't Blake," Drew started. "I'm his son. You see, something has happened, and my dad is currently unavailable. The strange thing is he left his phone here at home. I haven't been able to hear from him for hours. So, I went through his phone to see if I could find anything to help me. He did mention you a couple of times so I thought you might have an idea where he is."

He finished talking and his friends nodded. He confessed the right thing, not revealing too much because they still weren't sure if the investors knew about his dad's abduction.

"Well, kid, I don't know where your dad is. Maybe you should go to the police," the investor responded.

Disappointed, but not willing to back down, Drew spoke more forcefully, bending so close to the phone that his nose was touching the screen.

"We can't go to the police. There has to be something you know. Please try to remember," he pleaded.

There was a moment of hesitation from the investor, then he

sighed.

"Okay. I seem to remember one thing. There's this sci-fi convention taking place near downtown. It's been there for over a week now. The name of it always slips my mind...it's something-con. I met your dad there a couple of times. Maybe he's in the area."

Drew looked up at the others. He raised his eyebrows. Levi shrugged and Sumi made a cutting motion. He nodded.

"Alright. Thank you so much, Mr.—"

But the investor was gone. The call had been disconnected.

Drew sat back in his chair. By now, they had all finished eating, and the waitress came over again with the bill.

"Don't even think about it," Drew told his friends as they both made motions towards pockets or wallets. He took out some money and paid the waitress then looked at his friends.

"So, what now?" Levi asked.

"Do we go back to Nox's mansion, the convention center, or your place?" Sumi asked, looking at Drew.

Drew got to his feet and stood for a moment, thinking hard. "We've come this far. The investor is suspicious. He seems to know more than he's letting on. He doesn't know we've been to the convention center already. I think we should go back to the mansion, see what we can find."

With that, they trooped out of the cafe and walked in the direction they had come from. The decision had been made quietly. They would return to the mansion for answers.

The gates stood in front of them, imposing and distinctly ominous. It was getting late. Drew stood still, looking up at the place. There was a possibility that Mr. Nox was also involved in the whole thing but there was no sure way to know unless they went ahead and tried to find answers to their many questions.

The necklace was in Drew's hand, still glowing. He wondered if the radiation signature his dad had mentioned was somehow present in the mansion. Maybe his dad's tracker was there also.

"I think we should go in," he blurted out.

Levi and Sumi looked at him as if he had run out of his mind.

"You're kidding me, right?" Levi interjected; his eyebrows raised comically.

"Drew, we don't even know this guy. We can't just break into someone's house because some weird glowy stone led us there." Sumi cautioned reasonably.

Drew knew his friends were right, but he couldn't bear to turn back now. He had to do something to help his father. But how? Should he go forward or backwards? He had never been so confused before.

"Err...D? Care to share what's on your mind, bro?" Levi wondered.

"Y...Yeah, sorry," Drew stammered. "I'm thinking we have no other option. We should ring the bell and ask to see Mr. Nox. He might know something."

His friends looked at themselves, resignation mirrored on both their faces.

"Okay. We do it your way," Levi declared.

Drew nodded gratefully at them and turned towards the gate. As he walked closer, he saw that above the gate, there was a camera that was probably sending a live feed of anyone who approached the property to some monitor in the large house. Drew took a deep breath and raised a hand to the buzzer.

Hang in there, Dad. After this, I'm coming.

He pressed down on the buzzer. The crew weren't prepared for what happened next.

CHAPTER THIRTEEN

FAR FAR AWAY

It happened too fast. So fast that they had no time to react.

Immediately after Drew pressed the buzzer, there was a sound of running feet and the gate slid open as if it was being controlled by an unseen remote controller.

"What the-"

Several men trooped out of the property, all of them clad in black. There were no visible weapons but there was an air of danger around the men, something that screamed that they were hard and merciless.

"Um, hello. We're looking for—"

That was as far as Drew got before he was interrupted by a deep voice. A man's voice.

"Looking for me?"

The speaker stepped right into sight. He was a man of medium height and build, with light brown skin, dressed in a fitting black suit that subtly announced its worth. His shoes were also on the expensive side, as was the Rolex on one wrist. There was something about him that immediately put Drew on his guard. He couldn't quite put his finger on it.

Like the men in black, one could sense that this man too was a dangerous person, not to be trifled with. But where the men seemed violent and harsh, the man in the suit was like a snake, cold and calculating and more dangerous than all of the rest combined.

"Who... who are you?" Drew asked, finding his voice at last.

No, the phone call...that's...

The man smiled, a slight twitch of his lips, a smile that did not touch his cold eyes.

"You may call me Darian, my boy. All my friends call me Darian," He announced.

"Darian Nox?"

"The one and the same," Nox confessed with his hands extended out in arrogance, as if he was a prize.

Suddenly, realization dawned on Drew. He put everything together, seeing a pattern. His dad had probably come to this man. They had spoken about his dad's invention, maybe. Drew looked around at the men in black. There was no doubt in his mind. These were part of the same guys who had attacked them at the convention center. That could only mean one thing. The men in black worked for Darian Nox.

Drew reached into his pocket to hide the stone away. He knew he had to protect it by any means necessary. He couldn't let it fall into the hands of the bad guys. But even as he thought about this, two of the men surrounding them marched forward and pinned his hands to his back. As Drew struggled to get them off, one of the men reached into Drew's pocket and brought out the stone, which was still glowing, and took it back to Nox, leaving Drew restrained by the other man.

"Good. Bring them inside," Nox commanded and spun on his heel, walking towards the house. The men obeyed promptly. There was nothing the kids could do. They were well outnumbered. As Levi and Sumi stood there in silence, scowling at the guards with fists clenched, they could only think of one solution. Fight.

Suddenly, a scuffle broke up the stare down as a few of the men tried to restrain Levi, who managed to punch one of them in the face. He was rushed by many others and held firmly while cursing them out. Sumi glared at the men that approached her, silently daring them to lay hands on her. Something in her eyes must have warned them because they just formed a circle around her as she followed the boys.

They were led in the direction of the main house entrance, which Nox had disappeared into moments ago, the narrowness of the door forcing them to march in single file. Drew tried to call on the surge of strength that had saved him at the convention center, but he couldn't find it.

What is this...my abilities...did I do it wrong? Drew thought.

Maybe it only comes when I'm in immediate danger.

Drew saw that they were being led into a massive high-ceiling great room. The room looked like a large wood and stone built library, something they would've read about in a fairytale, with a large stone fireplace at one end and a formal dining and bar area at the other. A huge chandelier hung from above, and an enormous rhinocerous head can be seen mounted on the far end of the wall. Chairs were scattered across the room, but directly to the right of the rhino mount, there was a big leather chair that looked like it belonged in some kind of executive office.

Nox was seated in the chair. He watched them troop in, eyes focused on Drew, who was looking around for the necklace. The stone was nowhere to be seen.

"Welcome, Drew. Make yourself at home," Nox motioned.

"How do you know me? And why did you betray my dad?" Drew spat. His hands were held by two of the men in black. Levi and Sumi were also held to his left.

Mr. Nox shifted in his leather chair, the smile still on his lips, his eyes still cold.

"Why?" He scoffed, quickly shifting his disapproving look to a sinister smirk. "I believe that is the wrong question, my boy. To know why, you need to know how. And the *how* is so incredible, it would only provide more insight."

"Whoever you are, just tell us what we need to know!" Levi demanded.

Mr. Nox's eyes flicked to Levi's face and away. He looked back at Drew. "You, I know. But who are they?"

"These are my friends," Drew sneered through gritted teeth.

"Oh," Mr. Nox wondered. He looked at Levi and Sumi with something close to disdain. "You dragged these... humans into your problems, eh?"

"What do you mean by 'these humans', man?" Levi growled. "You some kind of racist?"

"Why are you trying to look down on us? We're all human here, so relax on the bigotry," Sumi protested.

Mr. Nox laughed out loud, catching them by surprise. It was laughter without warmth, high and cold. He threw back his head as he laughed, looking exactly like the villains Drew had seen in the superhero movies he liked to watch.

"A human. Me. How humorous," Mr. Nox chuckled. He rose

from the leather chair and started pacing with his hands clasped behind his back.

"My name…my real name…" he briefly paused. "…is Vozyr."

Levi gave Drew a sideways glance that seemed to say, *Yo, this dude thinks he's in a movie or some shit?*

Drew wasn't as skeptical as his friend. The name had a musical quality to it. It reminded Drew of the markings he had seen on the time capsule he had found in his attic. Some dormant part of his mind was whispering to him that the name had a meaning.

Vozyr means strong one.

He was sure about it. He was suddenly filled with great dread. Somehow, he knew some of the things Mr. Nox was going to say next, even though the mere idea was extremely suspicious.

"I know you'll find this difficult to believe, but I am not human. Not at all. I am what you humans would call an alien," he proclaimed.

Levi snorted. "Yo, I don't know what kind of drugs you've been on, but you need to stop man. There are no aliens. You're just rich, it's close enough though," he mocked.

"Look, there's no need for you to lie, okay? We know you're one of the people who captured Drew's dad. So just tell the truth and stop making up stories," Sumi asserted.

Drew did not speak a word. He just stared at Mr. Nox, dumbfounded.

"Humans," Mr. Nox hissed, affirming his hatred with an expression of disgust. "Filled with so much potential yet so annoyingly naive. You are a species that overestimates its own importance. Even though you have been blessed with great resources, you have not begun to scratch the surface of all the wondrous things you could achieve. You have made movies and written stories about UFOs and aliens and parallel universes, but whenever you're faced with the possibility of one of these things being real, your first response is not curiosity or wonder but stark fear and disbelief."

He stopped talking long enough to dab at his forehead with a white handkerchief. Then he continued.

"I tell you I am an alien, but you do not believe me. It seems I need to show you rather than tell you. That has always worked. Show, don't tell. It worked for my home planet. We were shown the terrors that were to come, not told. But by then, it was too late. Too late."

He paused again; this time apparently lost in thought. His eyes were fixed on something far off. Drew thought he knew that look. It was the look his dad wore sometimes.

"You bragged that you're gonna show us. Show us, then," Levi dared, snapping Nox out of his reverie.

Mr. Nox smiled and slipped a hand into his pocket.

"You might want to close your eyes," he casually suggested.

The three friends didn't obey until it was too late. What their captor brought out of his pocket was a ball of fierce light. It burned like a miniature sun. They closed their eyes quickly, but they could still see spots. Drew was especially affected. His eyes, which were now quite sensitive, felt like they had been pricked by thousands of burning needles.

"I warned you," Mr. Nox smirked. "You may open your eyes now."

They obeyed quicker this time and saw what laid on Nox's outstretched palm. It was not a star or a ball of energy. It was Drew's necklace. The rock was glowing brighter than ever, still too bright to look at directly.

"This is your proof. This is no ordinary rock, as your primitive minds might have guessed. This is a rock from my home planet. It is connected to a planet in a different solar system which means it is still part of that system. I know you don't understand. What I'm saying is, this rock has the physical and chemical properties of my planet's living things. There is a glowing effect when we walk close to these rocks. This fragment acts just like the whole. It glows when it comes in contact with one of my people. I suspect that's how you found me, yes? By following the glow?"

He didn't wait for an answer from the blinking teenagers. "So, there you have it. An alien. But as you can see, I am not two feet tall. I do not have one eye or blue skin. I look like any human. In fact, I might say I look better than most humans," he paused and chuckled. "I am from a superior race... One far superior to yours in technology. We are light years ahead of this excuse for a planet. We have always been and will always be. So, tell me, do you believe me now?"

He stopped pacing and stepped forward, looking at them, a wolfish expression on his face. His eyes were a different otherworldly shade from what they had been the first time they saw him. He seemed both taller and shorter than before. Somehow, his true alien form was somewhere under his skin. All that talk of who he was must have triggered his true self to surface, but he seemed to have it under control. He only let them see enough to erase any doubts they had left. The guards that held them remained still, seemingly unfazed by this revelation.

Drew looked around at his friends to see their expressions. Levi's face was white. He wasn't even struggling with the man holding him anymore. He looked like someone who had just gotten a rude awakening. He was very afraid and for the first time since Drew had met him, he had no witty remark to make, no snappy retort. Sumi's face was impressively impassive. She returned Vozyr's feral glare without flinching but somehow Drew knew she was also scared.

He realized that Nox, or Vozyr or whatever he was, had been right. Humans would always react with fear.

And what does that make me? I am human and I am not afraid.

He was sure about it. He was feeling many things at that moment but fear of the unknown alien standing in front of them wasn't one of them. He closed his eyes and tried to think.

We have to get out of here. It might be difficult, but we have to try. We need answers, dammit. I need answers. I have to be sure that I'm not—

"So? You believe it now? I want answers before I continue," Nox asked, seething on the inside.

The three of them glanced at each other and they all nodded slightly.

"Good," Mr. Nox retorted, looking completely human again. The fake smile was back on his lips. He straightened his suit and focused all of his attention on Drew once more.

"So, my boy. Where did I stop?" He paused, just for a moment. "OH, yes, humans. I've been here far too long. Well over 80 years."

Drew immediately thought about the picture he had found back in his house.

"We sought refuge here from an attack on our own planet. We couldn't defeat our enemies; they were much too powerful.

We could harness the energy of our stars, but they could do so much more. They were like demi-gods. In the end, we had no choice but to come here. The energy signature in this system was much too low for them to feel threatened. They will only go after galaxies with real 'potential.'"

This guy loves to hear himself talk. He must not have seen superhero movies before. Let's see if we can get him going some more, Drew thought.

"That doesn't explain why you want my father," Drew snapped.

"Yes. I was getting there. You see, I knew your father. In fact, you can say we are very…very old friends."

"What are you trying to say?" Levi shouted. "D's father is in on your scheme?"

"Levi!" Sumi barked.

Drew could not speak. He had already begun piecing the puzzle together.

"Ha ha! You humans are so slow! I may not look it, but I have been through very trying times here. When I arrived, it was such a horrible era. What you humans…you…these Americans were doing to people that looked like us. It was beyond our understanding. I learned of your…American history… and traveled across the country. I saw the impact of your ways towards one another. It was no different than what I saw in other places around the world. I realized that this was normal to you people. Hundreds of years of hate and bondage for people that looked and spoke differently, I felt compassion. I wanted to do something. I wanted to help. I joined the Civil Rights movement in the south. It was then that I came around to meeting-"

He stopped mid-sentence with a stunned look as if a surprising detail had just struck his mind. As his stunned look slowly turned into a menacing glance, he smirked at Drew. He looked at both Sumi and Levi and turned back to Drew. By the concerned look on Drew's face, he realized that the young man knew the truth, but was hiding something else.

Drew's heart started beating rapidly. He knew that at any moment the secret he has been trying to hide this whole time was getting ready to be exposed. While everything was extremely hard for him to grasp, nothing was more pressing than his friends learning about his very strange past.

Nox slowly made his way towards Drew. Levi and Sumi got riled up again, unsure of what he was going to do, but the men who held them didn't let them move.

Nox calmly reached over to brush Drew's face with his hand. He leaned over towards Drew's ear and spoke in a whisper.

"You poor kid. They don't know…do they?

CHAPTER FOURTEEN

BEYOND THE TRUTH

Drew didn't reply. He tried to act as if he had no idea what Mr. Nox was saying.

I must not let him know too much about me. This guy may be insane but he's dangerous.

"You didn't tell your human friends about your origins, eh?" Mr. Nox whispered in Drew's ear. "You don't trust them, boy?"

"What origins?" Drew muttered, feigning ignorance. Mr. Nox chuckled in amusement, not buying Drew's pretense.

"We've been monitoring you, we know what happened to your memories…how sad, if only you knew your…real potential."

Potential…what is he talking about…these…abilities?

"You must have at least found something by now, boy. Maybe

a note or a picture. Why didn't you show it to these dimwitted humans?"

So, he knows about the pictures? But how?

As if Nox could read his thoughts, he smiled and tapped Drew's forehead with his forefinger.

"I know, it still hasn't hit you yet, huh? We have met before. Oh, yes. I don't think you'll remember though. You were a mere child back then, in the fifties. You don't remember?"

Droplets of sweat began to nervously emerge from Drew's forehead as he took a big gulp to remain silent. Nox examined the boy's face for a couple more seconds and spun on his heel suddenly, walking back towards his big chair.

"Sometimes, even you humans can be right. Many times, you have come very close to uncovering tremendous discoveries that could change things forever on a cosmic scale, but your ignorance and ineptitude has always held you back from accomplishing true greatness. You know, in the fifties, there was this huge widespread alien invasion scare here on Earth. Humans ran around exchanging wild stories and reporting UFO sightings and stuff like that. It was to be expected, I guess. Even humans had to notice the number of extraterrestrial visitors landing in their backyards. Many of our ship's parts were found here and there, but never a full craft. We had to destroy the ships or hide them away; we knew humans were not ready to harness our technology."

Nox stopped talking for a couple of seconds. There was absolute silence in the large room. He had their attention, and he was taking a moment to savor being the center of it.

Dude should be a politician or a celebrity, running his mouth like this, Drew thought.

"Our arrival was noted in your news. Fortunately, as a *government conspiracy*," Nox continued. "You know, I still find it hilarious when

I hear humans say what they think my people look like. Your feeble minds think of us as beings with distorted features: bug eyes and antennas, sickly green screen, scaly skin. I don't blame you for this gross misinterpretation, of course. Part of the reason why we went into hiding was that you were not ready to learn from us. Even now, you are not ready. Maybe in the next hundred years, you humans will finally be able to harness what little potential you have."

"Whoa. Wait a minute, man," Levi blurted. "You keep talking about humans like we're scum or something. I'm sure the way you look down on us is exactly the same way those invaders in your galaxy did."

Nox laughed that same villainous laugh once more.

"You have no idea, boy," he replied to Levi. "If only you've seen the things I have. Oh, all the terrible things you humans do to each other. The invaders of our galaxy showered us with gifts and technological advancement for years before we realized what was happening. But in human history, any two new civilizations that met for the first time were welcomed with death. I have seen the darkest side of humanity, child. Not even the smartest among you are capable of understanding how small you all really are in the universe...No.... there was one...a rather smart human I met once, in St. Petersburg. He was a Russian scientist who had a working theory about other civilizations beyond the scope of Earth. There were several loopholes in his work, of course, but what he had been able to think up impressed me. I pretended to be a visiting professor of astrophysics from another school and over the course of my stay, I subtly influenced and inspired old Nikolai towards deeper truths about extraterrestrial life. I didn't go all out of course. He was exceedingly smart but still, he was only human. He's the one human who has ever had an inkling of the truth of life beyond Earth and maybe he would have been able to unravel all the truths, if he'd had more time, perhaps a couple hundred years. But he was human, and your species doesn't live very long."

Drew got a sudden chill on hearing those last words. If his suspicions were right and his entire family was also from Nox's planet...

How old is Dad, really? Hell, he could be as old as the dinosaurs! This is so crazy. I need to make him keep talking. Maybe he'll reveal more about his home planet. But I can't let Levi and Sumi know I might also be like Nox.

Drew thought for a long moment, then looked in the direction of Nox, who had stopped talking to drink a glass of wine.

"So, this so-called wonderful planet of yours, how exactly is it better than Earth? Without all your advanced tech, would your planet still be greater than Earth? What exactly makes you so special, huh?"

He tried to put as much anger into his words as he could, covering up the interest and curiosity in his mind.

"My people are special, even without our tech," Mr. Nox responded. "Before we made all those spectacular technological advancements, much like your father's device here... we were doing great things. I come from a Type II civilization."

Type II...Just like Dad was saying...Just like the box, Drew thought.

"I don't expect you to understand what that means. All you need to know is that overtime, our rapid evolution helped develop our biological nature even further. In human language, I guess you might say that we have superpowers."

Levi snorted in disbelief. Mr. Nox narrowed his eyes and glanced at him but looked away dismissively and walked towards Drew again.

Drew looked Mr. Nox in the eye and spoke.

"I've got another question for you. Since you hate Earth so much, why don't you just leave? Huh?"

Mr. Nox sighed. He walked back towards his chair. "Opportunity, boy. There is so much potential here and the risk factor is so very low. As long as I work from the shadows, the humans don't suspect a thing."

Mr. Nox sat in his chair and started fiddling with the communication module beside it, obviously trying to get it started.

Sumi frowned. She had been quiet all along, listening and digesting everything Mr. Nox had been saying. Some of the things she had listened to in the last couple of minutes were so unbelievable, she could have laughed at the absurdity, but some other parts were unmistakably true. There was one thing she knew for sure, though. Mr. Nox hated humans. So, when she saw him pressing buttons on the strange machine, she focused on him and spoke at last.

"Hey," Sumi called out. "What are you going to do with that? Is it part of some kind of doomsday device? Are you going to destroy us humans, since you hate us so much?"

Nox chuckled without looking up and made a dismissive gesture with one hand.

"Take them away," he instructed. "Put them in the basement."

The guards pushed the three friends out of the room and as they crossed the threshold to leave, they all heard Nox say one last thing that followed them as they were led away.

"*Survive, for now, children. Especially you...You will be especially useful to me.*"

CHAPTER FIFTEEN

THE LINK

The crew were being moved from the room where Nox was busy with the communication module and as they moved off, the guards demanded their phones and bound their hands behind their backs securely with cuffs. The guards relaxed their grips on the kids as they left Nox's presence and the three friends got the impression that these mercenaries, even with their armored vests and physique, were scared of him. Maybe he had given them a demonstration of his strange alien powers. Or maybe they were just scared of him because he was a crazy rich guy with delusions of ruling the world. Whatever it was, the guards breathed easier when they were out of his presence.

They were taken through a dimly lit stairwell that headed below the mansion. As the echoes of their steps filled the hollowed metal-sheeted passage, the crew noticed this area was fitted with multiple cameras and motion detectors. They knew they were most likely being watched.

Continuing their dissent down the stairwell, the crew were all in silent reflection. In many ways, Nox's speech was a combination of so many things. It was interesting, crazy, sometimes even boring but like his other friends, Levi listened attentively. He didn't want to miss anything that might help them in their possible escape later.

Somehow, we're going to make it out of here. We just need some kinda opening.

Despite their relaxed grips, Levi could not break free from the guard's grasp. They held him tight, and he could feel something digging into his waist the whole time. It was extremely uncomfortable, and he was confused for a while before he remembered what it was.

Man, I totally forgot about it.

Back at Drew's house, he had slid the remote they found in the backyard in the waistline of his trousers. There was no way he could adjust the remote without the guys holding him noticing and discovering it. If there was one thing Levi was certain of, it was that he definitely didn't want the remote to fall into the hands of a crazy guy like Nox.

It triggered some kinda weird reaction from Drew. Who knows what it could be used for in the hands of a maniac like this Nox dude? Maybe Drew can figure out a way for us to use the remote as a means of escape or something.

He tried to get Drew's attention, but his friend was lost in thought as usual, staring off into space, so Levi decided to wait until he got the perfect opportunity.

While he waited for his friend to snap out of his daze and look in his direction, he couldn't help but think about how weird this entire day had been. When he had told his folks that he would be stepping out for a while and called his bro to give him a ride, he hadn't expected the next couple of hours to involve finding strange glowing rocks in his friend's house, or being chased by mysterious men in black, or fighting for his life behind a crowded convention center.

Today went from zero to a hundred real fast, man.

Levi glanced sideways at his two friends to check them out and see how they were holding up. Sumi was listening to Mr. Nox intently as if he was one of the teachers back at Douglass.

Good ol' Sums. She's probably analyzing every bit of what this Nox dude has been saying in that amazing mind of hers.

He looked at Drew next. Drew was blinking as if rousing himself from a deep sleep.

About time, D, Levi thought. *Now, I just need you to notice the glow from the remote's "on" light and start planning how we're gonna bust from this place. C'mon.*

He didn't have to wait for long.

Drew was filled with mixed emotions, right from when Mr. Nox started talking until he gave the order that the crew should be taken to the basement.

What he had learned about his possible origins was a surprise to him, but the price seemed too steep. With all of Mr. Nox's big talk, Drew still wasn't sure what exactly was going on or what plans the rich otherworldly maniac had in store for them.

Also, my powers are still missing.

That last thought wasn't wholly true. He couldn't use his super strength or speed or see far distances. It was as if a switch had been flipped somewhere inside his body, taking all of his powers away. But towards the end of Mr. Nox's long rants, he had started feeling a flicker in his mind. It was so small that it was very easy to miss but somehow, he detected it.

It's like the signal isn't strong enough. Something wants to come out, some power maybe but the signal has some sort of interference. Sumi would know better.

He shook his head to clear it of thoughts and fell into a meditative mode. He knew that if his friends looked in his direction at that moment, he would have a distant look on his face, but he had to try to access his powers. It might be their only way out.

He focused for several moments and could feel his improved senses kicking in and out.

It's like I'm a TV or something and there's a problem with my antenna. But if I'm feeling so funny, what about my friends? How have they coped with all this stuff?

That was when he glanced at his friend and saw the glow. It was not like the harsh light of the stone that Nox had taken from them. It was more of a muted red glimmer and seemed to be coming from something under Levi's shirt. It seemed to be turning on and off every time Levi shifted his weight. Drew wondered what it could be, but he arrived at a conclusion quickly.

It could only be the mysterious remote that had briefly activated his powers back at the house. The longer he thought about it, the more sense it made.

The remote must be able to give out some kinda signal that activates my powers. But I haven't been able to use my powers since we entered this compound. Hmmm. There must be some kind of suppressing force on my powers; but maybe the remote can override the field of disruption.

They finally arrived at the basement level but were met with a huge door guarded by two additional guards. As one guard gave a command to the other, the door opened up to an underground bunker. They were all visibly shocked, but silent.

This guy even has a whole bunker under this mansion. How much money does he really have? And why would he need a bunker? This guy must really believe in this villain thing, Drew thought.

The bunker was crawling with guards. They stationed themselves at every entrance, corner and exit. Some sat in clusters, making jokes and sharing drinks. It didn't matter what they did, there were always two guards stationed in front of their cage. For the most part, the guards went about their business, totally ignoring the presence of the crew. It was obvious it wasn't their first-time putting people in cages. The cell was at the far end of the basement. It wasn't too big, but it was big enough and one could look inside through the thick steel bars. The guards pushed them through the cell door and locked them in, ignoring Levi's questions and protests. Two of the men stood guard outside the cage while the rest marched back up the stairs.

Once they were placed in a holding cell with one another, Drew's plan was finally in motion. Levi managed to catch Drew's eye at last. Drew made a gesture towards his friend's waist and the remote hidden there. He silently told him to press the activation button once again. Levi smiled in relief. He understood immediately and began leaning towards the side of the remote. This trick forced the pressure of his weight to switch the button on again, as he has been doing unaware this whole time.

Whoa...so I can feel something. Ok, let me see if this works, Drew thought.

Sumi saw them exchange several meaningful glances and realized that they probably had a plan to help them get out of the basement. She didn't ask them what it was though. She was aware of the proximity of the guards, just like the boys. She knew that if they spoke at all then it had to be about subjects that wouldn't rouse the suspicion of the silent guards. After several attempts to stretch the links of his cuffs to a breaking point, Drew was finally able to weaken them.

Sumi was shocked, unaware of how this was able to happen. Levi was also impressed, despite being the one with the idea. Drew's wrist burned with the effort, but he had managed to give his hands freer space.

Seems my powers are coming back. Good timing.

The first thing he tested was his telepathy, partly because he really wanted to hear his dad's voice again. He wanted to assure the anxious and worried part of his mind that his dad was okay.

He didn't look so good the last time I saw him. I really hope these clowns haven't hurt him or anything.

He focused on his mind and reached out to his father, wherever he might be.

Hey, Dad. Can you hear me? Dad, it's me. Do you copy?

There was no answer. Drew hadn't really been expecting a reply, but he still felt a slight disappointment. All he could hear was white noise. He was about to give up and try something else when—

A connection.

He focused harder and sensed it. He couldn't tell how he knew but he was sure about it.

Pops...he's coming.

He tried to screen his father's emotions for signs of anxiety or panic but found nothing. It didn't seem like his father was in pain. Drew dared to hope that everything was alright and that his father was unhurt and coming to save him, but he couldn't be sure.

Please, be alright, Pops. Please.

CHAPTER SIXTEEN

DEVIL YOU KNOW

There were few things in the world Blake hated more than being locked up.

He had been interrupted just before he could telepathically explain things to Drew and was knocked out by unknown men. Several times in the past few hours, he had mentally kicked himself for his complacency.

The look on his face when I denied him as my son...Alice...What kind of father have I become? I should have made sure that I wasn't followed home. I should have constantly watched my back. I shouldn't have let my guard down.

He knew that no amount of blaming himself could make things right but there was nothing else for him to do. He tried not to think of how confused his son must be.

I'm so sorry, Son. I know you can't hear me right now but I'm truly sorry for everything.

There were several shacks at the back of the convention center. After the kids were violently taken away, Blake's captors marched him over to one of the shacks and pushed him through the door, locking it behind him.

He sighed and looked around. The small space was bare. There was no furniture, just unpainted walls and a dirty floor. Since he had no alternative, he sat on the floor and waited. He didn't know what he was waiting for, but he used the time and silence to do some thinking.

Strange things are happening. That person on the phone, the one who spoke to me in the van, he seems to be the one behind all of this. He admitted that I may know him. He calls me his friend...It may be possible that this person... It has to be. I'll confirm once I speak to him again.

He didn't know how long he waited in that empty room; he estimated it was about two hours maybe, but he wasn't sure. At some point though, he started to get hungry and more uncomfortable. He was just about to lose control when the door slammed open and two of the men came in. They were both holding big guns and pointed them at Blake.

"Get up," one of them ordered. Blake obeyed with a sigh.

"Come with us," the same guy commanded. He walked out and Blake followed, the other gunman behind him. As they stepped out of the dim room, Blake looked up at the sky.

Doesn't seem like much time has passed, he thought. He followed the gunman to another of the stalls. The door was opened, and he went in with his entourage. This room was different from the one where he had been held previously. Unlike his first cell, this room showed signs that it had been recently occupied. There was a chair in the middle of the room facing the far wall where a large TV was mounted. Blake walked to the chair without waiting to be told and sat. He had thought about everything that had happened and most of his doubts about who was responsible were gone. He knew for certain that it was his old friend but what he didn't know was why his friend would betray his own people in this way.

While he was thinking of all the possible reasons why his old friend might have chosen this path, the screen of the TV flickered to life and a shadowy silhouette appeared. He already knew who it was, of course. The silhouette started speaking in a very familiar voice and the rest of Blake's doubts vanished.

"My friend," the voice boomed through the speaker, "...or should I call you... *Yaegr*?" Blake had not heard that name in decades and it felt strange to hear it now. It was the name he had been given at birth, in the advanced language of his people.

"Vozyr," Blake replied with a nod. "I see that you've changed a lot."

There was silence from the TV, so Blake kept talking. "What exactly happened to you? Huh? The Vozyr I knew was an honorable person. You were never the kind of man to resort to violence to settle matters or hide in the shadows while others did the dirty work. What happened? Why did you change?"

Vozyr chuckled in disdain.

"How could you possibly understand me? You have mostly been sheltered during all your years here on this despicable planet. You have not seen the things I have seen. You have not lost all that I have lost. My metamorphosis isn't a recent thing. I changed decades ago. When I arrived, at first, I was as naive as the rest of our people. The wiser ones among us tried to dissuade us from interfering in human affairs, but we pushed them away. I was one of the optimistic ones. The humans were a very fragile bunch. I wanted to bring peace to this chaotic world. I wanted to bring equality and prosperity. I saw everything as either black or white in those days, old friend. I was okay with fighting for the rights of the marginalized people. Maybe I saw the similarities between them and our own people. In a way, they were so much like us when we revolted against the Invaders of our galaxy. I couldn't just stand by."

The shadowy shape in the TV stopped talking for a moment. Blake opened his mouth to talk but before he could, Vozyr continued.

"Don't you recall? I was so passionate in those days. So... driven. I used all of my abilities to try to make good triumph over evil. But there was no hope."

"That's when you disappeared completely. Alice and I looked for you all those years... but you could not be found," Blake added.

"Yes, that was when the Vozyr you knew died, my friend. That was when I retreated into the shadows and became a... a mastermind, one who found more creative ways of getting money."

"So, you lost your morals and forgot all the things you stood for because you were disappointed by human behavior?" Blake countered, clenching his fist.

"Morals?" Vozyr laughed scornfully again. "What are morals? You are even more naive than I thought. All these years of mingling with humans and interacting with them has softened you. You do not think like one of us anymore. Your mind is no longer sharp and focused. I can feel it even from where I am. You are weak, Blake. You know nothing."

"Just answer the question," Blake growled through gritted teeth.

"Alright, then. After decades of watching humans destroy themselves and their pathetic world, I realized something. All the things I had experienced first-hand, like famines, genocides, economic collapse, wars, pandemics and so on were caused by humans. But it wasn't entirely their fault. They needed a guiding hand. You could say I took a cue from those madmen that invaded our planet. I decided to follow their example and attempt to subjugate a planet in order to usher its people into a new age of all-round advancement. I had learned a lot about humans and their systems. I first took an interest in their politics. Unfortunately, that backfired dramatically. But then, I took a particular interest in the economy and finance. There is a saying that interested me. *Money makes the world go round.* I realized that if one wanted to control the world, the one thing that could help was mastery over money. So, I started looking for ways to accrue more wealth. I got assets and bought stocks and made investments. It wasn't enough. I moved my investments to drug trafficking operations in South America. I seized control over a few illegal arms dealing operations in Sudan."

He continued, "I did it all--poaching, illegal pharmaceuticals, laundering, you name it. Because of my position in the shadows, competitors never knew who exactly they were dealing with and one by one they were either convinced to merge with my businesses or erased from existence by my men. I joined a group simply called *The Invisible Hand.* All you need to know about them is that they make sure that my hands are always clean of my dealings. I move with the times, you see. Until recently, I was exclusively interested in the tech sector. But the humans have started seeing the light at last. They are a long way from achieving total technological advancement, but they are several steps closer. They have realized that tech is the future. I saw this before most of them and began buying out small firms in the tech industry, amassing shares in the biggest companies, and later opening my own satellite communications firm. All the ads you see on TV about Nox Comms are just fronts for what we actually do. You see, my eyes have been opened. I have seen that the most important thing, no matter where I am or what I'm doing, is to make profit. And that is exactly what I'm doing with the company."

In some ways, you haven't changed at all. You still love the sound of your own voice, Blake thought.

"So, you delved into the black markets and turned into some kind of faux tech mogul? Do you realize that your black-market activities must have affected so many lives? You sold drugs and weapons and God knows what else. You sponsored terrorism. You did all these and you're talking to me about profit?" Blake asked in discontent. He wished his old friend was in the room with him or that he could at least see his face. He wanted to beat some sense into him.

"Once again you remain ignorant. I am not finished," Nox continued from the TV. "There are different types of profit, and some things are far more valuable than human currency. I pooled all my resources, gathered from decades of both legitimate businesses and black-market operations and started my company. But to date, we have not done a single job for a human, no. Our clients are more... out of this world."

He laughed at his own wordplay then continued.

"You see...Blake...all of our satellites and network towers are not used for local transmissions. We are using our satellites to communicate with the *Ascended Ones.*"

With this comment, Blake's jaw dropped. He couldn't believe what he just heard.

I had my suspicions, but this is too far, even for you!

Before he could put his thoughts into words and speak, however, the image on the TV continued his monologue.

"Yes, you heard right. The *Ascended Ones* are the new opportunity I have devoted my time and attention to. Their superior technology is better even than ours. There is so much possibility, so much that can be done by whoever wields their tech. It was because of this remarkable advancement that their empire was able to conquer our planet and take it for themselves. I used to wonder how we must have looked to them, scurrying about and fighting back with the most sophisticated weapons we had. We threw everything we had at them, but nothing worked. They are a *true* supreme race, my friend, and if there's anything I've learnt in all my years of human activity and this...capitalism, it is that the big guys always win. There is much more to gain from those who have already attained massive success than from 'prospects'. I didn't even have to think about it for long. I pledged my allegiance to them."

As he remained silent, Blake grinded his teeth and clenched his fist again, attempting to withhold his world of anger at bay.

You...Traitor! How could you do this?

"Oh, don't look so mortified," Nox retorted. "I know what you're probably thinking right now: The *Ascended Ones* destroyed our homes and killed our people and made us flee to this unremarkable planet to hide like rats. Yes, all of that is true. But I have survived this long not because I am the smartest or strongest, but because I know the secrets of this game. Stick with the powerful ones and you'll survive when others fall. It's that simple."

Blake feigned disinterest.

"So, you work for them. Good for you. I really don't care, really. You have shown yourself to be without a shred of honor or morality. I don't want to listen to any more of your crazed ranting, Vozyr. These are the things I want to know: why am I here, really? What is going to happen to my son and his friends?"

Blake tried to put as much anger as possible into his words. It wasn't difficult. He was very angry. He hadn't eaten in hours, he was anxious about his son, and mad at himself for getting captured so easily. Most of all, he was angry with his old friend and his crazy monologues. It was quite clear to him that Vozyr had become a threat to everyone in the world.

Even back in our own galaxy, he was always scheming. But at least, at that time, all the plans he was cooking up were intended to promote his people's welfare. Now, however...

Nox's annoying chuckle interrupted Blake's train of thought.

The billionaire who was actually an alien, the former leader of one of his galaxy's most prosperous sectors, the turncoat.

"You have no right to judge me, no no no. Definitely not. You abandoned your people. You took your family and set out for earth. There was never a shred of patriotism in you… and speaking of family, let's not forget what you let happen to yours… poor Alice… you are angry at me, and you think I need help, but you have bigger problems. Isn't that right, *Blake*? What sort of name is that, by the way? What does it even mean?"

Blake was visibly upset but did not answer and Nox's image continued talking.

"There are many words you could use to describe my position under my new… employer. You could call me an enforcer, I suppose. My job description is very simple. I am to find refugees like yourself. Those who survived the escape from our home and hide here on Earth. It's not as easy as it sounds, of course. Our kind are endowed with several interesting abilities and if they do not want to be found, it is difficult to find them. That brings us to why you are here."

"You're going to hand me over to your new masters?" Blake growled.

Even though he couldn't see Nox's face, Blake could hear the frown in his voice when he spoke next.

"I have no masters. I only do their bidding because it suits my interests at this time. When I stop finding them useful, I will move on to something else," he declared.

"Do you really think they will let you go?" Blake asked, his frustration increasing. "What's wrong with you, man? Can't you see that they're just using you? You think you can wake up one day and tell them you're no longer interested in working for them and they'll just let you walk away? You have witnessed the ruthlessness of these people firsthand. Do you really think—"

"Your prattling annoys me," Nox cut in sharply. "You are too much like a human. I am the one who should be asking what's wrong with *you*. You think this is one of those stupid movies humans watch? Now, don't interrupt me again if you really want answers to your questions."

He paused as if waiting for Blake to say something but when he didn't, the billionaire continued.

"The invaders of our galaxy found us because our galactic energy signature output acted as a beacon to them. The reason they have not been able to find us here is because our people on Earth are far outnumbered by the humans, so the signature is difficult to detect. You know all this. Everyone from the Canis Major galaxy knows this. But there's one other thing I know that you know. You know how to find the others. Your project, the one you've been trying so hard to keep secret. You will tell me the access code, my friend. Or else...I will unleash my wrath on Xaeon. Which would be such a shame, since he has so much useful potential that you don't even realize."

"If you touch my son, I'm going to kill you. You hear me?" Blake yelled.

"Fine... have it your way. You have delayed me enough. I have a lot to do. Let me make my phone call to the guards and---"

"Wait... I'll tell you where it is... and I'll tell you the code, just leave my boy alone."

"That's a good soldier! Just like the old days!" Nox mocked as Blake told him the location.

"And what of the code?" Nox inquired.

"A bargaining chip. You give me the kids back and you can have it," Blake responded.

The voice left the threat hanging and the TV went off. Immediately, as if they had been listening at the door, the guards trooped in and surrounded him. He stood up without a word and followed them out of the room.

He dimly realized that they were ushering him towards yet another stall, but he didn't pay attention. He was too busy thinking of his old friend's words, especially the part about seeing his son soon.

I hope Drew and the others are okay. That damned betrayer. I miss you, Son.

Outside the door to the new stall, the men in black checked his restraints to make sure they were tight and when they were satisfied that he couldn't break free, they opened the door and pushed him through.

They gave him a bottle of water and some food and also untied his hands. When they shut the door behind him, he could hear one of them telling the other to stand guard outside and be watchful.

What's there to guard? It's not like I'm a threat. I'm just an old guy who can't even use his powers anymore.

Blake sat on the floor again, resting his back against the wall, staring at the food they had given him. A loaf of bread and some cheese. He had lost all of his appetite, but he took a sip of water for his dry throat.

Blake sighed and closed his eyes. He knew he had to think about his next steps very carefully.

First, I need to get out of here.

But how was he going to do that? He ran a hand through his hair and sighed again. There were too many obstacles, too many moving parts. He had no idea if Drew and his friends had even made it out of the convention center.

If they made it to the house and found the capsule... would that be good or bad? All that information might be too much for Drew to process, especially as I'm not there to explain things to him in person. I hope he doesn't panic.

"Damn it, Blake," he muttered to himself. "What have you done?"

There was surely going to be some kind of information overload. He was sure of it. The pictures would be too much to process all at once. And the stone... would they know what to do with that?

Knowing nothing is better than knowing half of the truth. I've handed Drew and his friends a bunch of half-truths, incomplete facts that will only confuse them and put them in more trouble.

He looked down at the bread in his hand. He knew he had to eat to keep his energy up. He had always scoffed at the illogical heroes in the action movies Drew enjoyed watching. The heroes in those movies could fight battle after battle but they were rarely shown doing normal things. Apparently, in the movie world, heroes don't get hungry or pressed to use the toilet. Whenever he asked Drew about it, the boy just laughed and told him he was too old and just didn't get it.

Well, this is real life. The bread might be moldy, and the cheese might be a bit sour but it's all I've got. If I'm going to make any moves soon, I need to eat.

He tore a chunk of bread and cut a small piece of cheese and popped both in his mouth. Surprisingly, the bread was good, and the cheese was sharp and flavorful. Blake's stomach rumbled and he kept eating until all that was left were breadcrumbs. He untwisted the water bottle cap and drank the rest of the water.

He was about to start analyzing his options and was considering if he could make his escape the next time the door opened when he heard voices speaking from outside the door. It was definitely the men in black. He shuffled closer to the door and lay his ear against it, straining to hear the conversation on the other side.

"... yeah, they went to his house..."

"... stupid kids...think they called..."

"...the cops?... don't think so..."

"...so, we're going... the boss's house?"

".... yeah...so they won't escape again..."

Blake had heard enough. He backed away from the door. There was no time for thinking or strategizing, not anymore. It was time for him to act. There was no other choice.

He cleared his mind of every thought. It was extremely difficult. He was tense because of what he'd just heard and there were several other thoughts too... thoughts that were decades old... memories that he had never really forgotten...

The ship lurched suddenly. "Blake!"

He turned, looking for Alice but unable to see her in the sky through the smoke. There was a high-pitched beeping from the control panel, but he ignored it. The pod was already on autopilot mode. There was nothing he could do to avert the impending crash.

"Alice! Alice, come in. Where are you? Are you still in the air?" There was no answer. Blake's heart thumped. Somewhere in the pod, an alarm was blaring. But he had to find his wife, since they were tailing her. He looked down at his son who was scared. The two of them wondered—

No...no!

He couldn't even think about losing her. He forced himself to stagger through the smoke, arms stretched in front of him so he could find the backup radio.

"Alice, please be alive up there! Darling! Where are you? Please..." There was no answer....

Blake concentrated on clearing his mind but before a thought could be banished, it had to be brought forward first. It had to be reexamined before he could lock it away, leaving his mind free to act. Because of this, memories Blake thought were long gone swam up to the surface of his mind again and started to torment him. He could almost smell the smoke in the ship, could almost see the red light that had bathed the entire place, could almost hear the blaring alarm...

19...18...17...

He held on tight to his son. The pod was big enough for both of them to fit but they were heading down fast.

12...11...10...

The pod was counting down, its self-destruct option activated by the au-topilot. Blake guessed the control unit must have reached some sort of critical failure after that missile exploded near them. They were descending at top speed, battling the somersaulting of the pod as it hurtled towards the ground. He knew he had to time the ejection just right to leave the ship before it blew itself to pieces.

7...6...5...

As they prepared to eject, another missile exploded. This one was close *enough that it rattled the entire pod, separating Blake from his son. On the floor, blood welling from a cut in his head, was his son. Blake gathered the boy's limp form into his arms. He didn't think about the one glaring fact: he couldn't hear his wife. He didn't want to think... not yet. That would only slow him down. He reached for the escape hatch.*

3...2...1...

Blake cleared his throat and yelled, "Eject!"

The ejection seat shot out of the pod, and at the same time there was a boom, and an explosion rocked the night sky. It looked just like the last time they had escaped from somewhere using that ship. There was a ball of fire above them and they were running for it, afraid that it would catch up with them and consume them. There were differences between the two trips, of course. The first time, the ball of fire had been the planets in their galaxy, not a spaceship...

Blake pushed the thoughts of the accident out of his mind, but more thoughts came up. He saw Alice smiling somewhere in the desert, her hand in his, laughing at something he'd repeated. He saw Drew listening with rapt attention as he told him a bedtime story. He even went back to the first time they had found Earth...

"It's beautiful..."

She spoke in a singsong language, the general tongue of everyone in their galaxy. He was seated behind the control panel as usual. His wife stood beside him. They were both staring at the blue and green planet in front of them.

"Look at the monitor's analysis..." he suggested.

She did as he mentioned. They both read the intelligent ship's analysis of the planet before them. The air was composed of the same gasses that made up the atmosphere of their planets back home and about 70% of the planet was composed of water. There was abundant plant and animal life...

"It's perfect," his wife replied.

"What is it called again?" Her son asked.

"This is the Milky Way, and that planet is called... Earth."

"Our new home."

"You can do this, Blake. Come on. Come on!"

He focused his mind and delved deeper to access his forgotten powers. The pills that Drew had been complaining about were Blake's own design. He had created them after the accident so they could suppress his abilities. He had thought about it long and hard, but he had ultimately reached his decision. If Drew didn't have any powers, he would get the chance to live like a normal human kid. But Blake used the pills as well. He had created them with chemicals from their own galaxy, chemicals that couldn't be found anywhere else, the source of the strange taste Drew had often observed.

The pills were very effective. They dampened his abilities, which made it easier for Blake to move among regular humans without attracting undue attention. The pills also reduced the wavelength of their own energy signature, offering a bit of protection in case someone was to look for them.

Blake fought against the power of the pills. He was much more experienced with this part of himself than his son. The greater part of his life had been spent on different planets in his home galaxy and almost every day he had used his abilities so while it was a bit difficult to recall them, it wasn't as difficult or as slow as it was going to be for an inexperienced person like Drew.

Blake felt the power rush into him suddenly. His senses sharpened till he could detect even the smallest change in his surroundings. His eyes became both magnifying glasses and scanners. His ears were like sonar devices; he could hear every bit of sound even from beyond the door. His mind was picking up information, analyzing and storing it away at top speed.

This is what it means to be from a Type II world. I had forgotten how good this feels.

He took a deep breath and burst into action. He ran towards the door and struck it with one hand, tearing it off its hinges. The guard that had been standing by the door was too slow to react. Blake crashed into him and punched him in the neck when he tried to rise again. The man collapsed like a rag doll. Two more guards were in sight. They reacted quicker than their fallen comrade, but Blake was much faster. He covered the short distance between him and the two men in a fraction of a second, before they could even bring up the muzzles of their guns. He elbowed one of them in the face and while he stumbled backwards, he delivered a spinning kick to the second guy's neck that sent him to the ground. The first guy was up again and came towards Blake. His face was covered in blood, but he raised his gun and managed to squeeze off a shot at Blake's head.

Blake's improved senses made him see the bullet in a state of delayed time that exceeded even Drew's abilities. As the bullet flew towards his skull, he sidestepped calmly, and the projectile sailed past him harmlessly. To the guard, who watched everything with normal human eyes and senses, Blake seemed to have moved at an impossible speed to evade the bullet that should have ripped his head apart.

Still using his superspeed, Blake tugged the gun out of the stunned guard's hands and snapped it in two as if it were made of straw. Then he grabbed the front of the guard's clothes and slammed the guy against a wall till he fell unconscious.

"Stop right there or I'll put a bullet through your head!"

A fourth guard had emerged from one of the stalls. He had his gun out and pointed it steadily in Blake's direction. He was bigger than the others and looked tougher as well. His hair was closely cropped, which Blake took to mean he had some sort of military experience.

The guy didn't move closer. He glanced at his unconscious friends on the floor. He was apparently shocked by the damage a single man had done to three trained and heavily armed mercenaries, but he was smart too. He didn't want to end up like the others.

"DON'T MOVE!" He yelled.

Blake looked him in the eye, smiled and moved. It had been a while since he had used his abilities in combat, and he had forgotten how good the adrenaline rush felt in his bloodstream. When he moved with super speed, time slowed. He could hear the rotation of the earth itself. He could see everything sharply and fully. When he looked at the fourth guard, he saw the determination in the man's eyes.

This one won't be easy like the rest, he thought.

Even as Blake moved towards him, the guard started firing. His gun was a semi-automatic and he didn't lift his forefinger from the trigger. Blake dodged the bullets with ease—though one of them passed so close to his face that he felt its heat burn his skin. He reached the guy just as he ran out of ammo. Again, the guard reacted faster than the others. He reversed his grip on the gun, using it as a makeshift club and swinging it at Blake's head. Blake wasn't prepared for the maneuver, but his quick reflexes warned him. He was able to jerk his head backwards so that the gun's butt missed his face and struck his chin instead.

Pain exploded in his jaw. He let out a shocked cry and took a step backwards. There was a bruise already forming on his chin. The guard was advancing, his confidence increasing now that he had seen he could hurt his opponent. Blake growled angrily. He had been pulling his punches. Not anymore. Nothing would keep him away from his son when he needed him most.

He stepped forward, meeting the guard's charge and hitting him in the groin with a knee. The guard bent over by reflex, gasping in pain, and giving Blake the perfect opportunity to direct the same knee at his face. He heard the satisfying crunch of the man's nose as it broke. The guard staggered, trying to escape, but Blake reached out and grabbed him by the arm. With a violent twist, he dislocated the guy's shoulder, then rendered him unconscious with a quick chop to the neck.

The fourth guard collapsed and lay unmoving on the grass. He had been tougher than the rest, but he was still only human.

Blake looked around. Clearly other mercenaries hadn't been informed of his escape. He started walking towards the gate that led outside, the same one they had used when he was brought in.

It's been a while. Tapping in has always felt wonderful.

That was the term his people used for whenever they used their abilities. But there was a downside, especially for someone like Blake who didn't use his abilities regularly. There was a time limit. If he used his abilities too much, it was going to take a toll on him.

It was because of this time limit that Blake was running towards the gate. He had to locate Drew and he couldn't do that without the one ability he hadn't used yet.

He opened the gate and found the same white van that was used when the men in black abducted him. Luckily, the keys were in the ignition. He slid into the driver's seat and shut the door. Then he focused his mind on the single reason that had made him go through all the trouble of regaining his powers in the first place; finding Drew.

He tried to find his son telepathically by establishing a connection with Drew's mind. This would act as a sort of psychic compass that would lead him straight to Drew. It was the same way Drew had found him when he and his friends had shown up at the convention center.

Normally, it shouldn't even have taken him up to a minute to establish a connection with Drew's mind, but this time it seemed there was some kind of obstruction between them. He tried over and over, aware that he was running out of time.

Something's wrong. Maybe Drew has been captured and put under some sort of dampening field? Or maybe he's unconscious?

He tried not to think about Drew lying somewhere, knocked unconscious. He tried again and this time he was rewarded with a slight blip. He connected with his son's mind and started the car.

He knew what he had to do.

CHAPTER SEVENTEEN

CRASH

Drew looked around the room. It was really wide, but no attention had been paid to the decoration of the space. In the middle was a large worn-out couch and a wide glass table in front of it, and the paintings on the wall were peeling right off. It was a total contrast in comparison to the sight they had beheld upstairs. The space really was designed to look like a prison.

"How are you guys?" Drew asked the crew after trying to locate his father. He realized that all of this had been a lot for them to take in.

"What do you think, bro?" Levi replied but he was grinning to show that he was okay.

Sumi just shrugged and gave Drew a thumbs up.

"We're going to be okay," Drew promised to his friends, but his eyes were on Sumi. "Just stay with me and be ready, okay? I believe help is coming."

They were speaking in whispers and huddled close to each other so their voices wouldn't be heard by the guards. They took comfort in each other's presence and held hands without even saying anything. Sumi squeezed the boys' hands, putting in all of her relief and anxiety and even her gratitude that they had managed to survive so far. They were all well aware that their little adventure might have ended prematurely at the convention center. The guards had certainly planned to dispose of them one way or the other. Sumi didn't even want to think about whatever plans Nox may still have for them. She was just glad she had her taser on her. Everything Nox bragged about, especially about being an extraterrestrial, seemed too strange for her. It was all so illogical but the way the billionaire had presented the whole thing, he made it sound very credible.

But how can it be? Aliens and advanced intergalactic civilizations? Superpowers? Sounds like the script of a cliché science fiction movie.

"Hey, guys," Sumi whispered. "What do you think about everything that Nox was talking about upstairs? I mean, he seems kinda crazy and he's definitely some sort of racist but his stories… I don't know. I guess they have a ring of truth about them."

The boys nodded. It was clear that they were also trying to process everything they had heard.

"Man, I don't really know what's up," Levi responded. "I mean, all that stuff that he went on about escaping from his galaxy because of some invaders or whatever?" He chuckled and continued. "You gotta admit, it all sounds like Star Wars or something. He's like some kinda Sith Lord or whatever, with his own powers and everything. Sometimes, I think I'm dreaming but I don't even know what's going on, man. Did you see when he did that light trick with the stone? It didn't need no feminine touch that time, I tell ya."

Sumi grinned. Despite the situation in which they had found themselves, Levi had not lost his unique sense of humor.

"You're right," Sumi replied, frowning as she remembered the moment. "The stone suddenly started glowing like a miniature sun or something… it unnerved me. I was half convinced that the world was about to end. You know, like an apocalyptic moment. There was something tremendously alien about that moment. I couldn't even understand it. In fact, I think if I make any attempt to understand it, I might lose my mind. I was so scared. Even the guards beside me were trembling."

She shook her head as if that would clear it of the scary thoughts.

"Maybe I was kinda overreacting," she admitted, looking up at the two boys. "But you have to admit, that was a really bizarre scene."

Levi nodded. Drew just shrugged; his face squeezed into a brooding frown.

"What about you, Drew?" Sumi asked him, her voice sharp. Her analytical mind had been putting one and one together, juggling different thoughts and scenarios. She had come to lots of conclusions, most of them illogical. But the constant factor in all her speculations was that Drew knew one or two things that he might not be sharing. She didn't want to believe it, of course. He was her friend and they had helped each other out of tough spots more than once. But she knew in a deep part of her mind that he was intrinsically connected to everything that was going on.

"What do you think, Drew?" Sumi asked again, keeping her tone cordial.

Drew's face wasn't drawn with worry or stress. He actually appeared calm, as if he was having a sleepover at a friend's house instead of being trapped in a cage in a villainous billionaire's basement. When Sumi asked him the question, he just shrugged and spoke in a slightly confused tone.

"Uh… well, I really don't understand everything… I'm confused just like you guys." He hesitated. "But we really have to find a way out of this pla—"

"Hold on a minute, Drew," Sumi interrupted, holding up a hand. Drew stopped talking, confused.

"Look, I think you should come clean," Sumi demanded.

"Come clean? I don't understand—"

"Drew, I don't think you've been entirely honest with us," Sumi alleged, narrowing her eyes. "I think you know more about what's going on. Like, you probably have some sort of sensitive information about this whole thing. Maybe something your father told you. I don't know what you know, exactly. But I have my suspicions. I mean, upstairs, during the speech that dude was giving us, he whispered stuff into your ears a couple of times. It was almost as if you knew each other before. I don't know what's going on but if you know more than you've been telling, then this is the time to speak up."

"Look, Sums," Drew snapped, in a deeply frustrated tone. "It's nothing major, okay? It's not a big deal. I just think all our efforts right now should be concentrated on how we're going to get out of here and maybe find out what Nox is planning to do with my dad's invention."

"Yeah, that's right," Levi chimed in, reaching out to place a hand on Drew's shoulder. "But you gotta be honest with us, man. For real. Is there anything you're not telling us?"

Drew remained quiet. He appeared to be struggling with a big decision.

"Look, we're your friends," Sumi added. "There's nothing you could ever tell us, no matter how strange or disturbing, that will change that. We'll stick with you till the very end, no matter what happens. I know you're scared. I'm scared too. But the silver lining is that we are all together and that is our real strength."

Levi was nodding the whole time as Sumi spoke to show that he agreed with everything she was saying.

Drew looked at his friends and sighed.

Where do I even start from? How will I tell them that the less they know, the better? At this point, knowledge can be dangerous. Nox doesn't really see them as threats because he knows they don't know enough. If I start telling them all my suspicions..., how will they even react? They'll have doubts, that's for sure. Is this even my real face? My whole life has been a lie. It's a lie I believed and which I lived every single day. My friends are somehow part of that lie. Why didn't Nox blow the secret upstairs? I was so sure he was gonna say something. If he had spoken, I might have been able to deny or say something to assure my friends but with the way things are right now...

"There are strange things going on," Drew confided, carefully measuring his words. "And these things are kinda dangerous too. I have a couple of ideas but nothing concrete. I just need you guys to trust me. I want you to know that I do not take your friendship lightly. I cherish you guys, for real."

Levi and Sumi exchanged a long look. They were both silently weighing Drew's words. He had been careful not to say too much while letting them know that he treasured their friendship. Levi shrugged after a minute.

"Good enough for me, man," he announced, then raised an eyebrow questioningly as he looked at Sumi.

"Yeah… yeah. I trust you, Drew," Sumi expressed at last. Drew nodded then beckoned them to lean closer.

"OK. I've got a plan that might help us get out of here," he asserted.

"I thought you promised help was coming," Sumi recounted.

"Yeah. But we have to be ready for anything, right?" Drew replied.

"So... what's the plan then?" Sumi asked.

Drew nodded and gestured to Levi who showed Sumi the remote. At another slight gesture from Drew, Levi repeated the process of pressing his weight on the button to once again activate Drew's abilities. Strength surged through Drew's body as his friend pressed on the button.

This energy rush never gets old. Damn.

He grimaced and, with extra effort, completely broke the weakened links and snapped his cuffs into two. They had been too loud though, and the sound of metal snapping was the last straw. One of the guards turned and walked towards them, frowning. They quickly sat apart from each other and tried to look miserable, which wasn't particularly difficult. To the guard, they didn't seem to be plotting anything or saying anything suspicious, but he watched them for a few more seconds before turning away.

The three friends let out sighs of relief and Drew moved quietly to Sumi's side. With a quick tug and twist, he broke her cuffs. He did the same for Levi and the big guy was able to hold the remote better in his hand, his thumb still pressed down on the button.

"What next?" Sumi asked.

"We will need some sort of distraction, but I don't know how that's gonna work," Drew answered.

Noticing the kids whispering to one another, one guard taunted them, making jokes of their situation. He continued nonstop and soon it began to crawl under Levi's skin. He tightened his fist and clenched his teeth.

"You're out there, we're in here. So, I can understand why you have the balls to run your mouth," Levi retorted.

The guard sharply turned his attention to Levi, "What did you say to me, boy?"

"I'm not your boy! And I'm saying why don't you come in here alone, and let's see how well you can run that foul mouth then," Levi blurted, rage in his eyes.

"Motor, chill!" Drew cautioned.

We don't need that kind of distraction, Drew thought.

Levi's comment rather pissed the guard off. He immediately pulled out his gun and pointed it at Levi. "Say that to me again, boy!"

"Levi, relax! He wants you to react," Sumi yelled.

All Levi could think about were the many times he'd been taunted by any kind of enforcement officer because of how he looked.

He called me "boy." I'm not letting that go. I'm tired of people like him thinking they can say whatever they want, Levi thought.

The rest of the guards paid no attention to the drama happening; they remained engrossed in their games. But the foul-mouthed guard couldn't help himself. Wanting to intimidate Levi further, he raises his gun towards Levi. Drew and Sumi both stand up in fear.

"Dude, what are you doing!" Drew shouted at the guard.

"Shut it! Let's see if your 'homie' has the balls to repeat himself!" The guard responded.

Fear gripped Levi but he showed none of it. He stood there, ready for whatever would come. He continued his response to the guard.

"I said-"

BOOM!

The rest of his words were cut off by a loud boom that seemed to come from somewhere in the main building. The guard and the kids looked up but before anyone could say a word, an alarm started blaring. He picked up his radio and clicked it on. At once, the voices of his colleagues buzzed through.

"...alarm set off... main house..."

"...locate the boss... security..."

"...remain on alert..."

While the guards communicated, Drew and the crew looked at each other knowingly. It seemed help had come at last.

Suddenly, a memory came to Drew.

CHAPTER EIGHTEEN

FROM THE BEGINNING

*"Far above the skies… Where the galaxies align… I will be waiting…
To show you the wonders of space…"*

The song trailed off. The voice was therapeutic and oddly familiar, but he couldn't place where it came from or who it belonged to. His eyes shut as he drifted off to sleep.

Then, just as quickly, he was pulled into another memory.

"How bad is it?" A woman's voice came as she stood in the hallway, addressing someone.

"In here, come," echoed the voice in response, wanting to move them away from listening ears.

Xaeon remembered moving towards the sound of the voices, trying to find *out what they were discussing. Just as soon as he got to the door, he saw his father with his back turned, talking to a woman… a familiar woman.*

Finally, alone with themselves, the voices resumed speaking.

"The threat grows stronger each minute. It has been decided by the Heads, we need to search for habitable planets."

"We have to leave?" The woman responded with her voice breaking slightly. "This is the only life we've ever known. How would we adapt? How would Xaeon adapt? How much do we even know about this planet?" She trailed off, a series of questions bogging her mind.

"The planet has yet to be decided upon. The Heads of the Resistance deliberate everyday about this. But it doesn't matter where they pick, we will find a way, I promise. As long as we are together, we will make it work."

"Dad? What's going on?" A young Xaeon called out as he moved closer.

His father turned around to find his son standing behind him, his hair an entangled mess. It seemed he was just waking from sleep. He moved close to his son and bent to his level.

"It's nothing to worry yourself with, Son, you should go back to your pod. Do that for me, okay?" He reassured him as he placed a kiss on Xaeon's head.

Xaeon strained, trying to make out the face of the woman his father was talking with.

His father signaled to one of the house assistants, "Take him to his pod." With that, Xaeon was pulled away.

Ever since he had abandoned his medication, memories he didn't remember having, had come flooding back. Drew sighed as he collapsed back into reality.

"Drew…Drew! Did you hear me? I think we have our distraction now," Sumi shouted, covering her ears.

Distracted by the noise, the guard in charge immediately signaled to some other guards, asking them to go up and check what the ruckus was about. The guard with his gun pointed at Levi was one of them and he hesitated for a moment, giving Levi the dirtiest of looks before succumbing. He returned his gun back to its holster and raced up the stairs.

Levi sank to the floor, his heartbeat hammering against his chest. His breath caught in his throat and his vision dimmed. He'd had his run-ins before, but never had he been in a situation like this. With the guard's gun pointed at his chest, he had felt only moments away from his demise. There was too much he hadn't done. He breathed loudly through his mouth, trying to swallow as much air as his lungs could manage.

The rest of the guards huddled in a corner; their voices hushed as they had a conversation. The crew was certain it was about the noise.

Noticing the guards were distracted, Drew saw an opportunity to talk to his friend.

"You okay, bro?" Drew asked.

"Yeah, I'm good, I just need to catch a breath. Man! I thought I was a dead man. I stared death in the face, you guys," Levi responded.

Sumi rolled her eyes, she understood what he felt, but she felt Levi always had a penchant for confrontation. He didn't have to challenge that guard. He should have just kept his big mouth shut.

The alarm cut off, but the guards could still be heard scrambling. It took Levi a few minutes to slow his heartbeat down to normal and regain control of his shaky hands.

"So, what's the plan now?" Levi asked.

"Do you still have the remote on you?" Drew responded. Levi searched his person for the remote, it wasn't on him.

His attention was drawn to where he had slumped earlier and there lay the remote, it must have slipped out of his pocket. He rushed to grab it. He examined it to make sure nothing was broken.

"I got it."

"Good, just keep it on you at all times. We're gonna need it to get out of here," Drew responded.

Sumi, who had stayed quiet the longest, decided to chip in. "What does this remote do exactly? I still don't understand it."

"Well, I don't know exactly myself. But I really believe Nox set up some kind of field disruptor around the building. It's stopping me from doing or sensing anything. Having the remote feels like a loophole, a chink in the firewall. So, when the remote is active, I regain my...abilities..." Drew explained

"Nah, you mean your supernatural abilities," Levi corrected.

"What?" They both asked, surprised.

"Supernatural sounds cooler than just *abilities*." Levi explained with a shrug.

"And how did you get these supernatural abilities? Do you have any idea?" Sumi asked because her confusion lingered. She didn't understand how her friend had just manifested such bizarre abilities.

Drew furrowed his brows as he thought for a minute. He really could not remember where it had come from. Shaking his head in denial, he responded "I don't really know. They just started when I stopped taking the pills my father gave me. I don't know what to make of it. It's just as confusing for me."

"My theory is... and hear me out... I believe your father must have performed some kind of freak experiment on you as a kid or that you were exposed to some high-level chemicals that should have killed you but instead, it turned you superhuman just like in the comics!" Levi suggested with a childlike glint in his eyes.

"Be sensitive, idiot!" Sumi scolded, as she lightly smacked him upside the head. "Yeah, Drew's father is a little odd, but he wouldn't do that to his son! It must have been something else."

"Well, D is my boy too, but I still maintain that it's a possibility," Levi replied as he rubbed the back of his head.

Another loud noise came from upstairs, and the trio's attention turned upwards. They wondered what was going on. The sound of objects smashing into other objects… or possibly people? There were loud screams, grunts, and the sound of gunshots filled the air. They wondered what was going on up there. Were the guards at war with each other? No, it was more likely an intruder. But who was it? And whose side were they on? Sitting around and thinking about it did no good for them.

"Guys, we really have to make good use of this opportunity, now that everyone is distracted… or possibly dead or dying, we need to leave here!" Sumi suggested.

"I don't see an exit down here; the only way out is up. And up is where the bullets are flying. It sounds like people are being thrown into furniture too… I think. I am not going that way. Did you see the furniture up there? There's nothing cheap in the whole house. Nah, I'm not dying today," Levi replied.

"Stop being such a wuss! If we stay here, we just might die too. What if a gunman comes down here to finish us off, what then? I am not going to just sit here like a lamb waiting for slaughter. I am taking my chances out there and you are coming too!" Sumi demanded.

Every now and then, they bumped heads with one another like siblings, those two. An outsider would not believe they were such good friends when it happened.

"Guys, I think…" Drew's breath caught in his throat. His eyes shone a very bright white, and his body began convulsing aggressively.

The lights flickered on and off as if reacting to him. He pulled his hands up to cover his ears as they rang so loud, he felt they would explode; he couldn't hear anything but loud ringing. The surge travelled through his toes, all the way up and settling at the base of his spine. He twisted and turned on the floor, a dull glow seeping from underneath his skin. With his eyes firmly shut, he muttered words in a strange language. The more he spoke, the faster the light flickered. Some bulbs gave out and exploded.

Levi and Sumi stood there confused and worried, shielding themselves from the shattering glass. They were too afraid to move close or touch him, not knowing what the repercussions would be. They considered calling for help but with such a racket upstairs, no one would hear them. And if they did, who was to say they wouldn't be offered swift deaths?

Knowing they could do nothing but watch in the hopes that he snapped out of it soon, they called out to him, asking for any indication that he was alright. Or even hearing them.

After several seconds of thrashing, he stopped abruptly. Drew laid completely still. The lights had stopped flickering. The slow rise and fall of his stomach was the only indicator that there was still life in his veins. The bright glow underneath his skin had dissipated completely. He was back to looking like a teenage boy.

They rushed to his side, panic evident in their voices as they asked — begged him to speak.

"You know you shouldn't go in there," a hazel-eyed child with the curliest hair he had ever seen blurted out.

"Nobody's going to know. Just be a lookout!" Xaeon responded as he pulled himself into the vent.

He crawled into the vent on all fours and moved through the tight space. He was trying to sneak his way into the kitchen, the cook always let him help in the cake making, but his parents disapproved of him being in the kitchen.

He was almost at the end of the journey when he heard voices down below. Xaeon looked through the holes in the board. He saw a group of men sitting at a round table, discussing. Looking closer at their attire, he realized they were

The Heads of the Resistance. They made ultimate decisions that were binding for all that lived. Moving slower in a bid not to make any noise, he turned to his friend and pressed his index finger to his mouth and then pointed downwards. He would very much like to not be caught.

She looked down to find what he was talking about, and immediately got the message. They moved more carefully.

"Brynr was captured yesterday," one head announced to the dismay of the group.

"They are taking us out, one after the other. We cannot wait any longer. We have to decide and decide quickly! Anyone could be next."

"What is the decision of the collective?"

One head stood, scroll in hand as she read its contents.

"The collective, having weighed the situation and thoroughly deliberated, has decided that the next line of action would be to evacuate. Our people are to be moved to a different planet.

However, not one in this galaxy. They are to be moved to another. A few planets will be chosen, but for now, we have just one, it is considered the most habitable. Their technological intelligence is nothing like ours. As much as that has its disadvantages, it has its advantages too. For one, it is almost impossible for them to detect alien life forms on their planet.

In time, we will have selected a few other planets for our people. It is expected that this information be sent out to the selected families; they are to make preparations immediately."

"And what is this planet?" One head asked.

"It is called Earth..."

Xaeon repeated the name in his head. He wondered what this Earth was and why they were all going there.

He felt someone squeeze his palm and call out to him.

Back to reality.

"Drew, what happened? Are you okay? Say something to us!" Sumi pleaded as she squeezed his palm in hers.

Levi stayed on the other side of Drew, monitoring his breathing. Eyes still shut, Drew began mumbling. Levi moved his ear closer to Drew's face to make out the words he was saying. "What did you say?"

"My father is here," Drew repeated, his voice now barely above a whisper. He still felt a residual tingling dancing under his skin. His eyes fluttered open and ever so slowly, he pulled himself up.

"Bro, what just happened? Everything good?" Levi asked.

Cupping his face in his palms, Drew replied "I don't know, I just felt a strange power surge through me. It was unlike anything I've ever felt before and it consumed me, but not in a bad way. It felt like I was getting introduced to a part of myself that I've never met before or at least, I don't remember meeting. I know I sound crazy, but it's just hard to explain…" he made a deliberate decision to not mention the flashbacks he'd had.

"What triggered it? Was this feeling like the last time? Was it the remote? Do you know?"

"Umm… I don't think so. My guess would be my father, if that makes any sense."

"And it just made you know that he was here?" Levi continued his interrogation.

"Umm… maybe. Maybe not. I just know that he's here. I feel his presence and I also know he just might be a part of the disturbance upstairs, if not the cause of it."

"So…"

"…Guys, chill," Drew snapped. "No more questions. I'm just as confused as you, if not more. I don't know what's happening to me or why it's happening…these blackout moments…these random shocks…I honestly don't know what's going on inside of me, since I got off my pills."

His shoulders slumped in frustration. Sumi could tell that he couldn't make sense of what he was feeling. They had flooded him with questions without considering how he himself was feeling about the changes happening with his body. She placed a hand on his shoulder and offered him a warm smile. "I can only imagine how this affects you. But I know we will figure this out, I promise."

"What if we find something bizarre? What if I am like Mr. Nox and also on some sick agenda to take over the world? What if that's what's awakening inside of me? I don't think I would be able to live with myself."

"Well then, we will take over the world together. People will bow to us. Think of all the free stuff we'll be getting!" Levi injected playfully, trying to lighten up the mood.

It seemed to have worked for a little bit and Drew smiled at the thought of it. But it was short lived as Drew went back to being somber almost immediately.

"You're a good person and you know that! You don't care about world domination or any of that nonsense. I have seen how you treat people, and animals too. I'm sure it's something else. Maybe you are the one to stop Nox and his ridiculous world domination scheme. Maybe you're just a random guy with superhuman abilities. But whatever it is, we are here for you always and we will figure it out together. Do you hear me?" Sumi asked, to which Drew gave her a slight nod of approval.

She continued, "Good, now if you're done sulking, let's find our way out of this dump!"

Drew stood to his feet, rubbing his palms against each other, and nodded at Levi. Levi in turn pressed on the remote and Drew felt power surge through him. It felt like a veil had lifted from him and his body tingled.

His strength felt amplified, and he was ready. He tugged at the lock that kept the gate in place. One… two… three! The lock pulled from its hinges, like paper torn from a book, returning back to them their freedom. Drew led the way, following his intuition to his father. The closer he got, the stronger he could feel his father's presence.

They maneuvered their way through the bunker, which was surprisingly large. They turned several corners, trusting Drew's judgment and silently praying that they didn't bump into any guards. That was when it hit Drew, a deep energy surge. He could feel his father's anger clearly like it was his own, he felt his worry too and a slight hint of fear, but anger remained the stronger emotion.

Soon they stood before a door, and Drew hesitated. This must be it, the only thing standing between him and his father. Reluctantly, he grabbed the knob, turning gently but still holding it firmly in place. He didn't know how to feel about his father. Since their last meeting he had found out too much about himself that his father had kept secret. The emotions he felt were conflicting. He had so many unanswered questions.

"Drew, you've been spacing out a little too much. What is going on? Are you sure you can do this?" The sound of Sumi's voice pulled him out of his reverie.

Blinking back to reality, "No, sorry, nothing is wrong. I'm fine. Let's go in," he replied as he pushed the door open. A sudden bright light from the room filtered through, harassing their vision and causing them to squint and protect their eyes.

CHAPTER NINETEEN

THE SEARCH

They had been underground in the dark for too long, so it took them a minute, but once their eyes had adjusted to the light, they scanned the room. Drew's father wasn't in it, much to their disappointment. He had been so sure he'd sensed his father up here, maybe he was wrong.

Before them was a lab, heavily equipped to the teeth. It had just two chairs put in place, obviously meant to be manned by two people. They stepped in, scanning the environment for anyone. When they confirmed that they were alone in the room, they closed the door behind them. The room bore such advanced technology; it was unlike anything they had ever seen before.

Projected monitors graced the air space, each one bearing parts of what they pieced together to be… the globe. Earth's globe.

The screens were littered with red dots blinking all around. The number of dots seemed to be increasing by the minute. Every part of the globe had red dots, some more than others.

"Wow! Look at all this stuff. What do you think they do here?" Levi asked as he ran his fingers over some of the tech close to him.

"Well, my guess is that this is a lab of some sort, but what kind of experiments they carry out, I can't say that I know. It doesn't look like the kind to dissect people, at least," Drew responded.

"They're tracking people. That's what the red dots are. Look, this part actually documents their names," came Sumi's voice as she pointed at a separate box on the screen. For each new red dot that appeared, the box recorded a new name.

"So, they are keeping tabs on people? Are they newborn kids? Are they rich? Are they convicts?" Levi asked.

Knowing that the crew relied on her hacking skills for answers, Sumi pulled out a seat and began typing away on one of the keyboards. Computers were her thing, and she knew a thing or two about getting information that people didn't want to be gotten.

"I don't think you should be touching tha…" Levi tried to object.

"Shsssh!" Sumi voiced, not wanting to be distracted. She resumed her typing till she was able to decode the content on the screen.

"These are names of people from all around the world. There are so many of them, hundreds of thousands, I'd say. Just random people going about their daily lives, so far. Chances are they could be totally unaware that they're being tracked. I can't see a connection between them at all, well not yet anyway. Why would Nox keep track of people from all over the world that have nothing in common? It makes no sense," Sumi buried herself in thought.

"Unless they're some kind of sleeper agents for his crazy plans," Levi suggested.

"Maybe you're right, maybe not, but no theory is too absurd at this point. There just has to be a connection between Nox and these people, our setback is that we just don't know what it is," Drew proposed as his gaze remained fixed on the monitor. "Why would he keep tabs on random people if there's no connection? Whatever his reasons are, we'll uncover them. But why this many people? We have to figure out what this is all about."

Drew wondered if it had to do with the stone and communication device that was stolen from his father. It couldn't be that important... could it? The questions ran ceaselessly through his mind as he tried to make sense of things. Sumi continued her typing, determined to find out more.

She stopped abruptly. "You guys, you're not gonna believe what I found."

"What?" Asked Drew.

"Come take a look." The crew gathered beside Sumi, eager to know what she had discovered.

"Look," she repeated as she pointed to a name on the screen.

"That's my father's name..." Drew confirmed. The thoughts began raging through his mind again, but he soon regained composure. "If this is live tracking, could you find out where he is? If he's here?"

"I can try," Sumi noted as she busied herself once again. "Yes, he's in this building. And he's close."

A voice from the hallway boomed through the entire floor, causing the crew to stop dead in their tracks. Someone was coming their way.

"Get the van ready and take two guards with you. I want the goods here safely and quickly. Is that understood?" The voice questioned as the footsteps moved closer.

The voice belonged to Mr. Nox. Chills ran down their spines. They wondered if he was headed their way. Did he know they had escaped their cell? They looked around for the best spot to hide themselves.

A loud racket was made slightly above their level, and it seemed to infuriate Mr. Nox. The noise had been happening on and off.

"What is that noise?" He questioned.

"Sir... we are still dealing with the little disturbance that happened earlier," a guard responded.

"Little disturbance? I told you to get it under control, your team assured me they would. Does that sound like it's under control? So incompetent."

"I promise sir, we will neutralize this disturbance," the guard asserted.

"How many are there? These intruders," Mr. Nox asked.

"I am unsure as of yet Sir, I haven't gone up there. I will go immediately to see what's going on!"

"No," he calmly responded. "Send someone to do that. You go check on the kids and get back to me. We will put off getting the supplies for now."

The guard hurried off to carry out his new assignment.

The crew heard footsteps coming dangerously close to where they were and they did their best to return the room back to the way it was, turning off the lights and readjusting the chairs. They found a small closet in the wall. It looked like it was used as a changing room. There were old lab coats bunched up in a corner, while some were hung on the wall. Whoever was in charge of the lab must have spent a lot of nights there. The crew huddled in the space, shut the door and prayed they wouldn't get caught.

A door creaked open, from the sound of it, it was a different entrance from the one they came in through. The intruder stepped in, walking slowly and surveying the room. The lights came on and there the intruder was, standing right in front of their hiding spot.

Their hearts sank as they saw a shadow looming. There was silence for the longest of seconds, the intruder did and spoke nothing. They just stood still. The crew did their best to breathe as little as possible. There was no way to tell who it was but since they had more foes than friends in the house, they would take no chances.

Then, a second person rushed into the room, panting and in a hurry to deliver whatever message he had come bearing.

"The kids are not in their cell, Sir. Their cuffs were destroyed and so was the lock on the gate," the voice reported hurriedly.

As soon as the voice spoke, they realized that who the voice was addressing must have been Mr. Nox. He had been standing in front of their hiding spot all this time. Did he know they were behind him?

They hoped not.

"And the guards assigned to their cage?" Mr. Nox asked.

"There was no one at the post, Sir. I believe they went up to handle the disturbance," the guard responded.

"Gather everyone, whoever is left. I want people stationed on every entrance and exit in this building. Send some others to search for those kids. They are still in this bunker somewhere. The rest of the guards, send them up, I want these intruders squashed quickly!"

The guard rushed out. Mr. Nox stood still in the same position, scanning the lab. Then he pulled out a seat and typed for several seconds. When he was done, he stood up immediately and without looking back, he left the room and shut the door.

The crew gave it a few more minutes before they came out of hiding, clutching their chests in their palms, catching up on the air they had starved themselves of as they each took big gulps.

They were too afraid to go back to typing and finding out information from the lab. There was no telling if and when he would come back. They stared at the monitors, but they looked different. All the information they had earlier seen and accessed had become cryptic. They could not make sense of what they saw; it looked like it had been rewritten in a strange language. Mr. Nox had encoded the files.

"We need to get out of here before someone comes back!" Levi whispered loudly, fear evident in his voice.

They hurried towards the door, peeping through to make sure no one was stationed outside. Once they confirmed that the coast was clear, the crew decided to leave. That was when a file caught Sumi's eye. "Guys! Look at this. This could give us some of the answers we want!"

They brought their attention to the file that lay on one laptop. Its title read "Operation Prey," written in bold letters. A little ray of sunshine, they thought!

"There's no time to read it, Sumi," Drew dismissed as soon as Sumi reached for the files.

"Then we take it! We can read it when we get to safety. Find out their deepest darkest secrets and expose them with it. We could find out why your father's name is on it too," Sumi resolved as she stashed the file in the pocket of her jacket.

"I want to find the truth out too but what if we get caught?" Levi challenged. "Taking it means they will know we were here in this room. We don't know the premises, they do. That makes it easier for us to be discovered. We are safer with them thinking we could be anywhere in the building."

"And if we don't get caught?" She countered. "Even if we do, we can always use the file as a bargaining chip. It's obviously important to them. It would be foolish of us not to take it," she concluded as she led the way and proceeded to open the door, not entertaining any objections.

Sumi was stubborn; as much as she was open to other opinions, whenever she made a decision, she stuck to it regardless of the consequences. In school, her stubbornness had saved them a lot of times and got them in just as much trouble. But either way, they were uninterested in arguing with her.

Blake was beginning to lose his strength. It had been quite a while since he'd engaged in physical combat with anyone. He had taken down one too many of Nox's men and his strength was beginning to wane. They were no match for him, undoubtedly, but he was beginning to wear himself out.

He swung at yet another guard that charged at him with a piece of broken wood. As soon as his fist connected with the guard's jaw, he collapsed to the floor, making no further movement. Blake himself had felt a deep pain surge through his rib cage. His side had been bruised from being smashed into walls and furniture and a large splinter had pierced through his side, leaving an open wound. He trusted his bruises to heal in no time but his strength however, he needed rest to regain that. He couldn't rest yet, he reminded himself. Each moment he delayed could have dangerous consequences for his son. He could not bear the thought of losing him too.

Quickly, Blake brushed the intrusive thoughts aside as he focused on the battle before him. He needed to get to Drew and that was all that mattered to him.

Another guard charged at him; Blake could see how shaky he was. He already knew he was going to be defeated but he pressed on anyway. As swiftly as he came at Blake, he was sidestepped, and a quick kick landed in his nether region caused him to collapse and wince in absolute pain. Blake bent over, pulled the guard up to a sitting position. "Where is my son?"

The guard kept quiet, nursing the pain that rested in his groin area.

With a lip busting jab to the guard's mouth, Blake grabbed his collar to ensure he was taken seriously this time.

"I repeat! Where. Is. My. Son?"

"You don't scare me," the guard spat.

"Is that right?" Blake snarled as he stood up, pulling the guard by the hair and slamming him against the wall. "Well, let's see if I can convince you otherwise."

Blake pulled out a pocket knife, tore the guard's shirt open and slashed his side. The guard screamed in pain.

"Be quiet, we are just getting started. You see this incision I made; it isn't life threatening but it hurts like hell. From your facial expression, I can tell that you've figured that part out."

"Go to hell," the guard retorted, keeping up his bravado.

"Oh, I have been there. Don't worry, I will try to bring as much of it to you as I can." Blake threatened.

"Wait!" The guard replied, his voice weak and doused in panic.

Blake's plan had started to work. He didn't want to have to kill the guard. He was very aware that would be the consequence of cutting him up some more. Thankfully, the guard couldn't handle the pain anymore and was more than willing to squeal. It only took one slash to provoke the snitch in him to spring to the surface. He admitted that three teenagers had been brought into the mansion and were now below the bunker. Two boys and a girl, while he didn't know which one was Blake's son, he was certain that they were unharmed.

He confessed that he had been one of the guards stationed to watch the teenagers in their cage. That was until Blake broke into the building and he had to come up to handle the issue.

Blake shoved the guard aside. Having gotten what he needed, he proceeded down the stairs. As soon as he got to the floor below, a new set of guards awaited him, ready for battle.

"It feels like we've been going around in circles. Each corner we take leads to more corners. Are you sure about this, D?" Levi asked as he paused to take a breath.

"I think this is the right path. I can't sense my father as strongly as I did before, but I still feel him, and it's this way," Drew offered.

"Maybe we moved too far away from where he is? If you no longer sense him strongly," Sumi suggested.

"Or maybe he feels drained and is conserving his energy, only to use it when absolutely necessary. This way is the only corner where I sense his energy at all. I'm sure that he's searching for me telepathically, and if he is doing it in a mansion rigged with field disruptors, it must be taking too much from him."

"How do you know this, Drew?" Sumi asked, still clinging to confusion.

"I don't know how, I just do. Since I stopped taking the drugs, I've been getting these flashbacks that are mine I think... but I don't remember anything about being a part of them. I also know some things that I don't think I'm supposed to know. Does that make any sense?" Drew asked.

"Well, it makes *some* sense," Sumi assured him.

"Do you think you can maybe sense a way out of here?" Levi retorted.

Drew smirked as they moved on.

A guard rushed into Mr. Nox's office. He looked like he had been struggling with someone or something. His clothes were torn in odd places, blood trickled down the side of his head, and his left eye was sporting a bruise that was beginning to turn a dark shade of purple.

"Sir!" He screamed. "The intruder is making his way down to this floor as we speak. We tried to get rid of the threat, but he was too strong. We have lost a lot of…"

Mr. Nox raised a finger, signaling he wanted the guard to be silent. The guard obeyed immediately.

"Correct me if I am wrong, in your explanation, you mentioned "he". Am I right?"

"Yes, Sir."

"So, this means there was one intruder and not a group of them like I was led to believe?" He continued.

"Yes, Sir but he was too stro--" Again, Mr. Nox cut him off.

"So, one intruder took out a group of supposedly highly trained guards? Do tell me why I shouldn't finish you off myself?" He asked, his voice remaining ever so calm.

"I know I do not deserve your mercy, Sir. But before you do, the intruder Sir, he came looking for his son. I overhead him asking a guard where his son was. He has unnatural speed and agility— like he's on steroids. We were no match for him."

Mr. Nox's eyes lit up instantaneously. He would have never guessed it was Blake, not immediately anyway. Blake was not one prone to violence, much less doing something as irrational as taking on a whole army of guards.

He remembered the times he had seen Blake so passionate in a fight, back when they worked together. They were few and far between. Losing his wife had thrown Blake back into his shell. He reduced himself to a lab scientist, trying out several different experiments and projects. Never confrontational. Even when the stone and communication device was taken from him, he didn't so much as make a fuss.

And all of a sudden, he is taking out trained guards? Maybe that is what loving a child does to a father, makes him mad.

He felt bad for Blake: his love for his son had led him to his inevitable demise.

"And that's why I don't have kids," Mr. Nox blurted out.

"What was that sir?" The guard asked.

Bringing his attention back to the guard in his office, he smiled and continued, "Go tend to your injuries, I will take care of this intruder."

The guard was extremely relieved, he hadn't expected mercy, but he got it. He didn't want to linger any longer before his boss changed his mind. And with that, the guard excused himself.

The noises they heard above them had died down drastically and Drew hoped his father was okay. They had been moving around for quite a bit and had not bumped into anyone. Not one guard was in sight. They remembered Mr. Nox instructing that guards be stationed in every part of the bunker. So, it was strange that they didn't find anyone. They had no intention of doing that, but they also dreaded the eerie quiet that consumed the halls.

"Guys look at this," Sumi called as she showed them a page from the file she had taken. "The information on here dates back several years ago from the Astronomer's Today Academic Journal. It's by Nox. It talks about people from a more advanced civilization stranded here on earth. They had been forced to flee their homeland by a species more advanced than theirs."

"Isn't this what Nox was going on about earlier when we were upstairs?" Levi asked.

"You're right! And after what we saw him do, I'm not surprised, and there's more to it," Sumi continued. "Some fled, some became slaves of these colonizers and others got killed. They picked Earth as a place for most of their refugees, scattering themselves around the globe because they were too afraid to be seen in clusters. It also talks about how they live among us and blend easily because they look just like us." She looked at Drew for a brief second and then looked back at her paper.

As Sumi continued, Drew thought to himself, *So these new memories are…*

"Here it also says that there are theories that these aliens were once inhabitants of Earth, several thousands of years before. They were just like us until they had a breakthrough in technology, becoming more superior to the rest of the humans on Earth. They moved to a different galaxy where they lived and thrived, but the climate on their new planet altered their biological composition. Their bodies had to adjust to fit in."

She read some more; eyes skimmed through the paper with speed. "It also says here that they have a more advanced body system. They work faster, move faster, their brains accumulate faster, and some can even heal faster and communicate telepathically."

"Some?" Drew asked.

"Yes, that is what it says here. Not everyone evolved the same. But even the weakest ones are much stronger than a human on earth."

Levi peeked at the paper she held to read more of its contents. She handed it over to him and pulled out two other pages of the file, handing one to Drew and keeping the third for herself.

"Apparently not advanced enough if they had to flee invaders," Levi mocked.

Levi's comment slightly got under Drew's skin a bit as the thoughts of his memories began to connect to him more.

Unaware of Drew's annoyance, Levi began reading his paper to the others, skimming through the section titled *Type II*.

"So, Nox proposes that these *Type II aliens* were chased out of their homes by much higher-level beings. Man, if they couldn't fight back, how would we even hope to defend ourselves if these higher-level beings just decide they wanna come down to Earth? According to this document, Earth is classified as a Type 0.7-- not even a one yet. He says it would take us another 250 years before we are even considered a Type I! 250 years? Are we really that primitive?"

"Not to mention if these are aliens that look like humans, how many more other species are there? Humans aren't the only sentient life forms. There are beings more advanced than us. Stronger, faster, better. Should they decide to take over Earth, we're powerless against them. This is freaking me out, guys," Sumi expressed.

Levi continued. "This part talks about subjugating the human race. Nox says humans are lower functioning species lost in the endless cycle of trying to control and destroy one another. According to this, these aliens have been studying humans for a long time. Nox believed if humans on Earth knew better, they would do better."

"Hold on guys, this paper gets much worse," Drew interrupted.

Both Levi and Sumi crowded around Drew's paper as he continued.

"This one seems to be some kind of manifesto and plan by Nox. He says many of his kind tried several methods to help humans transcend into a more evolved race. But none of them worked and so as a last resort, he's decided that the solution is to dominate earthlings. He's decided that humans on Earth were and still are incapable of advancement on their own. He says we are slowly destroying nature and since they live on Earth now too, they will not let us bring the planet to ruin. According to this, the plan is already in motion and has been for years. It talks about a new world order that would bring stability and give purpose to human existence. What's *AO*?"

"So, he's like a psychopath trying to do what he thinks is right for the human race?" Sumi asked.

"That's what it looks like," Drew continued. "It also says they've been keeping tabs on the aliens that came down to earth. There are a lot of them."

"They live amongst us, and we will never be the wiser," Sumi lamented.

"My paper says they can and do live for hundreds of years." Levi pressed his palm against his face. "This sounds like some weird sci-fi bullshit. Is there a hidden camera somewhere because this isn't funny anymore. But all of this… is so crazy and kind of overwhelming to grasp. Are we believing all of this?"

Having to take in all of this information, it became so much clearer to Drew about his father's connection to the situation, especially with what had been happening to him physically. However, seeing how his friends were handling the news, he wasn't so sure if they would be ok with the possibility that—

I'm one of them, he thought.

"Let me ask you guys a question. Do you believe that we should be approaching the situation judging *all* of these aliens? I mean, we talk about being judged and mistreated because of who we are and what we look like all the time. How are we any different if this is how we're feeling about all of them? I mean, we just read these papers. They have been oppressed to the point that they were chased out of their entire galaxy. More than anyone, we know what happens when people are afraid of what they don't know. They create hate. But they are refugees. Many of our own families have had to deal with that. Besides, he is just one guy with some evil plan."

Sumi and Levi both reflected on Drew's words; they rang true for the both of them. Sumi realized that it may affect him more because of his growing connection to all of this and the possible connection of him and his father being similar to Nox. Both Sumi and Levi nodded in agreement with Levi placing his hand on Drew's shoulder and apologizing.

Just then, Sumi came across another piece of key information.

"Drew, it says something here about a stone and communication device that is a key instrument in tracking down these people. Didn't your father lose a communication device?" Sumi asked.

"It may just be the same thing. Plus, one of the guards took that stone from you, didn't he?" Levi wondered.

"Yeah, that's true, here let me take a look," Drew remarked as he read the paper. "Yes, I think it is the same one. My father talked about it being a prototype. There's only one in existence." Drew felt more convinced that his father had a role to play in all of this. Everything pointed to it. He hoped his father was not a part of the world domination scheme.

"Could that be why your father came here? Maybe he is trying to save us and take back the device?"

Drew responded, "Dammit man, I just don't know anymore!"

"He's here for us, Drew. Don't let your anger and frustration about all of this make you doubt your father's love for you. Do you hear me?" Sumi pleaded.

"Yeah. Sure," Drew shrugged.

"I still think we should talk to your father, or at least you should. You need to get some answers. If he created a device this advanced, he must know a lot about these aliens... but how do we find him? We've been going around for quite a bit and still haven't found anyone or anything," Levi lamented.

"You're right Motor, my link to him has been going back and forth, I think we should just push back towards the bunker entrance. We just have to be careful that we don't run into any guards in that direction.

They all agreed as they continued looking around.

CHAPTER TWENTY

ONE MORE TRY

A guard slammed into the door, pulling it clean off its hinges. It was a swift battle, none of the guards came close to defeating him. The door crumbled to reveal Mr. Nox standing there, arms folded like he already knew what was going on behind the door. He looked down at the unconscious guard and a wicked smile possessed his face. He raised his eyes and pinned them on Blake.

"That must have felt good, didn't it?" Nox wondered as he side-stepped the guard and entered the space.

"Where is my son, Nox? What have you done with him?" Blake asked, breathing heavily.

"Oh, nothing too damaging… yet. I'm more interested in his father. I must say, I'm impressed to see you like this. When was the last time you were in the throes of battle? The adrenaline rush you feel now, tell me, did you miss it?"

"I am not playing your games Vozyr, I swear by the gods if you have touched a hair on his head!"

"Yes, yes, I know, you will kill me and all of that cliche nonsense. Oh, I am shaking in my boots."

Mr. Nox walked away from him, reaching for the bottle of wine poised on the shelf and pouring himself a glass. "Drink?" He asked casually. When Blake gave him no response, he smiled and continued "Okay then, more for me." Nox downed the wine in one sip.

"Take a seat, Blake. You see, I am not going to sugarcoat this or pretend about it. The truth is, I need you on my team. You are a crucial part of this project. Your generous contribution to our cause has boosted our work speed by 30%!"

"You mean what you stole from me." Blake corrected.

"I am more than happy to give it back when we complete the project. I remember when you came down to Earth. You and your wife."

Blake twitched a little bit, he didn't know if he liked the idea of Nox talking about his wife.

"I was here twenty years before you showed up with your family. I joined the Naval forces in Britain alongside the Allied Forces, and I fought in the World War, risking my life for them. I fought like I was trying to save my own people. When the constant fighting didn't bring any of the change that I wanted, I moved to America. Still determined to help the life forms on Earth, I helped create a movement for the reform of civil rights. You remember that, don't you?" Nox asked, to which Blake lowered his gaze. "Of course, you do. That was how I reconnected with you on Earth. You were always a vibrant young man, you had an active mind, so full of life and purpose. I could see it in your eyes that you wanted to do good, make a difference in this world, just like you tried in our home world. That endeared me to you immediately. Finding out that you ended up in the same galactic quadrant as I was made me so happy, the stars truly did align for us." Nox continued, attempting to flatter his old friend. "The relief I felt to find someone else like me, I felt less alone in this world. You were someone that understood, someone that reminded me of home. I knew I had to help you and your wife immediately! And so, I pooled together my resources for you, helped you settle in undetected."

"And I have always been grateful for that.--"

"Let me finish Blake," Nox interrupted, as he stared down at his glass. "What you don't realize is that I fought tooth and nail for them. I even joined in their politics to gain enough leverage to bring the change they didn't know they needed. And what did they do?"

BOOOOM!!!

With a thunderous pound on the table by the force of his fist, a frustrated Nox continues.

"THEY SPAT IT RIGHT BACK IN MY FACE! THE NERVE OF THESE MAGGOTS!" Nox shouted. He pauses to regain his composure.

"They intentionally rigged the elections. I saw this for myself. Despite this, project after project, I tried to help the earthlings. Each attempt failed just as badly as the last, if not, worse."

He turns to Blake hoping to appeal to his logic with a sincere tone.

"All these humans do is destroy nature, collapse their economies, instigate pointless wars again and again, slaughtering each other like sheep, causing disasters all over their globe, damaging nature even more. The list is endless. These humans have continued this cycle for as long as they began to exist. If they are not subjugated, they will completely destroy themselves. How am I the bad guy if all I want is the betterment of Earth and its inhabitants?"

"Maybe the point was never to have interfered in the first place," Blake interrupted. "Maybe the point was to let humans on Earth grow at their own pace. Who are we to decide how they run their planet? They have chosen war and violence for several centuries, yet the species endures. We were supposed to simply take refuge here, not dominate."

Blake continued. "You remember when the *Ascended Ones* came to our galaxy? They offered us peace, they improved our daily lives, they even gave us the technology we know and use now. We thought they were sent from the gods. Surely, we were not destroying our natural resources or engaging in pointless wars, but we were still less advanced than the *Ascended Ones* and they used that against us. They integrated themselves into our society, slowly taking all the positions of power and started their journey of domination. Maybe they had the right intentions, maybe they saw that we weren't thriving as much as we should, maybe they thought they were helping. But the truth remains that we were doing just fine without them; yes, maybe less advanced but we still thrived. Look at what they did to us. We lost our homes and now have to live down here. How does it not feel like the same thing? Leave them be. Let them grow at their own pace."

"How do you think we can go back to our home if we are stuck down here with these lower life forms?" Nox countered. "They do not have the capacity to protect themselves from an invasion. The *Ascended Ones* are up there building better civilizations, advancing their technology even further. How will we ever defeat them and take back our home? Coming down to Earth has set us backwards by centuries. I am just trying to quicken the pace. Humans cannot think for themselves, history has proven that they cannot do *anything* for themselves. This cause benefits everyone, WHY DON'T YOU SEE THAT?"

DREW TYPE 2: COMING OF AGE

"You have lost your way Nox. Your intentions are far from pure and your approach is flawed. You have been responsible for so much pain and suffering. Subjugating this planet is vile. How do you take from people their free will?"

"A small price to pay for a greater good. Every utopian civilization has a price to pay, old friend."

"You stole my technology. It was my only chance to establish a stronger secret communication with our lost people here on earth; you kidnapped my son! I would not say we are friends. You have lost your way and you are willing to drag everyone down to Hell with you."

Nox took in a deep breath. "I did not lose my way; you are just too blind to see my path."

"You know it's not too late to do what is right," Blake tried to convince him.

"Save the emotional bullshit for someone who cares. I turned off empathy a long time ago. What I do not understand is what you see in these pathetic humans. We have tried everything to make it work. You and I both have tried to help them. We risked our lives, energy, knowledge, resources and what did we get? Nothing! ALL OUR EFFORTS MADE NOT ONE DIFFERENCE!" Mr. Nox roared.

"We did not come here to fix Earth, that is ultimately for the humans to decide. Can't you see that you're trying to do to them, what was done to us?" Blake asked.

"What I can't see is why you are so keen on these lower life forms. You lost your wife on this planet, because of these people, why does that not upset you? What have they done to you to make you so pathetic? I almost can't differentiate you from them. With your technical know-how, we could bring about a new world order faster than the rate we are going even now. But you *choose* to be average. Here I am, promising you a place at the top, not to live this miserly life any longer and yet you turn me down adamantly. Don't you miss home? We can recreate all that with our power. We can bring home here and have our people reveal themselves."

"Where is my son?" Blake asked, cutting him short, already tired of the conversation.

"You can both be a part of this new world, Blake. Just join me. I would hate to see such greatness go to waste." He offered his hand.

Blake chuckled. "You cannot be this gullible. So what if you dominate the humans on earth? If you bring advancement and call more of our people down here and we start all over, then what? You will doom this planet too. Our people revealing themselves will be a beacon to the *Ascended Ones*. Like a sore thumb, we would stick out. It would be the disaster that swallowed our planet all over again."

Mr. Nox met Blake at eye level and maintained contact. "You see that is where you are wrong *Yaegr*. We have a plan in place to ensure none of that happens and that is why we need you on board. All that the *Ascended Ones* require from me is the capture of the *Rebel Faction* that escaped to this planet all those years ago. That is our deal. Your device will help find them all. So you see, I'm just a collector. After a few of our older colleagues are taken away, we could make Earth the perfect utopia, under our control!"

"You are a bounty hunter against our people, traitor. I won't be a part of anything that steals from any beings' free will."

Nox sighs. "Well then my friend, I am afraid this has to be goodbye." Mr. Nox pulled out a gun from his drawer and aimed it at Blake. He turned off the safety and clicked the gun in place.

Moving swiftly, Blake slapped the gun out of Nox's hand. "So, the hard way then…" Mr. Nox concluded as he positioned himself for one-on-one combat.

Nox slammed Blake into the ground and without hesitation, he rained punches down onto Blake's face. He lifted Blake up and slammed him against a nearby coffee table, continuing with his flurry of punches. The blows were enough to break the wooden legs supporting the table.

Blake was quick to protect himself, avoiding most of the blows. He connected his knee with Nox's groin; a low blow, he admitted, but it did the trick. Nox rolled away from him, clutching his nether region in pain. And just like that, Blake had gotten the upper hand in the battle.

"Where the hell is my son?" Blake screamed as he squeezed around Nox's throat as tightly as his arms could permit.

"I guess you'll never know," came the response. Nox felt his blood circulation cease; his eyes bulged and his vision blurred as he began to pass out. He extended his hand, reaching for something, anything and soon the tips of his fingers touched a broken piece of wood from the coffee table. Without hesitation, he smashed it on Blake's head. The sharp edge cut through his flesh and blood gushed out from the side of his face. Blake staggered backwards, struggling to find his footing. He looked to the ground in a bit of a daze and also grabbed a piece of the wood that broke off from the blow.

Nox saw an opening and took it, he charged at Blake, hitting him several more times with the piece of wood. Before Blake lost consciousness, he plunged the wood deep in Nox's thigh. Unable to stand on his feet anymore, Blake fell on his back, blinking in and out of consciousness.

Mr. Nox grunted as he yanked out the shaft buried in his thigh. Tossing it aside, he stood and walked towards the corner Blake was bunched up in. Nox stood towering above him, equally bloodied but still with most of his strength about him.

"Pathetic," he spat as he turned around. He looked for the gun where it had been tossed earlier. He picked it up and returned to the table where he had left his wine. The weapon in one hand, wine in another, he took another gulp and pulled up a chair for himself.

He called in a guard to bind Blake's hands and feet. His energy had depleted, escaping was not an option.

Blake sat in a corner of the room; he had finally recovered from his near unconsciousness. His face was bloodied from the deep cut on the side of his head; it was healing, but much slower than it normally would have. His energy had been drained from all the fighting and how much blood he had lost.

Mr. Nox rolled up his sleeves as he spat some blood out of his mouth. The blood came with a tooth Blake had knocked loose. He hissed at the slight pain it caused. Then he smiled and jested to Blake, "Well it's a good thing you didn't take one from the front. I would hate to have you ruin my smile."

He looked at the sorry sight that was Blake, bloody and broken, and shook his head in disappointment. "You used to be so much of a fighter, resilient, dogged but now you are just... I don't even know what you are. Weak. You are no different from an earthling."

Blake fell silent. He had lost this battle; he knew what was to come and he would not beg for his life.

"But I know you Yaegr," Nox continued. "You are as stubborn as you are now weak. And that will prove troublesome for me eventually. So, I will have to end this quickly. You have already caused enough destruction. And my partners don't take too kindly to delay."

"You can do whatever you want to me, but just remember, our kind does not die easily," Blake countered.

Nox threw back his head and let out a loud sinister laugh at

Blake's remark.

"What's so funny?" Blake responded.

"You are… answer me this, what do you even remember about our abilities at their full potential?"

Blake spat out a bit of blood. He looked at his bound wrists. "Is this really necessary?"

"Well, I'm waiting," Nox contended.

"I don't even know where you are going with this," Blake responded faintly. "There's a lot to Type II abilities, I don't know where to start. They are stronger, obviously but then there are Type II's that have tapped into their abilities and are so advanced that their bodies can morph into a rare, berserk, creature-like form called a "Nomu". The morphing is temporary anyway, they can return their bodies back to humanoid at will."

"And?" Nox urged.

"When they are in transformation, they are stronger than a Type II. Their strength then is only comparable to the *Ascended Ones*. Even on our planet, we rarely ever saw anyone with the ability to morph. I was told it occurred only a few times in a generation. In all my years, I only saw one of our kind that could do it. I was a kid then, his name was Hamza, one of The Heads at the time. He was very revered but also very old. He only transformed once and even then, it was amazing, unlike anything I had ever seen. Even in his weakened state, he was still stronger than the average Type II. It's incredible how much strength comes with that advancement. If only we had half of our population with the ability or even a quarter, we would have had a much more even fight with the *Ascended Ones*. We might have saved our home. My point is, if you do see a Type II human with the ability to turn in a Nomu, you should never engage them in combat," Blake concluded.

Nox let out a laugh, one so deep it came from his stomach.

Blake looked at him, confused; he didn't remember saying anything funny. He let Nox have his laugh.

"You believe Hamza was the only advanced Type II of our kind?"

"If there were more, why didn't they speak up or do anything to help? Besides, we would have noticed," Blake responded.

"Well then, I guess your observation skills need a lot of work," Nox admonished.

"What do you mean by that?" Blake asked.

"You, my friend, have grossly underestimated your son after all of these years. And that is fine. But underestimating me? That's a really horrible mistake you made," Nox snarled as he began to loosen his cuffs and take off his suit jacket. "Let me refresh your memory, help you remember what it's like to witness the power of a Nomu."

Nox's eyes glistened as they began to morph. His pupils dilated and became bloodshot red. He threw his head back as an other-worldly groan escaped his throat. His shirt began to stretch out and rip as his body grew bigger and bigger. Nox fell to his knees, digging his hands into the earth as talons sprung forth from where his fingers had once been.

Blake scooted far away from him as the enormous shadow of the beast closed in on him.

The crew moved cautiously, doing their best to avoid being seen. Drew was sensing less and less of his father. They were either moving far away from where Blake was, or something had happened to him.

"My feet are killing me," Sumi whispered.

"Take those shoes off then," Levi suggested.

"What? Are you crazy? These chucks are my favorite shoes; I can't afford to lose them in this madhouse. If I'm going to die, then I would rather die in them," Sumi lamented.

"Then why are you complaining?" Levi countered.

"Guys! Shhhh!" Drew paused, raising up a finger. He could hear some guards coming their way. He pulled both of his friends into a room and closed the door. They peeked through a small opening as two guards walked past, guns on their belts as they discussed the current situation. Once the guards moved to a safe distance, Drew spoke again. "We really have to be careful, you guys. You can't just go about starting arguments in the middle of a situation like this. We need to find my dad and then find a way out of here. Do you think you guys can focus until we sort that out?" He asked.

"Yes, sorry. Levi just gets on my nerves sometimes," Sumi scoffed.

"Hey! I'm right here," Levi complained.

"I know," Sumi sassed, rolling her eyes.

"Okay, let's go," Drew instructed as he led the way. Those two were always fighting. He decided leaving them alone together would cause everyone to be immediately discovered, thrown back in the cage, or possibly killed.

Another guard came along, this time he had heard footsteps and was out to investigate the cause of the noise.

Luckily for the crew, another door was open, and they went in, each one picking a different spot to hide in, since huddling together would make them that much easier to find. The guard entered the room, scanning it for intruders.

He didn't seem in a hurry to get it over with, taking his time to properly search. The crew were afraid of what might happen if he found any one of them. The guard moved close to where Sumi had hidden herself. He turned on a flashlight and he could see the shadow of a person looming behind some crates. He pulled out his walkie talkie. "Team 3 to all units," he advised through the speaker.

Drew knew they had been found out. He knew he needed to do something... but what?

He remembered it. The day he spent quality time with his father... They had set out on a fishing trip that cool evening. He followed his father almost all the time, but never once did he actually participate in the fishing. Drew just enjoyed being around his dad; even though he was terrified of the fish, it was a small price to pay for his father's company. He had realized quite early that showing interest in the things his father loved was one way to get him to pay attention.

He didn't think his dad was bad at parenting, he just thought of him as overly passionate about his job. He really enjoyed figuring things out.

His father had been quiet for a while, obviously buried nose deep in whatever he was working on with the fish. He thought to start a conversation.

"Why do you catch the fish, take pictures and just throw them back, Dad? It feels like a waste of time."

Not looking up from his oversized journal, Blake responded. "It's for an experiment I am carrying out, son."

"Oh, what is it about?"

This time, his father looked up, amused that his son had any interest in what he was doing. He patted Drew on the head and proceeded to explain further.

"You see, if I can figure out this fish's movement, eating patterns, behavior, how it reacts to changes in climate, how the tide affects it, I can predict and track every other fish like it. It's incredible! And once this experiment is successful, I will move on to more advanced species!"

"Like people?"

"Yes, Son... like people."

"I am not as brave as you Dad, I can't even touch a fish. They scare me."

Blake pulled up a fish from the water and offered it to his son. "Come, touch it."

"But I'm afraid."

"Yes, well you see, fear shouldn't stop you from trying out new things. If you touch this fish, your fears might come true, you could totally hate the experience and move on to never touching a fish again or... you could touch it and find out that it is just a fish and it is nothing to be afraid of. But it is up to you to decide. No matter what you choose, it makes no difference to me. So... what do you want to do?"

Drew thought about it for a second and then moved close to his father, eyes shut and stretching out his hands in acceptance. He wanted so badly to be a part of what his father was working on. He didn't want to disappoint his dad.

Blake placed the fish in his hands. "Well?"

"It's... it's cold and slippery." Slowly he opened his eyes to examine the life form in his hands. It didn't look so scary. Almost immediately, the fish started flapping aggressively and Drew dropped the fish purely from the shock of the sudden movement. Then he let out a giggle.

Blake picked the fish up and returned it to the water. "The fish was out of the water for too long, it was trying to tell you to put it back. So how do you feel?"

"It's not so bad."

"You know, there is this saying that I heard, and I just love it so much. 'Not everything that is faced can be changed. But nothing can be changed until it is faced.' "

It made absolutely no sense to him, what his father had explained. He was just so excited to have pleased him and conquered his fear of fishes.

"Team 3 to all units... Do you copy? Over," the guard repeated.

Drew knew then what he had to do. It didn't matter that he was afraid, he was going to protect his friends either way. He sized up the guard, checking for weaknesses and strength. The guard was of average build. He looked no taller than 5'9" and he didn't have a gun like the rest. Registering this information, Drew crawled from his hiding spot, sneaking up behind the guard as carefully as he could manage.

In the instant the guard noticed a presence behind him, his face was met with a heavy blow that knocked him off his feet. One more hit and the guard was out cold. Drew snatched the walkie talkie from him and handed it over to Levi who had also come out of hiding.

"Sumi, man the door. Make sure there are no other guards headed this way," Drew instructed.

Sumi rushed out of her hiding spot and did as she was told. "Team 3, what is your status? Over," a voice came from the walkie talkie.

The crew looked at each other. Levi cleared his throat and tried to mimic the guard as best he could.

"The issue has been resolved. Over."

"What was the disturbance? Over."

"One of the intruders came down here but the threat has been apprehended. Over."

"What floor are you on? We will send reinforcements just in case. Over."

Levi threw the walkie talkie to the ground and smashed it with his feet. "We need to get off this floor," he urged the crew.

"One moment." Drew paused as he proceeded to strip the guard of his vest. "Here, put this on." He threw the vest at Levi.

"Dude, no! What do we know about his hygiene? We don't know what they experiment on down here. He could have some horrible diseases for all we know!" Levi protested.

"Put the damn thing on and stop whining!" Drew demanded.

"Well, if I die, let it be known that you killed me," Levi remarked as he started donning the vest.

Drew proceeded to tie the guard up, gagging him so he wouldn't scream for help when he awakened.

"Let's get out of here."

CHAPTER TWENTY-ONE

SOMETHING MORE

The third batch had been scheduled to set off for Earth and the capsules readied for take-off. The families were given their final moments to say goodbye to their friends. Not all were headed for Earth; they didn't want to overpopulate the planet in such a short time. Some were to be scattered across other galaxies. So, chances remained that they might never get to see each other again.

"No Son, we can't."

"Dad please."

"You can't go with her, and she can't come with you either."

"Mom... please."

For the first time since he had started having these memories, he remembered his mother. Not her face but her warm hands pulling him into an embrace, trying to assure him that it would all be okay.

They had begun their journey to Earth, it was chosen as the most suitable planet and they were one of many families headed there, each assigned their own capsule. They couldn't risk putting more than one family in a capsule, the smaller the travel groups, the higher their chances of leaving undetected and the higher their chances of survival.

The kids did not understand why they had to be separated and each parent could not afford to let their child go into the care of the other. Earth was new, they didn't know what to expect. Each family had to stick to their own. Naturally.

Xaeon stretched out his arm, reaching for friends who in turn had tears welled up in their eyes as they reached for him too.

"No, please let me go," Xaeon begged.

Their pleas and tears fell on deaf ears as they were all pulled into their different capsules, doors shut as they launched for Earth.

Drew shook his head, the memories were becoming too frequent and each time they came, they left him with a slight ache. He almost missed taking his medication.

The crew decided to split up to cover more ground. With Levi wearing the vest for protection, they were to reconnect with each other when they got to the last room on the floor.

Drew had searched as many rooms as he could find, but no one was in sight. The floor seemed secure enough. He wondered if the absence of guards on that floor had anything to do with his father. He found an office and immediately concluded that it belonged to Mr. Nox. It was way too sophisticated to belong to anyone else. Even with Nox being absent, his cologne remained a very strong presence in the room. The seats were made with thick, clearly expensive leather.

He stepped on a tiger skin rug, noting how real it seemed. He stooped to touch the fur of the animal and that was when it dawned on him that it was an actual tiger. Its skull was still in place in its head. "Creepy," he muttered. With his eyes focused on the open laptop that lay on the table, he walked to the other end of the room to grab it. Once he had completed the task, he doubled back and went to join the rest of the team where they were waiting on him.

"Did you find anything?" Levi asked as he spotted Drew. "No, nothing. But I think we should stay alert," Drew replied. "I did find a laptop in Nox's office. Maybe we can find things on it that can be helpful to us."

Levi reached out to grab the laptop, but Drew pulled back, not intending it for him.

Handing it over to Sumi, Drew said, "See what you can find about these experiments. Why they are tracking these people and where the stone and communication device could be. No pressure. Just find and report whatever you think will be instrumental in figuring this out."

Drew turned to Levi, "Motor, remember our phones were taken so when we split, let's not stray too far away. We'll meet back here."

Levi stood immediately and handed Drew the remote that he was still holding onto.

"You never know when you'll need this, bro," Levi advised.

"Not from inside your pants though," Sumi blurted in disgust which prompted Drew to snicker.

Levi saluted the two and hurried to carry out his task. Drew was naturally a leader, without even trying, although he had his moments of reluctance. His friends had always looked up to him to come up with plans to get them out of a sticky situation and he always came through.

As soon as Levi left, Sumi buried herself deep in the task she had been charged with, hoping their hiding spot was safe enough for them to work from.

Her search on the laptop caused her to stumble upon several

files containing information of more individuals. The file they had acquired earlier only contained a fraction of what was available here. Here she could see what connected the people, why they were important enough to track: they all came from outside Earth.

For Sumi, it was scary to find out that there were several thousands of aliens on her planet. For centuries, the aliens had trooped onto Earth in small numbers, not enough to call any attention to themselves. But if the aliens were so horrible, why didn't they attack? They had been here for centuries; it was more than enough time. She allowed that little speck of hope to glimmer, maybe they weren't all bad. Just then she received a transmission from an unknown source. The message was encrypted. Normally she could find a way to decrypt messages, but this one was much more difficult. She decided to save the transmission for later when the crew gathered again.

Meanwhile, Drew sat nearby, eyes closed, his focus rested on establishing communication with his father. Blake had become harder to sense. Sometimes it felt like he wasn't in the building at all.

"Dad... can you hear me?"

Nothing.

"If you can hear me, please say something."

Still, nothing.

"We need your help. I have no idea what I'm supposed to be doing and the crew is counting on me to come through."

Drew was becoming frustrated with the constant silence he was saddled with.

"At least... please be alive. Don't die on me," came his final plea as he got up to his feet. It was up to him now to figure it all out. He was going to have to protect his friends with all he had.

He walked up to Sumi, "Will you be okay by yourself for a few minutes? I need to move around a bit, see what I can find and also see if there's an angle that lets me communicate properly with my dad. I can't seem to feel his presence anymore."

Looking up from the laptop, Sumi gave him a small smile "I'll be fine on my own, just please don't be too long."

"I promise I won't," Drew replied. He gave her shoulder a light squeeze and then went out the door.

Sumi continued digging; Nox hadn't really bothered with encrypting this sensitive information. He must have been so confident that nothing would go wrong. Then, she discovered Mr. Nox wasn't working alone. For years, he had amassed associates that invested a lot of money to his cause. In the files, these investors were referred to only as *"The Invisible Hand."* From what she could gather, they represented a very powerful population, stronger than any government body.

They had no names or faces, they remained completely anonymous. Even Mr. Nox had no clue what they looked like. They only communicated using voice warping devices. So, their voices too, could not be pinned to anyone. They really put in the extra effort to stay unknown, Sumi tried to work out if it was possible to not only discover their identity but to expose them.

They had funded every project Mr. Nox had carried out in the past. Operation Prey was not the first, several others had failed before it. This new project showed signs of success after the stone and communication device were introduced. It was the missing piece they'd needed but so, evidently, was Drew. Sumi paused to read the sentence again and her eyes had not deceived her, the documents made clear mention of Drew.

What could they need him for?

She feared it might be one of their experiments.

Drew's ability to sense his father, his thing with the remote, his superhuman strength and, of course, that time bright light glowed from under his skin... It wasn't that much of a surprise that they wanted him for their experiments. Maybe they want to understand the inner workings of his body, what caused him to do all that. But the files didn't say much about Drew or what exactly they planned to do with him, only that he was important to their work.

She needed to tell Drew what she had found, he was like a cube of sugar in an anthill. The longer he stayed, the more danger he was in.

Levi had searched several wings of the bunker and he felt terribly exhausted. He entered the room closest to him, shut the door and took a seat. He was going to take some time to recuperate before returning to his search.

He rocked the chair back and forth for a bit, letting his mind wander. This was one hell of an experience. If he did get out of it alive, he was going to tell his story to all that were willing to listen, he thought to himself. *What if Drew is really an alien?* He caught himself thinking. As much as he didn't want to entertain the thought, it lingered in his mind. It certainly wasn't a normal occurrence for a human to glow, with light shining through from underneath their skin.

It was also not normal for him to have superhuman abilities amplified by a remote. He had broken chains with his bare hands and a steel lock without getting even the faintest bruise on his person.

As much as he had tried to act cool about it, he couldn't shake off the thought. He knew Sumi felt the same. Drew was either an alien or the victim of some crazy experiment by his father. He didn't think Drew was a danger to him, he was confident there was nothing to fear from his friend. But he still needed answers for the questions that raged in his mind.

Levi, getting carried away, swung both legs up on the table. As soon as they came in contact with the desk, he heard a click and the groaning of a moving wall. It seemed he had accidentally opened a hidden doorway in the mansion.

Immediately going on alert, he made his way to the door, walking ever so cautiously to it. He pushed it open, peeping in.

"Is anybody in here?" He paused before walking into the room. It looked deserted; cobwebs clung to every piece of furniture in the room, as if it hadn't been touched in years.

"Of course, nobody's in here, what was I thinking, asking a stupid question," he reprimanded himself as he went on to survey the room.

It looked like an old, deserted lab. Unlike the one they had seen earlier, this lab had a lot of testing equipment: several hospital beds, dead heartbeat monitors and human sized tubes.

Why would they have human sized tubes? The floor was littered with shattered glass, doused in some brown substance.

Levi was fairly certain it was dried up blood. It was truly some kind of a Frankenstein laboratory.

He remembered the files had talked about previous experiments that had failed.

Were they experimenting on people?

"Of course, they were," he replied to himself.

He walked over to a file cabinet. Pulling it open, he found a series of files arranged in alphabetical order. They must have been the names and information of the victims of their experiments.

They were several files, all dusty and some hadn't stood the test of time too well, as mites had eaten through them. He picked a file labeled Potential Nomu Designee (PND) and read:

PROFILE

Name: Dryana Xyra

Earth Name: Jessica Lawrence Occupation: Teacher

Family: A partner and two adopted kids (boys)

ABILITIES

Strength: 73.5%

Tolerance: 56.1%

Speed: 70.2%

Healing: 81%

FINDINGS

Day One: Subject was brought in sedated. Once consciousness was restored, the subject began to fight against restraints, almost breaking free. Almost. Subject is sedated, too unstable to begin tests.

Day Two: Subject still rebels, biting and thrashing aggressively. Subject is sedated.

Day Three: Subject is calmer. She understands now the futility of trying to break free. Subject refuses communication still, only asking, rather, begging to be set free.

Day Four: Subject is promised freedom if she co-operates. Because of the false hope given to the subject, she participates in all activities willingly.

Day Eight: After a series of tests, the subject's strength and abilities have drained significantly. Subject exhibits weight loss. Subject also shows signs of degradation to both long-term memory and short-term recall.

Day Nine: Subject has returned to thrashing around, begging for freedom.

Subject is not nearly as strong as when she first came in. More and more of her memories are fading away. Subject has no idea who or where she is. Subject no longer remembers anything about her family.

Day Ten: Subject is totally complacent. Subject has no willpower or reason to fight for freedom.

Day Eleven: Subject was released and asked to go. Subject chose to stay. Subject knew not where to go or who to call. Subject submits herself for more experiments.
Day Twelve: Subject has lost all advanced ability and has become completely normal for her species. Subject's body could not handle the tests and is now in critical condition.

Subject expired on Day Thirteen at roughly 18:00 hours.

RESULTS
Successful

CONCLUSION

Tests resulted in the total suppression of the Nomu, reducing the subject to the same functioning as a normal Type II.

Subject's body failed to pull through experiments.

Levi closed the file and returned it back into the drawer. There were several others like that. Random people were snatched from their families, and it always ended in the test subjects dying. The word "Nomu" would often show up, although he could not find the connection as to why.

Each had vastly different experiences. Some showed such strong will that they fought to break free from Day One to their last. Some expired almost immediately.

The common denominator was that they all always died in the end. There was not one single file that suggested anyone made it out alive. But if there was, then it must have been top secret. They had killed one too many people for nothing.

He searched for more things he could find in the hidden room. There was so much dust to wade through. He made his way deeper into the room and discovered a cage similar to the one they had been locked in earlier. But this cage was bigger, much wider. There was no lock to keep anyone out, so he went in, still as cautious as possible. There were little inscribed sticks poking out of the ground in different parts of the cage.

He yanked one stick and read what was written on it. The stick simply stated, "Subject 1." It wasn't quite clear to him, so he picked a different stick and it read "Subject 7." And it continued like that, each one he took out had inscriptions on them.

That was when it dawned on him, they had used this space as a makeshift burial ground for their victims. Maybe disposing of their bodies would have led back to Mr. Nox and that's why they chose to hoard them instead.

They were never offered a proper burial and their families still thought of them as missing.

Discovering he stood just above another grave, he screamed and jumped to a corner. The sand in the cage was shallow. The victims couldn't be that far below the earth. He expected there to be a foul smell to envelop the room but there was nothing. He theorized that chemicals must have been used to dissolve the bodies, leaving only the bones. Or it could also be that their intestines were removed and thus they couldn't smell. He had watched one too many crime movies on TV but whatever was done, he didn't much like the idea of standing in front of or above a corpse.

Uninterested in exploring any more for fear of finding more bizarre stuff, he returned the sticks that served as tombstone markers as carefully as he could, walked out and shut the cage behind him. He made a mental note to thoroughly wash his hands in as much soap as he could find. And so, going back out, he decided to focus on searching the open room for useful information.

Taking a chance in the hallway, Drew went in search of a place that provided a better connection to his father. Blake always knew what to do and he really needed someone to tell him what to do.

He took a turn and just as quickly as he did, he hurried back to the corner he came from. There was a guard there, Drew hadn't noticed his presence. He peeked slightly and saw that the guard's back was turned to him. Relief. He hadn't been seen.

The guard stood alone, pacing sometimes but mostly standing still. He was the only guard in the corner, at least as far as Drew could see and the guard stood in front of an exit door. It must lead to another floor in the building. He knew he and Sumi would need to get past that door soon enough.

Drew went into one of the rooms, looking for something, but he didn't find anything worthwhile. Then he remembered coming across a game room earlier in his search. Slowly he went back down the hallway. He walked swiftly past the room Sumi was in. She saw him walk past and whispered his name.

"Drew, I'm here."

Giving her a quick look, he responded, "I know, I need to get something first."

"What? Wait, I have to tell you something," she whispered again.

"When I get back," he responded as he hurried off, the urgency getting the better of him.

Sumi stood there at the door, peeping to see when he would return and also scanning for any guards coming her way.

Drew came back out, a couple of ping pong balls in his hand as he walked past her door again.

"What are you doing with those?" Sumi called as he just walked past her, focused on where he was going. "Has he gone crazy?" She asked nobody in particular. Once again, she hunkered down.

"I swear to God, if I find any more secret doors, I'm out of here for real. These people are the crazy kind of evil!" Levi lamented. Talking to himself was a fond and soothing habit of his. He had done it for as long as he could remember, and he very much didn't care who was listening or who thought of him as crazy. If he felt the need to converse with himself, then that was exactly what he was going to do.

It didn't take him a long time of looking around before he came across a small box containing a bunch of DVDs, each one labelled with the name of a victim. They must have been recordings made during the experiments. There were at least fifty of them. There was a video player plugged to a black and white TV.

For a second, he thought about what to do with the DVDs, he was too traumatized to watch them, much less in the room where everything had happened. He packed up the contents of the box; he was taking it with him to show the crew. Whatever horrors were on those recordings, he was not going to watch them alone.

But hey, more dirt to pin on Mr. Nox, he thought triumphantly.

As much as what he came across was a really good find, Levi knew he still needed to find the stone and communication device he'd been looking for in the first place. So, he decided to bunch up all his findings and stash them in a corner of the room while he went ahead to look for the power source.

Drew returned to the spot he had stood earlier when he saw the guard. The guard stood there still, pacing every few minutes but standing in place for the most part. Drew took two ping pong balls and tossed them across the hallway towards the guard whose back was turned to him.

With urgency, the guard turned towards the location of the noise, his baton ready for assault. *No gun,* Drew mentally registered. It seemed the possession of guns was restricted only to high-ranking guards.

The surprised guard studied the balls for a brief second before speaking. "Who is that? Who did that? Come out with your hands up," he threatened.

Drew maintained his silence, hoping the guard would approach him. Nothing. Drew dropped a few more balls, this time closer to where he was standing. It seemed to work as the guard began to move closer trying to investigate the source of the noise.

"I am fully armed and will not hesitate to shoot. Come out this instant!" The guard barked with a commanding bass to his voice.

Drew backed away slowly, taking refuge in one room but leaving the door completely open. He needed to make sure the guard came in through the door.

And like a lamb to the slaughter, the guard entered the room. It was dimly lit but Drew's eyesight did not falter. Just as quickly as the guard entered the room, Drew used the remote to help activate his abilities and snuck up behind him, one hand yanking the baton from his grasp and the other one pressed against his mouth to prevent him from screaming.

Drew covered the guard's nose alongside his mouth, gripping tightly as the man struggled to break free. It took a few moments before the guard passed out from lack of air. Drew slowly deposited him onto the floor, taking a few zip-ties from the guard's waist to bind him. Drew then gagged him with one of the guard's gloves. He couldn't believe himself; he had taken out two guards with ease in one day. He didn't expect navigating the bunker to be this easy, but he was proud of himself and how willing he was to toss fear aside when it came to protecting himself and his friends.

The guard was taking too long to awaken. Drew kicked at the guard's feet. "Hey! Wake up!"

The guard's eyelids fluttered open slowly, his eyes bore confusion, then realization slowly hit him, and he began to struggle against his restraints.

"It's no use trying to escape. You're firmly bound." Once the guard had calmed down, Drew resumed speaking. "I have a few questions to ask you, if you cooperate with me, this will all go smoothly for both of us, and nobody will get hurt. But if you don't... well your dentition will make a beautiful collection for my shelf."

Drew moved close to him in an attempt to remove the gag. "Do you promise to be calm and not cause a scene?" The guard mumbled something inaudible through the gag.

"Nod your head for yes, shake it for no," Drew instructed.

The guard nodded his head vigorously.

Drew pulled down the gag and as soon as speech was restored to the guard, he began threatening Drew.

"You're as good as dead boy, you have no idea who you're dealing with."

"Nox? I have met who I am dealing with."

The guard shouted and Drew gagged him again. "I told you not to scream! If you don't comply, I will be forced to rid you of all your teeth," Drew threatened as he menacingly whispered in the guard's ear.

"Now I'm going to ask you a simple question. Where is my father?"

The guard mumbled under the gag. Drew pulled it down once more, giving the guard a dirty look to remind him of what would happen if he did scream.

"How the hell am I supposed to know where your father is? I don't even know who he is!"

"Don't play dumb with me," Drew warned, as his eyes pierced through the soul of the guard.

The guard began laughing vigorously, choking on his own breath. "You really suck at this. You kidnap a random guy and expect him to know where your father is?" The guard taunted.

Triggered, Drew kicked him in his side, causing him to wheeze as he collapsed to his side. "I am not playing with you man. Where is my father?"

"Dude, I don't know!"

For a second, Drew paused and thought. "Where is the intruder that is causing the disturbance?" He rephrased.

"That's your father?" The guard asked, a mocking smile adorning his face. "Well, you might as well just be looking for his body instead."

Drew's heart sank to his stomach. Dead? He couldn't be.

"What do you mean?"

"The boss went to take care of it. Anything that the boss takes care of, stays taken care of, if you catch my meaning. Besides, it has been a lot quieter, no more noises. So, put two and two together," the guard smirked.

Drew furrowed his brow and squinted at the guard. "So, you don't know that he is dead. You just assumed he was, because you heard no more noises? Explains why you were tasked with guarding doors, even that you fail at."

The guard started to make a retort and Drew punched him square in the face. "Shut the hell up."

The guard was taken aback by the blow, but he did as he was told. He couldn't believe the strength of the punch and was not willing to take another lest he get knocked out again.

"Where does the door you guard lead to?" Drew asked.

"Level two," he responded.

"And what is on level two?"

"More rooms, more guards. Offices and a lab," the guard blurted out.

"Where is the stone and communication device?"

"You expect me to know that?" The guard countered.

In truth, Drew didn't expect much from the guard, but he could only hope. "If it would be anywhere in the bunker, where would you suggest?"

"If I had a guess, why would I tell you that?"

"Maybe because you don't want to get badly hurt for information you are going to give to me anyway," Drew sneered in a vile tone.

The guard gulped. "If it was to be in any part of this bunker, I would say the power room. I overheard the boss one time talking about a device that consumed a lot of electricity. That's all I know."

"And where—"

"Don't ask me where the power room is, because I don't know. Only the boss and a few of his top guards know where it is," the guard interrupted. "What are you going to do with me?"

Drew ignored the question and gagged the guard once again.

He mumbled and cussed but Drew paid no mind. There was nothing further he could tell him.

"Sorry man, but you are going to feel this one, later," Drew said as he used all of his strength to knock the man unconscious again.

Walking to the door, Drew peeked to see if there were any guards outside. Once he had confirmed they were alone, he picked the guard up and carried him over his shoulders while he walked down the hall to where he had left Sumi.

She saw him coming with someone on his shoulder and she rushed to open the door for him. "Who is this?" She asked as soon as he entered.

"The guard stationed at the door," Drew answered, hunched over.

Drew dropped him in the same space as the first guard they had bound, with both guards in their underwear.

"I couldn't get much out of him but—"

"There's something I have to tell you—"

They both spoke at the same time. "You go first," Drew offered.

"Okay, so I was going through the files, and I found a bunch of stuff. This operation wasn't their first, they had done others before this, and they tested on humans too. He works with a group called *The Invisible Hand*, but they're nameless, faceless and they don't even use their own voices, completely anonymous. But the crazy part is that I saw your name in one of the files," she paused.

As expected, Drew was confused. "What do you mean you saw my name?"

"It didn't say in what capacity they needed you, but it was labeled under *PND*," she explained with a pause, hoping he understood what that meant.

"Why would they have my name on it? What is a PND?" Drew inquired, "It doesn't make any sense at all. That would mean they knew me long before now. I could as well have been one of the red dots they were monitoring."

"Maybe. But I don't think it's safe for you to be here," she warned. "Hey, what did you want to say?" She asked, recalling his comments earlier.

"Yes, the guard. He wasn't much help, but he did say Mr. Nox had captured my dad, well he actually emphasized 'killed', but he has no proof of that so I'm sticking with captured. Maybe that's why I can't sense him so strongly," Drew concluded. "He also told me chances are that the device is in the power room, but he has no idea where the power room is."

"Can you sense your dad at all?" Sumi asked.

"Very faintly," Drew explained.

"So, I have an idea. Can you try sensing Levi?" Sumi asked.

Drew sat in a corner and tried to envision Levi in his mind. He hadn't practiced targeting anyone or anything outside his father's connection. He was not even sure he could do it. After taking a few minutes, it finally happened. A bleak, but stable vision channeled into his mind, though briefly.

Wow, this is crazy, but it really hurts my head. I guess if I don't already have a connection it takes up more of my energy.

"So…do you feel anything yet?" Sumi asked, eagerly waiting.

"Umm… he is spinning on a swivel chair?" Then he opened his eyes. "I saw him in an office."

"Spinning himself on a swivel chair," Sumi sighed, cracking a smile on her face. "Good, and you did it in a fair amount of time. Can you try finding the power room?"

"I don't know what it looks like, Sumi," he complained, still feeling the toll from locating Levi.

"Well, it can't be that hard, I guess. If it's the power room, it's where all of the electricity comes from. Maybe try sensing the room with the most energy. Can you try?" She suggested.

"It's worth a shot," he groaned as he tried focusing again.

Drew envisioned himself walking through a hallway towards a brightly colored door. The colors on the door seemed to bubble and bounce like they were reflecting some light. He moved closer and closer. When he had closed the distance between himself and the door, he stretched his hand to pull the handle, but it moved away from his reach. Confused, he tried to reach the handle a second time and it moved again.

Then the door creaked open a little, revealing a pitch-black darkness that loomed over him. The darkness seemed to have noticed Drew's presence and it slowly started spewing out of the door in Drew's direction.

A strong fear engulfed Drew. He had never felt anything so dangerously evil. Blood trickled from his nose, and he forced his eyes open.

Sumi rushed to his side, abandoning the laptop she was charged with.

"Drew, can you hear me? Are you okay? Sorry for putting so much on you like that."

He nodded slowly, still unable to form words. He was shaken to his core. When he had calmed himself down, he muttered in fear.

"There is a great evil in this place," Drew cautioned. "Nox did not mention everything in those files, there is something terrible here that he didn't talk about. You need to leave."

"You need to calm down," Sumi instructed. "What happened, what did you see?" She inquired as she wiped the blood from his nose.

"Sumi, I do not want to put you in any more danger. You and Levi have gotten into enough trouble because of me. This is too dangerous to drag you into, but I can't leave without my father."

"Spare me the pep talk Drew, it won't work and I'm sure it won't work on Levi either. We are well aware of the consequences of staying with you, so you're not getting rid of us that easily. Besides, leaving you doesn't guarantee our safety. Who's to say we won't still have to be on the run? Who's to say Mr. Nox would let us get away?"

Drew couldn't help but agree with her, she did have a valid point. They were already in too deep to consider running away. He knew he had to think up a plan and do it fast. "You're right. Look I'm sorry I dragged you into this…"

"Hush! Now's not the time," Sumi interrupted. "We need to come up with a plan, do you have anything in mind yet?"

"I believe I might," Drew responded. "It's not fully formed and I'm still trying to figure out all the details, but I am certain it will work."

They decided to wait for Levi's return before they executed any plans. Sumi went back to her research, working twice as fast to find any more important information.

Levi had descended the last set of stairs. He had started his search from the topmost floor and gradually worked his way down. It was the most exhausting and exhilarating experience he'd had in a long while. With as much exercise as he had done since he started the search, he should be excused from school extra-curricular activities for at least a month.

The last two rooms were another waste of time. He had found nothing there either. Just chairs and tables, not much in them, but he had come across a bar a while ago. The room was dimly lit, with lights flickering back and forth. The shelves were fully stocked with books and wine, but there was no one in sight. He immediately stood up and adjusted the swivel chair, trying to make sure there was no proof that he had ever been here.

"Might as well take one for the road," Levi joked as he grabbed a bottle of wine on his way out.

Crossing the barricade again, he headed back into the main room to try one last door.

There he stood, at the front door of the last room.

If it wasn't in that room then it must be outside of the building.

He couldn't have missed it, he was thorough.

The door came open quite easily. When Levi entered the space, he was met with emptiness. No chairs, no tables, nothing. Even the walls were painted white. It looked like an asylum. Then, he looked downwards, the floor was the only decorated part of the room.

There were different floorboard designs lined out and they intertwined with each other. The designs were very intricate, he could not deny the magical genius of whoever designed the floors.

But why just the floors? Why not anywhere else? Levi suspected that there might be a secret door somewhere. It would make no sense for there to be a room like this with nothing in it. He walked around, touching the walls to see what part of it would make a sound.

He continued round the room, touching and tapping every part of the wall. Still, he was met with nothing. It must be something else then.

But what?

Levi went back to the door and this time he started knocking on the walls and placing his ear on them to listen for whatever part of the room sounded hollow. Even that didn't work. He was a hair's breadth away from total frustration.

"What if this is just a torture room? What if there's nothing special and Mr. Nox is just a psychotic freak that locked people in white empty rooms to see how long before they broke?" He asked himself.

A slow humming from beneath caught his attention and he turned slightly to his side. Pressing his ear against the floorboards, he listened again for the humming. And there it was, the sound again.

He knocked on the floorboard and it gave a hollow-sounding echo. There was something underneath. Levi didn't know whether to feel excited or frightened by it. He felt both. Moving on all fours, he kept knocking and rubbing his palms against the floor, looking for a way in.

He crawled over to a painting of a lion, its open mouth marking the entrance to the place beneath. A clever hiding spot he thought. He pulled the floorboard that represented the teeth, and it gave way, making room for a handle that led to another hidden spot. Levi pulled it upwards. It was quite heavy to open as the door had been made of a rather sturdy metal. It creaked and complained until it was finally opened at full capacity.

It hid a few more stairs leading downwards. At this rate, he would not be surprised if he bumped into the devil himself. He had descended so many stairs today that he should already be in Hell by now or at least close enough to hear the screams of the damned, Levi thought.

Again, he began his descent down with the bottle still in hand. There was only one source of light and it shone brightly, lighting his path and leading him to where it was emanating from.

A sigh of relief escaped his lips as he came face to face with what could be nothing but the power source he had set out to find. It was a power grid system. Several different wires stemmed from it. It looked like a large square video game console with lots of wires as its branches, leading to different parts of the building. At the center of this power grid nested the communication device with a glowing stone that blinked a bright red color.

He was careful not to get too close, the whole premise was buzzing with electrical life. He was one wrong step away from being the main character in an obituary.

Carefully, he stepped back out, climbing the stairs out of the basement. He was going to tell the crew what he found. His search had finally paid off. He had done enough thinking and decision-making for the day, he would leave the rest of the deciding and planning for his crew.

Levi walked into the room his friends were in, box of DVDs in hand, his sudden appearance causing everyone to turn in his direction.

"Guys, you won't believe all the crazy shit I found. Mr. Nox is one crazy mofo," he blurted out as he dropped the DVDs on the floor.

"We are just glad you're back bro!" Drew chirped. "What are those?" He asked, pointing to the DVDs.

"Well, it turns out Nox used to experiment on people. Testing on them until they couldn't take any more and they gave up. He buried them in the same room. The DVDs might contain video proof to incriminate Nox. I didn't bother watching them, I've gotten enough trauma for one day, maybe you guys can. Oh, and the files of the victims were all labeled under *Potential Nomu Designee.*"

"PND!" Sumi and Drew both repeated much to Levi's confusion.

"Yea...how do you guys know that?" Levi asked.

"We ran by that label as well in our research," Sumi explained as she turned to Drew. "Do you think maybe that's what they plan to do to you too?"

"I don't know, could be. But judging by what Motor is saying,

I'm sure whatever they are planning, it won't end well for me," Drew suggested.

Drew then turned to Levi to ask a few more questions about the DVDs before putting the box in a corner. They would need to settle down to go through the whole box."

"Why is there a bottle of wine in here?" Sumi added, looking through the box.

"You're asking the wrong question, Sums," Levi replied.

Smiling lightly, "Ok. Did you find the power source?" Drew asked.

"I found better!" Levi professed. "I found the location of the stone *and* the communication device. It's hooked to the power source, like the heartbeat of a huge power grid console sitting at the center of the room."

"Great work, Motor! Your detective skills coming in clutch!" Drew complimented. "We need to get to it quickly."

Levi stared at the bound guards, there had only been one when he left. He lost interest in them just as quickly, turned, and did as he was told. The crew went on their way down to the room, commending Levi for being so observant and finding the power source.

Once they had entered the basement and found the stone and communication device just as Levi had described, Drew tried again to connect to his father to relay the information telepathically. But just like the last time, no response.

Please be alive, Dad.

"Guys, this thing is massive. How do we even get close enough to it? It looks really dangerous," Sumi asked.

"There's got to be a switch to turn it off or something," Levi suggested. "Let's just try to find a switch, guys. But don't get too close to the device."

They searched for a little bit, coming up with nothing.

"Why would you think they'd leave a giant *POWER ON* switch out here for everyone to see, detective. Wouldn't that be a stupid thing to do? Now we've wasted even more time we don't have. Great thinking!" Sumi spat.

"Listen, I don't see that techie brain of yours coming up with a better idea!" Levi responded.

Sumi mimicked him, making a face at Levi. "At least I don't come up with stupid ideas."

"Guys! Not here, not now!" Drew barked at them both as they quieted down, with their eyes hissing at each other. Drew stood still as he began communicating with his father telepathically.

"Dad, we are in the power room. We can see the device. What do we do? Now would be a really good time to say something." Again, he was met with silence, but Drew was uninterested in giving up. He tried again and again, each time trying harder than the last until he made a breakthrough.

"Nox…" came his father's voice, as low as a whisper. Relief washed over him as he heard his father's voice. *"Are you okay dad? I was so worried about you."*

"Listen to me," his father pleaded, ignoring the question.

"What is it dad, what's going on?" Drew asked.

"Nox is not who you think he is… get as far away from here as possible. Run." It sounded like he was using the last of his strength to communicate.

"I am not running anymore and even if I would run, I won't leave without you," Drew replied.

His father stayed silent for a moment; Drew feared he might have lost the connection with him. He tried again to communicate, and soon his father's voice came back. He must have taken a few moments to rest. Telepathy was draining.

"It's not safe, son," Blake continued. *"They are trying to find you. You*

must not let that happen. All will be lost if they do."

"Tell me what to do," Drew insisted.

"You need to find a…"

"A what? Find what, Dad?"

And just like that, the communication ended. Drew tried intensely to connect back with his father, but it proved futile.

Nox must have discovered he was communicating with someone. He had no idea what he was supposed to find.

Find a… He repeated in his head as he tried to fill in the blank. Nothing was coming. It could be anything at all.

Giving up, he turned to the crew for help. Maybe they could figure it out together.

"My dad got cut off before he could tell me what we needed to do. All he mentioned was "find a…" Before he could complete the sentence, the communication was lost."

"That's not helpful at all. It could be anything. Did you try again?" Levi wondered.

"Yeah, I did, and it didn't work. So, do you guys have any other ideas?" Drew asked. "I could use an idea right now because according to my dad, the guards are searching for me, and it will only be a matter of time before they're headed this way."

"Well, I would say we find a way to overcharge this device, push it to the max and cause it to burn itself out. Or maybe we could mess up the connection, wrongly rewire a few things so that it explodes, starts a fire or something," Sumi suggested.

"That is not a horrible idea," Levi admitted, much to Sumi's surprise.

"It isn't horrible?" Sumi asked.

"No, it is not a bad idea at all. In fact, I am just thinking about how much risk it comes with. We don't know how the wiring works; we do not have enough knowledge of this stuff to toy with it. If we do anything wrong here, it could have serious consequences for us too. We could be digging our own graves. We need to find a safer way to destroy this thing," Drew deduced.

Above them, the noises had started all over again. The guards were loud, and they obviously weren't bothered about who heard them. The crew knew they were being hunted and the hunters knew the crew members were aware, there wasn't much need for subtlety.

The footsteps got increasingly closer. They could not risk being caught; all their efforts would have been for nothing.

"So... what do you guys think our last moment will be like?" Sumi asked hesitantly, as she glared at the ceiling.

"You know, I was low-key thinking the same thing," Levi responded.

Drew had stayed quiet while the duo lamented about what they expected their last moments to be. Then something finally came to him.

"Aha! That's it!" Drew exclaimed and he began smiling to himself.

"SOOO...You know how we're gonna die?" Levi asked.

"Nobody is dying here, at least not us," Drew assured the crew.

"What. What is it?" Levi asked.

"I think I finally have a plan. If all goes well, I promise it will all work out for the best. But this time, we are no longer going to be on the run."

"Oh lord, thank you God! We are not going to die today!" Sumi exclaimed as hope surged through her chest once again.

He huddled close to them, explaining the intricate details of his master plan.

The guards closed in on their hiding spot and the door creaked open.

CHAPTER TWENTY-TWO

TAPPED IN

Drew had given the crew hope again. He scanned the room, this time, away from the power grid. He examined the doors and the walls while his friends stared in wonder. Whatever he was doing, they hoped it would save them.

"Look up there," Drew voiced as he pointed towards a box hanging from the wall. "That has to be the control switch. The generator is also down here, we will use it to control where and when in the building power will be supplied. Levi, I want you to man this station and I will tell you when and what to turn off. Just wait for my signal."

Without question, Levi rushed towards the box on the wall, prying it open to indeed reveal a control panel hidden underneath.

"You know guys, since our time here, I've noticed something," Drew announced. "The doors…they're electrically charged. Not all of them but the ones for important rooms like the first entrance to this bunker or the lab doors. If the power stops being supplied, everything goes off. Including the doors. If you're in, you're locked in… if you're out, you're locked out."

The crew pondered on his observation.

"I also suspect there are steel enforced bunker doors. The roof of this door has some spacing in it. I suspect they also did this for only the important rooms in the building. I cannot say for sure that it's in every room. But I am sure I saw it when we were in the lab." He paused. "Since this is the main power room, Sumi, I want you to overcharge the computer motherboard with the list of people being monitored by Mr. Nox. Find a way to direct an excess surge to just that device in the room."

Contemplating for a few seconds, she nodded, "I think I can pull it off. But back to what you mentioned earlier, there's no telling where all the guards are in the building or if they're all in the same place. I'm sure there are several teams scattered, trying to hunt us down. How do we pull this off?" Sumi asked.

"I can move faster than normal, that's why I have to be the one to go. I will try luring the guards into the lab. If they truly need me for whatever crazy plan they have, I trust they won't shoot me on sight. Their goal would be to capture me, and that'll be their mistake," Drew explained.

"But won't you be trapped in there with them?" Levi asked.

"That's the point of being fast…"

"You'll be able to run out of the lab quickly before the door closes," Sumi completed.

"Exactly!" Drew agreed.

"This still sounds dangerous," Sumi added.

"What escape plan isn't? You are in control of the power now. I also need you to access the cameras in the building, you'll be my eyes on the way up," Drew instructed.

It was not until Drew called their attention to it, that the crew noticed there was a corner of the room with a large screen TV displaying different parts of the building. A surveillance channel. They had been too engulfed with the power grid to notice anything else.

In all fairness, the monitor was not placed in plain sight. It was several feet away from the power source; for safety purposes, they assumed.

This was where Sumi was to work from; she studied her new position, pulled a chair out and sat.

It was only several moments ago that they'd been looking for an off switch on the device. It would have been a ridiculous discovery if they had indeed found such a switch. For a building drenched in sophisticated technology, putting a switch to turn off and on the most important thing in the building would be a very stupid thing to do. Panic had frozen them in place, causing them to forget all logic, but Drew had still remained calm and observant. She was grateful for how he was able to maintain his composure.

"Wait!" Sumi shouted as she remembered something. "What do you mean I'll be your eyes? If you are out of this room, there is no way to communicate with you. We have no phones, no walkie talkies, no means of communicating."

"Aren't you *REBL*, the best computer genius and hacker we know? Gain access to the cameras first. If you have full control of the cameras, I am sure we'll be able to communicate just fine. I know you are worried but you got this Sums. You are one of the few people I'd entrust with my life," Drew assured her with conviction.

Sumi was left speechless, with a hint of blush, at his impassioned words. She immediately got to work gaining access to the system.

"They are closing in quick, guys," Levi remarked.

They could still hear doors swinging open and things crashing into the ground. The guards were still on their aggressive search and the noises were becoming increasingly close, it was only a matter of time before they were on this floor. Even though Drew was sure not all the guards knew about the location of the powerhouse, he wasn't going to gamble with that.

"I have access!" Sumi beamed, as her celebratory declaration shifted back to focus in a manner of seconds.

"Sumi the *REBL* is now activated!" Levi cheered. Sumi shook her head with a smirk.

The screen lit up with several live video feeds. She could see rooms all over the building.

"Great! So, the cameras, what functions do they allow?" Drew inquired.

"Well, some are movable. They can turn left or right. Like this one," she answered as she demonstrated by moving one camera's focus left and right. "But some aren't movable at all."

"Can they do anything at all?" Drew asked.

She typed away for a few seconds before speaking. "Nothing important, I can just turn the light in the lens from green to red and vice versa."

"Perfect. We should be able to communicate now." Drew affirmed. "I need you to be my eyes, Sumi. You'll either guide me to safety or to my capture. The movable cameras, I need you to use them to tell me where to go. The direction with no guards, or at least the smallest number of guards. For the ones that aren't movable, use the green light on the side of the cameras for safe, and red for not safe. I'll be looking at the camera every turn I make. We got this, Sumi," Drew concluded.

"I'll do my best, I promise," she assured, turning back to her typing as she started the process of overheating the circuit board. "Done." She expected it to take a few minutes to completely overheat and begin to melt, quietly hoping there wasn't a backup anywhere else.

Drew then turned to Levi who had been silently manning his position. "Motor, wait for my signal, not a moment sooner or later."

"You got it, D," Levi replied.

"By the way, do you still have the remote on you?" Levi asked.

"Yea, it's on me somewhere." Drew searched his pockets. "Ah, here it is," he verified.

"I guess that's settled then. Be safe out there, bro," Levi cautioned as the two dapped each other.

"I will. You guys do the same," He said, saluting to them. "Sums, what routes should I take?"

Sumi proceeded to explain the routes that were the freest and the ones that led him straight to where the most guards were. Once again, he pleaded with them to stick to the plan, no matter what.

Then he made for the exit, leaving them to their tasks.

It wasn't long before Drew popped up on one of the cameras, he stared directly into it and Sumi directed him, signaling where to go. Drew made his way up the stairway, it was the one they had used in going down to the power room. It wasn't as quiet as they had left it. He heard a footstep above.

Drew moved slowly, trying to make as little noise as possible. It was just one guard, pacing the floor. He spotted the lab; it was right there but just one guard wouldn't do the trick. He needed as many of them as were available.

Standing up straight, Drew called the guard's attention to himself. He had already pressed the button; he was ready should the guard try to attack him. The guard turned to him, shock filling his eyes as he saw Drew there. Taking his walkie talkie, he yelled into it, calling for the rest of the guards. This wasn't a foe he wanted to face alone, he needed reinforcements.

Drew knew some guards would come through the stairway and he didn't want to be standing with his back turned to them when they did. He sped past the guard, going close to the lab door but not so close that it was obvious what he was doing. He made a hand gesture, daring the guard to come at him. He was fairly certain the guard would not, but he didn't want to just stand still, the guard might figure it was a trap.

"Come on then! What are you afraid of? Come at me! Don't tell me you need backup to handle a kid," Drew taunted.

"Surrender now and I will make this easy on you," the guard replied, taking a few steps back.

"Who says I want it easy? Give me everything you've got." The guard didn't respond so Drew continued taunting him. "You must be a coward 'cause I'm standing right here, unarmed and you still need help? Pathetic," Drew spat, really trying to rile the guard up.

"All teams to level two, over!" The guard yelled into his walkie talkie again.

He noticed the camera positioned adjacent to him; the angle was perfect. He moved close to it so he could easily signal the crew when the time came. His hand still remained on the remote in his pocket, gathering as much charge as he could.

The guard stood, baton in one hand and walkie talkie in the other, but he made no attempt to come close to Drew. He must have been warned about him. His hand shook a little and Drew could see the impatience in his eyes as he awaited backup.

Footsteps rushed down the stairway, signaling that backup had arrived. A few guards rushed behind the first one. Behind Drew, another set of guards emerged, pinning him in the middle. Drew sized them up, counting them. There were ten of them. Five before him and five behind him. Some had batons, while a few others had stun guns. He was certain it would hurt really bad if he got on the wrong end of one of those but besides that, they had come down with nothing lethal. He was right. Their aim was to capture and not kill him. So far, everything was going according to plan.

Drew pulled out his hand from his pocket, leaving the remote switch on. He rubbed his hand over his face as if wiping dirt off it. It was his signal to Sumi who he trusted was watching. It was time.

"You have nowhere to run to kid, surrender!" The first guard declared. This time, it boomed with confidence.

"Come on then, show me what you've got," Drew taunted.

"You're in for a world of pain boy, this is going to hurt like hell," the guard replied, slapping his baton against his free palm lightly.

"Get him!"

Drew focused on the energy, the buzzing sensation that surged through his veins, he was ready. The guards closed in on him and as soon as they had, he sped off. It was a speed unlike anything they had seen. Around him, the wind gushed, knocking off balance anyone that stood too close to him.

Drew stopped only seconds away from the door to give Sumi the signal to close it. The guards wasted no time in following him. If he went into the lab, there was no escape for him. Quickly, one of the guards shouted into his walkie talkie for a guard to lock the other exit to the lab so they made sure Drew didn't escape.

"Do it now, close the door!" Sumi yelled to Levi.

Without hesitation, Levi pulled the switch, causing the door to start closing.

Drew smiled to himself as he heard the guard. They'd walked right into his trap. As soon as he walked through the door, he felt pain surge through his body from his leg, traveling up his spine, crippling his muscles. He had never felt anything like it before. He collapsed to the floor, writhing in pain. The head guard had sniped him with an electroshock projectile while his back was turned. His body shook in pain as he felt like he was being burned from the inside out.

He rolled his body further into the lab, creating distance between himself and the guards that were fast approaching him. By the time the guards arrived at the door, the opening was too narrow to fit anyone through. Soon, the door closed completely, trapping Drew inside. The steel bars posed an impenetrable ally for Drew, taking away completely the option of breaking into the lab.

"Damn it!" A guard yelled. He picked up his walkie talkie again. "Bravo-2, do you copy? Over."

"Yes, over," came the response.

"Get some guards with you. The hostage has locked himself in the lab on level two. Gain access through the back door," the guard commanded.

"Copy that, over," Bravo-2 replied.

Levi held Sumi's mouth shut as she screamed, kicked and tossed. He kept whispering to her, trying to calm her down or else she would cause them to be discovered and they could not be of any help to Drew if they got captured too.

That seemed to quiet her down a bit, but her eyes still welled up, tears trickling down the length of her cheeks.

"You need to open the door, Levi! Get him out of there."

"I can't. Not right now. The switch runs on power. Each time it's used, it has to recharge. Even if I wanted to, I can't open it now. Besides, he's hurt. There are guards stationed just outside the door. What chance would he have?" Levi asked.

"He's not safe in there either! The circuit could overheat any moment now! He'll die if he stays in there!" Sumi screamed. "We have to do something!"

Levi held her close. "We will figure something out. I promise. You need to calm down, I need you to have your head in the game. Can you do that?"

Sumi nodded slowly.

"We need to come up with a plan for when the device is charged again. How to get him out of there safely. Let's figure that out first, okay?" Levi asked.

She nodded again, faster this time. If the doors were opened again immediately, then what? Drew was already hurt. She doubted he would be able to fend the guards off. They would capture him for their crazy experiments. She wiped the tears from her eyes and turned back to the computer. She worked, determined to figure something out.

"Bravo-2 to head guard, do you copy? Over."

From the other side of the door, they heard a guard pull his walkie talkie from its holster. "Yes Bravo-2, status report. Over!"

"The back doors are barricaded with steel. We can't get through. There is no way in or out. Over," Bravo-2 reported.

They heard a guard cuss under his breath. "Roger that. Over," he concluded and returned the walkie talkie to its holster.

From the power room, Sumi watched the guards pace around the entrance to the lab. One in particular spoke into his walkie talkie a lot and then made to bang furiously at the steel door. She had no audio access yet so she couldn't make out what he was saying. She pressed her fingers up and down the bridge of her nose. She'd had so much faith in the plan, she didn't think it would go awry, at least not so fast. Drew was hurting and he needed help and she couldn't do anything about it. She hated the feeling of helplessness that washed over her.

"Wait... what is this?" She asked nobody in particular as a particular piece of footage caught her eye. A camera had caught some action from a corner in the upper level.

It looks like a man wrestling a… beast? She was sure her eyes were deceiving her, and she needed to confirm what she was seeing.

"Levi, come take a look at this," she called.

He came to her side "What is it?"

"There," she pointed to the screen. "This is a part of the upper level, I think. Look at it and tell me what you see."

"It's blurry," Levi squinted. "Man, when did they last clean these cameras, there's dust all over it."

"Levi! What do you see?" She called his attention back.

"It looks like a fight… a man and… what is that thing? It's too big to be an animal," he described as he looked closer.

"So, you see it too! Let me try and see if I can zoom in," she replied.

The creature seemed to notice the camera as it momentarily let go of its victim and turned to look directly at the lens. They couldn't figure out what it looked like or see its eyes, but they could feel it glare at the camera. Its mouth opened wide, and an otherworldly shriek reverberated through the walls. She had not gotten audio access yet, but they could hear the creature's scream throughout the house. It emitted such a high frequency that almost immediately the camera exploded, disconnecting the crew from the feed in the room.

"What the——" Levi yelled, surprised by what had just happened.

"Oh, my god! Do you think it saw us?" Sumi panicked.

"I don't know, but I'm certain it was aware that it was being watched."

"What if it's on its way down here?" Sumi asked.

"Focus. If we hear any sound heading this way, we'll activate our steel doors, okay?"

"Okay."

Levi studied her facial expressions and then asked, "Do you want me to take over for you? Take some time to clear your head maybe?"

She shook her head even before he completed his sentence. "I just need a moment to breathe, I can handle it."

"Are you sure?" Levi emphasized, knowing her tendency to overwork.

"I do need help gaining audio access into the lab."

Levi smiled at her, excited to be of help. He pulled up a seat beside her, burying himself in the task assigned to him.

He stood at the window, backpack strapped, his lunchbox in hand, fully clothed for school. He stared as the school bus pulled up. A woman stood there, back turned to him. She had her hair tucked in a headscarf. Another woman stepped out of the bus, and they started talking. The lady in a scarf was talking with his teacher. His heart sunk; he knew nothing good was going to come from the discussion.

They spoke for several seconds and soon, the teacher gave a nod of understanding. She had noticed him peeking from the window, she offered him a warm smile and waved at him. He didn't wave back; he didn't like the feeling he was getting. He looked into the bus and there was his best friend, looking right back at him, wondering why he wasn't boarding the bus with them. Tears welled up in Drew's eyes as his teacher boarded the school bus and it drove away with the rest of his class.

The lady in the headscarf walked back in. Her face cloaked in sadness as their eyes locked. Her eyes… They were just like his, as deeply bronze as the sun in the wee hours of the morning.

"Why did they leave without me?" Drew asked.

"Honey, you can't go there anymore," she replied, bending to reach his height. That voice, he had heard it sing him to sleep a number of times.

"Why not?" He asked as he moved a step away from her.

"You'll learn at home now. Your dad and I will get all the textbooks you need…"

"No!" He interrupted as a fresh batch of tears streamed down his face. "I like my school just fine! I want to go learn with my friends! I don't want to learn from home!"

"Xae… Drew, it is not safe for you to be there anymore. You are still too young to understand it. But I promise, in time, you will. I am just trying to keep you safe," she reassured as she pulled him close, enveloping him in an embrace.

His hands fell limp at his sides, and he didn't return the hug. Her palms were soft and her embrace warm. He loved the sweet lavender smell that she always had. But he was too upset to enjoy her embrace. "You don't want me to be happy! You're taking my friends away from me. I don't want to be around you!" He yelled as he shoved her and ran up the stairs.

She remained on her knees, not entirely surprised by his outburst. She'd expected it. She didn't know how to explain the situation to him or if he would even understand it. He aged differently from the humans on Earth. The life expectancy for earthlings was about a hundred at best, for their kind, it was triple.

Drew's classmates had started losing their baby teeth, growing taller, having slight changes in their voices as they neared puberty. But Drew, he had stayed the same, not ageing a day. It had been the same for the last three classes. It would not be long before brows were raised, and questions were asked. She didn't want her son to be considered a freak or discriminated against even more, since that landmark Supreme Court decision for school integration happened. She saw the news and what was happening to the young black students all around the South. She had to school him at home. Even that would have to be for only a little while. They would still have to move to a different city where he would blend in and continue his schooling. She understood the effect the cycle had on Drew, but they didn't know any other way to stay undetected.

"Honey, come back," she called after him. "Drew!"

"Drew!"

"Drew! Can you hear me?"

Again, he emerged from the memory. A voice kept calling his name. He pulled himself up, pain still searing through his body, but it felt more bearable.

"If you can hear me, say something," Sumi called. The smoke emanating from the room made it difficult for her to see him clearly in the lab.

Scooting over to the device the voice came from, he responded, "Yes… I'm here. Sorry, I blacked out again, didn't I?"

Sumi let out a giggle of excitement. She gave Levi a high five.

"We have two-way audio access on the cameras now!" She proclaimed to Levi.

Turning her attention back to Drew, she reported, "Drew, I am going to stop overheating the circuit, it could explode or start a fire any minute now. We have to come up with a plan to get you out of there."

"No Sumi… please. Stick to the plan. Don't stop overheating," he muttered in a weakened voice.

"Uhhh...Drew, could you say that again? I don't think I heard right the first time," Sumi responded.

"Sumi… please… the plan… it's still in motion, see it through to the end," Drew pleaded, still trying to recover.

Sumi's eyes bulged as she gave Levi an astonished look. "Am I hearing wrong?"

"No, I don't think so," Levi lamented.

"I think he's out of it. The shock from the stun gun, all the smoke in the room, they all must have gotten to his head and impaired his thinking. I say we get him out of there," she rambled, trying to compose herself after feeling a wave of emotions.

"Sumi…" Drew squeaked. "Trust me… This is not a suicide mission… The plan will work. Please, stick to it."

"You're awfully quiet!" Sumi snapped at Levi.

"Sums, I think we should listen to what he says and stick with the plan," Levi reasoned. As Sumi was getting ready to explode, he cut her off before she could speak. "Now before you snap at me, you need to understand that Drew is not the same dude we are used to at Douglass. He has these abilities now… I'm starting to believe he can handle much more than we think. You should have a little faith in him, just like he's had in you this whole time," Levi concluded.

"It's not that I don't trust Drew…I'm just afraid to lose him… like Yuna," she admitted. Levi understood exactly who she was referring to. When Sumi was about eight years old, her best friend Yuna had died of cancer. Her hair began falling off and she had to cut it all, including her brows. She had to stop school completely and focus on getting chemotherapy. Her skin turned pale, and her lips became chafed. But she wore a smile through it all. She was so strong, even with the terminal illness. But Sumi watched her friend slowly deplete into nothingness, and she'd felt totally helpless.

It was that same feeling of helplessness that consumed her now. Sumi's eyes began to glaze. "You better not die on me, or I swear to God I will look for you in the afterlife and whoop your ass!" She yelled at Drew with tears streaming down her face.

He laughed lightly. "Yes ma'am. Thank you for trusting me with this."

All the while, the guards had remained in front of the lab, pacing back and forth, with the head guard shouting commands into his walkie talkie. Now that they had access, Sumi and Levi could hear them speak.

Two guys rushed down the stairs, carrying a weird looking device. They mounted it on the door and handed a little speaker box to the head guard.

"Drew… is it?" The guard spoke.

The voice pierced through the steel door; Drew could hear every word clearly.

"I am sure you can hear me. And as cliche as this may sound, you are actually surrounded. There are guards on either side of this lab. You have no way out," the guard taunted, repeatedly slamming his baton on his hand. Drew offered no response.

"Earlier, we were unaware of what you are. Well, not anymore. Now, we know. Don't you wonder why the pain hasn't subsided yet? You were shot with enough current to take down an elephant," the guard chuckled. "I just thought you should know; in case you permanently lose the functioning of a limb."

"That bastard!" Levi swore under his breath.

"We are definitely going to kill him. This one has to die," Sumi fumed with conviction.

"What? No comeback? I thought you had a smart mouth not too long ago. Or are you dead now, weakling?" The guard continued.

Drew concluded that they must have gotten a two-way communication device if the guard was expecting feedback from him. He had to find a more subtle way to communicate with the rest of the crew.

He pulled himself back into a lying position, the pain still crippling. He had nothing left in his bag of tricks. No way out.

CHAPTER TWENTY-THREE

MORE THAN HUMAN

The creature shrieked and slapped Blake with the back of its enormous paw, sending him flying halfway across the room. It stood seven feet tall, eyes bloodshot red and giant fangs sticking out of its mouth. The length of its body was covered in fur. Razor sharp talons replaced fingers and its ears stood pointed towards the sky, turning slightly to pick up sound waves. Its legs were bent backwards and each step it took, dug into the concrete floor. A tail wagged behind him like a predator stalking its prey.

It growled in anger and began charging at Blake again. Blake had depleted most of his energy, so he shifted from defense to avoidance, doing his best to evade the creature. He had come to realize during the course of the battle that the creature protected its underside. It's chest and stomach were sensitive areas and so Blake only waited for an opening to strike. The beast always recoiled in pain whenever Blake did that. He also noticed that those areas took a longer time to heal. So, Blake had decided to try again, this time using the sharp end of a broken piece of furniture. The beast, catching on to what he was attempting to do, protected his vulnerable area, causing Blake to miss and stab its arm, which seemed only to enrage him more.

The creature was swift, leaping in the direction it had earlier flung Blake to. Blake rolled just as quickly, moving his body away from harm. Its hind legs landed on the floor where Blake lay just moments before, creating a huge dent in the floor. The rest of the guards had already made it downstairs towards Drew, spurred on by the fear of becoming casualties in the bloody battle.

The creature swung its talons, slashing away at Blake, who avoided the blows as best he could. Broken bricks crumbled to the floor from where the creature's talons collided with the wall.

So, this is the power of a Nomu... Vozyr, I would've never imagined you could do this, Blake thought.

He was deliberate in studying it for any other weakness he could exploit. The creature had become just a little bit slower, maybe it was starting to wear out, he assumed. But it was going to be a long time before the creature was tired enough for the fight to be even. Blake gathered some sand from the broken bricks that littered the room, careful not to alert the creature to what he was doing and as soon as the creature neared him, he flung a handful of dirt in its eyes. It stopped momentarily, screeching in anger as its sight was temporarily impaired.

It wasn't a long-lasting solution, but it would buy Blake a few much-needed seconds to catch his breath.

Drew shifted to his side, studying his leg. A large bruise had formed around the spot the stun gun had hit him and the skin around the area looked like it was burned. His body was healing slowly but it didn't do much in alleviating the pain, he was still in a lot of it.

Meanwhile, the crew heard the head guard assign another guard a task, telling him to bring back a saw that could cut through steel. Sumi watched the guard leave immediately to do as he was told, walking through the driveway, getting into a car and speeding off.

"This is not good. It's not good at all," she stressed to Levi.

"We need to distract them somehow," Levi suggested as he shuffled around. "Do we have audio access to the hallway?"

"Yes, I think we do. What do you have in mind?" She asked.

"Well, we tell them that we have possession of the stone and communication device," he devised. "I mean... we kind of do, right?"

"Then what?"

"I don't know. We just work with it," Levi professed. They both agreed it was worth the shot.

"Hey assholes!" Levi barked, voice resounding through the hallway.

The guards turned their attention upwards, looking for the source of the voice. The head guard's eyes stayed pinned on one of the cameras.

"We have your stupid stone and communication device!" Levi continued.

"Is this your pathetic attempt to save your friend's life? There's no way you have the device," the head guard asked, mocking them.

"Why don't you come and find out? Or are you scared of a group of kids?" Levi taunted.

"You know, your friend mentioned the same thing before we took him down and he is a far more formidable foe than the both of you. But look how easily he fell. You're just bugs, waiting to be squashed," the head guard replied. "You see, your mistake was alerting me of your presence, now I know where you are and how to find you," he turned to the door. "You hear that, Drew? Your little friends just told me how to find them too."

The crew fell silent for a bit, fearing they hadn't thought it through. But if it came down to it, they could lock themselves in.

"You see, the truth is that the boss is only interested in you, Drew. Your friends are just minor inconveniences that we will take care of soon enough. Once we've opened this door, they're as good as dead." Turning back to the camera, he added, "For now children, enjoy the show."

The crew watched through the cameras as the car pulled back into the garage. The guard had returned, much sooner than they had anticipated.

Drew's body was burning up, sweat puddled around him and his lips quivered. Shivers ran up and down the length of his body. He felt so cold, yet so warm. He was blinking in and out of consciousness, fighting the urge to let go. Numerous times he came dangerously close to the edge and each time, he struggled to stay awake. He was slowly losing the will to hold on, the pain was messing with his mind. He closed his eyes in surrender to whatever might come.

Chants possess the air, filling his ears with words from a language that is unfamiliar to him.

"The chants… and drums… like in my dreams," Drew recalls.

Men and women adorned in ceremonial robes dance in the clouds. Each one with a staff in hand and an oddly oversized African-like tribal mask resting on their heads. He says nothing, watching them perform whatever it is they are doing.

Then she stretches out her hand, one of those in ceremonial robes. She looks like she is in her early nineties. Her eyes hold such warmth and a smile rests on her lips. "What are you doing here, Son?" She asks. It is the first time he has heard any of them speak in English. She extends her hands to him as a greeting. He stretches out his own hand, offering it to her and she pulls him up into the sky.

He stands there, looking at these strange people. One with a scar on his face catches his attention. He has the same jawline as his father. He figures he will have to ask his questions out loud if he is going to get any answers, since everyone is focused on their dancing and chanting.

"What is this place? Am I dead?" Drew asks.

"Oh, you silly boy. You are not even supposed to be here... But you managed to land here somehow, traveling through your memories... Yes... I see now. You've been here before. So, you are the wild seed boy... You still have not found your soil, I see. You know not of your past or your future. You are so busy trying to figure these things out, that you now no longer have a present either!"

"I... I don't know what you mean. I mean I do but... what do I do?"

"Make a decision already!" The lady shouts in laughter.

"What decision?" Drew asks.

"To fight for your present. Your past reconciles with you eventually, and your future will find you. It's your present... your now... that needs you the most," the lady replies.

"Fight for my present—My friends! My dad! They need me. Please, how can I get back? You never told me if I was dead or not."

You are neither alive nor dead. You are in the in-between," one person responds.

"In the in-between? What does that even mean?" He asks in shock.

"Well, down on earth, time has frozen. When you make your decision, everything will return to normal," another says.

"*Who are you people?*" *Drew asks as more questions form in his mind.*

"*We are your ancestors from ages past. We were once just like you, with the unique abilities of a Type II human. We were protectors of our people. We fought wars when the need arose, we made our lands better,*" *one remarks.*

"*But I thought Type II humans were all aliens from another galaxy,*" *Drew wondered.*

"*You have much to learn, Wild Seed!*" *Someone called out.*

"*Some of us lived in a more advanced time, a time that had no need for wars. We had figured it out, how to live peacefully, ended scarcity and suffering. It was truly peaceful,*" *another speaks.*

"*I don't understand what that has to do with me,*" *he insists.*

The man with a scar finally speaks up. "*Xaeon, you are a part of us as much as we are a part of you. You carry in you our history, our stories, our strength. I know it might be hard to understand now, but I promise you that you are stronger than you will ever know. Inside of you, lies the strength and wisdom of a thousand ancestors. All of us here. All we are, all we have, it's inside you, Son, to use as you see fit. Wake up to your power. You are nothing ordinary!*" *The man yells.*

"*Well, you still have the option to stay here if you choose,*" *the first woman whispers to him.*

"*What is your decision, Son?*" *The man with a scar asks him.*

"*I want to go back. I want to go save my friends and find my father,*" *Drew responds, a new conviction setting in his heart.*

"*Then take with you the strength of a thousand ancestors and fight like you have an army behind you! Because you damn well do!*" *Her voice says as Drew slowly descends back into the earth. The ancestors resume their chanting and dancing as they become harder to make out in the clouds.*

"*Drew?*" *A warm voice calls at him. He smiles almost immediately.*

It is that familiar voice again. "*Mom?*" *He asks.*

"*Open your eyes baby,*" *she replies.*

He has no idea he had shut his eyes and he opens them just as quickly. He looks around, the place is brightly lit, pictures of him hang on the wall. He looks so young in those pictures and the clothing… he needs to speak to whoever dressed him up in those pictures.

"It's your old pod, back home. You might not remember it," she admits.

Drew's head turns swiftly in her direction. "Mom…" It is his second time seeing her. This time, she doesn't look like the woman who spoke to his teacher. She has let down her hair. It is blessed with texture and has curls that run all the way down to her waist. Her eyes hold such light and fierceness. She looks every bit a strong warrior.

She reaches out and intertwines his palm with hers. There it is again, that softness he enjoyed. How could she look so fierce yet be so warm?

"Do you remember the time you contested in the brawn tournament? Everyone thought you were crazy! The other kids were at least two decades older than you, but you were so adamant, you really had to be a part of it."

He smiles, bits of the memories flooding back.

"And each time you got knocked down or beat, you stood up, you would not accept defeat. You had a bloody nose and one of your teeth came loose. I was so afraid, I wanted you to stop but you had the stubborn will of your father," she replies.

"Dad always recalled you were the one with a stubborn will," he interrupts.

"Ssshh!" She hushes. "I'm the one telling the story. And even as beat up as you were, you won the tournament. You didn't exactly play fair." She winks. "But you were determined to win, and you did. You had the biggest smile on your face. I almost laughed because of the missing tooth."

Drew lets out a little laugh as more and more of the memory comes back.

"Son, look at me," she says, her expression solemn. "I learned something from you that day. It doesn't matter if the odds are against you. As long as there is a beat in your chest, breath in your lungs and determination in your mind, you are unstoppable. No matter what my darling, you keep fighting! Fight through the pain, fight till you get what you are fighting for!"

He goes into her arms, accepting a hug from her. "I love you mom," he cries.

She hugs him tight, placing a kiss on his head. "You are my entire world. It's time to go baby," she says as she slowly fades away.

The guards had gotten a tool to saw the steel open and they spent several minutes sawing a big enough hole to allow them to enter. The crew watched helplessly from the power room, fearing this was the end. This was Drew's plan; he had told them to stick with it till the end.

The guards trooped into the room, one after the other, once they had made an opening big enough.

Suddenly, Drew's consciousness returned to his body. His eyes came open, and they shone pure white. His body began jerking once again, his hands twitching, and electric discharge pulsated from under his skin. The guards moved away from him, creating distance between them. They suspected it was somehow the effect of the stun gun and so they gave him space for it to die down.

The crew worried too, this was like the time when they were in the cage, and he had blacked out. Was he sensing his father's presence again? The questions ran through their minds.

Drew let out a loud scream and his jittery hands began to mutate. The transformation looked painful as Drew continued to writhe; he didn't stop screaming. The guards were stunned, barely believing what they beheld.

Then his screaming died down, his body still mutating slightly. Still aware that the crew was watching and listening, he calmly instructed them.

"Kill the lights."

Without hesitation, Sumi turned off all the lights in the lab. Leaving them in pitch black darkness, even the crew could no longer see what was going on in the room.

"Find the switch!" The head guard yelled, and some guards scrambled to the walls, touching around the area for a switch.

Drew left his lying position and crawled up in a corner, like a predator stalking his prey. His vision was better than perfect, he could see them clearly, scrambling around like rats in a cage. Now they knew what it was like to be hunted.

One guard stumbled slowly to where he stood, watching them. As soon as the man came close enough, Drew pounced on him, knocking his head toward the wall in one pull. The sound of screaming caused the others to scramble and panic even further. Drew watched as one tried to make for the exit. With speed unmatched, he lunged at the guard, throwing him towards the door headfirst.

"What kind of coward fights in the dark!" The head guard yelled. "Turn on the lights and face us!" He tried desperately to hide the panic in his voice.

"The same kind of coward that waits for a person to turn their back and then shoots," Drew responded, with a deep hiss reverberating in his voice, as if it were scratching his throat, attempting to claw at the air when he spoke.

The head guard immediately shot in the direction of the voice. Drew moved swiftly away from the electric field that came his way. In that brief moment when the electricity surged, the guards caught a glimpse of Drew's face. His eyes glowed with a reddish hue, while small fangs protruded from his mouth and his eyes held a hunger for violence.

Shrieks and screams emanated from the room as one by one, Drew took out all of the guards, saving the head guard for last.

"Coward! Show your face!" The head guard screamed.

"Okay, since you're so eager to see... Turn on the lights!"

He instructed and just as quickly, the lights came back on.

The crew gasped in shock. There their friend stood, looking

somewhat like the creature they had seen in the footage earlier. He still looked human. But he stood a full foot taller; his clothing seemed to be having a hard time containing his body, especially his arms, which had completely transformed into something like a werewolf. Silently, they watched.

The head guard, coming face to face with Drew, pulled out his stun gun and aimed it at Drew again. Drew rushed at him in anger, slapping the gun away from his wrist. "You never get tired of pointing that thing at me, do you?" He asked.

"You're an abomination, you don't scare me!" The head guard retorted.

Drew slapped him across the room. "That is for threatening my friends." He walked up to the guard to continue his assault, but the man had already been knocked out of consciousness. Drew dragged his unconscious body and tied him to a steel beam inside the lab. He was going to be there for a while.

Drew came out of the lab, turning to one camera in the hallway, and began to speak. "Can you hear me, guys?"

"... Yea. Sure, we can," they hesitantly responded.

"I know you must be wondering what's going on, what I've become and who I even am. I promise you that I am still the same person. I don't fully understand what's happening to me yet. I am sorry. It's not that I knew about all this and kept it a secret from you guys. I mean there were some things but I... I just didn't want you guys to judge me. I hope you can forgive me. I don't want you to hate or be afraid of me. You guys are my only friends in the world. If I lose you both, then I will be totally alone, and I can't even imagine what that would feel like. I barely get to really talk to my father... But I also can't make you stay with me; the choice is ultimately yours. I just want you to know that I am truly sorry for all of this," he concluded.

He was met with silence. The silence unnerved him and he didn't know what it meant or what to make of it. He bowed his head in defeat and turned to leave when Levi's voice filtered through.

"Ain't nobody scared of you! My mom back slaps harder than what you did there. I am sure she has supervillain powers."

None of them could help the sudden snickering that evolved into laughter of relief.

Sumi joined in on the joke, "We still have a project to complete after all this craziness, those giant arms of yours better not be an excuse not to do your part, because I don't care if you have to use your tongue to type, but you're doing your part of the project."

The crew laughed again, and relief flooded through Drew, knowing he still had his friends' love and acceptance.

"Are you still in pain?" Levi asked.

For the first time since Drew's mutation, he thought about the pain. It had receded into a dull throbbing in his foot and by now it was just a mild discomfort; no real pain came from it. In this form, his healing seemed to be several times faster than when he was in his human form.

"No, the pain is gone," he replied.

"That's so cool, bro," Levi praised, excited at his recovery speed.

"There are guards on the other side of the lab, so you can't use that exit," Sumi reported. "Like before, I'll have to guide you through a different route. I will use my voice to guide you through for the most part but also watch the cameras, there may be times guards would be around and I won't be able to use my voice to guide you through."

"Yes ma'am," He affirmed as he began following her directions.

Sumi did her best to lead him through the least dangerous routes. As she scanned for the next turn for him to take, her eyes caught something quite disturbing. A body lay bloodied against a wall in the hallway. There was no way to confirm that whoever it was still had life in him. She called Levi's attention to it. She zoomed in on the picture and that was when they figured out who it was. "Isn't that Drew's dad?" Sumi asked, to which Levi nodded in affirmation, his expression grim.

"What should we do? Should we tell him?" Sumi asked.

"I don't think we have a choice," Levi replied.

"Drew, can you hear me?" Sumi spoke.

"Yes, loud and clear," he responded.

"I found something while I was looking through the footage…"

"Okay... and?" Drew asked, still focused on silently navigating his way through the route.

"I think it's your dad," Sumi remarked.

Drew stopped immediately and turned to the nearest camera. "My dad? Where is he!"

"He's directly two floors above where you are. But I don't know if he is still… alive. He looks pretty bloodied and tied up, I could barely recognize him, and he's made no attempt to move from that spot," she informed him. Rage and fear consumed Drew.

Arrgh!!... No Dad, please! It can't be… you can't be. I need you, please.!

He immediately changed route, abandoning the plan and moving in the direction that led to his father.

"I must add," Sumi warned, "that it might just be a trap."

"I don't care!"

CHAPTER TWENTY-FOUR

SINS OF THE FATHER

Drew's blood boiled under his skin, a new anger forming in his chest.

If he doesn't make it, I'm going to rip Nox's head clean from his neck!

His talons elongated further, sharpened and ready for battle as he sped up the stairs at animal-like speed.

I can feel him... but barely... Dad... I'm coming!

He arrived at the upper level, leaping through the hall like a cheetah zeroing in on its prey. He made no hesitation to turn the final corner. What he immediately saw across the hall melted his anger away like steel near a raging furnace. Extreme distress took the place of rage as the first thing he saw was as Sumi described: his father against a wall, bound and covered in blood. Never in his life had he ever witnessed a bruise on his father, let alone blood. Yet here he lay. Despair settled in Drew's being, clutching at his heart. In a shaky voice, he whispered, "Dad?"

Blake opened his eyes and raised his head slightly to see his son standing there. As soon as Drew spoke, Nox came out of the room too. He had been expecting Drew. Nox had suspected that Drew and his friends had gained control of the surveillance cameras and had used it to bait them.

Well… would you look at that, Nox thought.

Blake stared at his son, surprised at the new features he wore. Now it made sense, what Nox had noted about his skills of observation.

Son… you… a Nomu… so he was right… I had no idea, Blake observed, struggling through his pain.

However, the moment of awe at his son's evolution was quickly overshadowed by the simple fact that he was able to see his son again. Wondering if it was a dream, he called out to him.

"Son, is that really you?"

"Yes, Dad. It is. I don't know why all of this is happening to me. I can't make sense of it… but I am going to get you out of here," Drew responded.

"I am afraid you cannot do that. Your father belongs to me now. He's not going anywhere."

Blake didn't seem fazed by any of it, he simply replied, "It's all going to be fine, Son," and closed his eyes again, spent.

Drew returned his gaze to Nox, giving him a deadly glare.

So, I see… you too, Drew thought.

He was somewhat surprised at what Nox had become, a full-on beast. They looked alike in a lot of ways and at the same time, different. Nox too felt a bit of surprise; he knew Drew was a rare Type II as well, but he hadn't expected that the boy would be able to become a Nomu so soon.

Nox suddenly started laughing, as if he had heard an inside joke. Drew looked at him, confused. Suddenly he pulled Blake up by his shirt like a ragged doll. This infuriated Drew more and he charged at Nox.

"Let go of my father, Nox, you bastard!" He yelled, running into him with the ferocity of a bull. Nox swung at him, and Drew immediately went into defense, blocking the hit. The force however, pushed him several feet back.

"My name is Vozyr! Do not address me as Nox!" He yelled.

Drew charged at him again, this time avoiding the blows before they hit. Vozyr tossed Blake aside, needing both arms for the battle. They began to fight, clawing at each other furiously, though Drew stayed mostly on the defense.

The fight continued into the room, wrecking it even more as dust and debris filled the air. Drew managed to get close enough to Vozyr's face and he slashed it with his talons. Blood trickled from the cut and Vozyr raised his hand to his face, touching the injured part that had soon begun healing. His eyes lit up in amusement. "You have no idea how exhilarating it is to meet another Nomu, much less to be in a fight with one!" He remarked, grinning. "This is going to be epic."

Drew didn't care at all for any of what Vozyr was saying, his only interest was in getting back his father. "Let my dad go! What is your hold on him?" He yelled.

"He has a job to do Xaeon. I can't let him go just yet. It must be completed. He's the only one that can properly run my system," he admitted as he continued the fight.

"You are not allowed to call me that name! We found out all about your plan. All the people you're tracking. The Type II humans... do they even know that you're watching them?"

Vozyr offered no response, still attacking Drew, who did his best to avoid the blows. He was knocked back out the hallway but recovered quickly. "We have the files; we have proof of all the experiments you've done down here, and we will expose you to the world!" Drew shouted.

Vozyr stopped his attacks and began laughing hysterically again. His laughter was beginning to piss Drew off all the more.

"How ignorant are you?" Vozyr asked Drew. "Humans on Earth do not believe in aliens. That's not a real thing. It's just what you see in movies, it's good for entertainment. Go ahead and tell the world, nobody will believe you, proof or not. Humans on Earth want to believe so desperately that they are the only sentient life forms and they will attack anything that threatens that mindset. So tell them, I dare you. All you will gain from it is permanent residence in an asylum. And should you show them any of what you can do? The government would commit you to a facility where they would experiment on you, trying to find out all they can about you. You can't win! You can't stop this either," Vozyr concluded.

Drew could not deny there was truth to what Vozyr was saying, but he refused to believe there was no way out. He lunged at Vozyr who sent him flying with his hind legs.

"Instead of fighting against me, you should join me. I can help you make sense of all of this. Everything happening with your body. I can teach you about your Nomu heritage... our heritage. Your father lied to you, kept you in the dark, he failed in his duties as a father. I can change all that, help you see the world the way it truly is," Vozyr appealed, sneakily hiding his true intentions to make use of his abilities for DNA research.

"My father has never failed me!" Drew yelled back. "Yes, he kept me in the dark, he didn't tell me of my heritage, but it was all to protect me, it didn't make sense before, but I understand it now!"

His voice softened. "He didn't want me to be a part of all this fight-ing. He didn't want me to carry the burden of a whole other galaxy, he wanted me to have a normal life. But in truth, the fight never stops, it's not restricted by time or space. It doesn't matter where in the universe you live. The fight is always inherited by those who are simply willing to stand against oppression. It doesn't matter if it's a civil war, a world war, or a galactic war, as long as there are people like you looking to dominate, destroy and control others, there's al-ways going to be people like my father, fighting back against them," Drew responded.

Blake, still bloodied and curled up in a corner, felt his eyes well up. He didn't imagine Drew would have that much faith in him. He knew he had not been the best role model to his son and yet there he stood, defending his honor. A tear escaped his eye.

Vozyr scoffed. "You have such blind faith in your father, it's almost admirable." He let out a small laugh. "If he is such a great tool in fighting against oppression, such an upright man, ask him why he was trying to leave this planet. Ask him why he spent several years trying to create an escape route."

This new information fazed Drew, he turned to his father look-ing for some kind of feedback. He wanted him to deny the claims Vozyr made, but Blake's head remained low, he did not object.

"Oh! He didn't tell you about it?" Vozyr called out feigning shock. "Were you just going to leave without him, Blake? Or de-ceive him into coming with you? How long did you plan to keep lying to him?" Vozyr taunted.

Again, Blake offered no response.

"I guess he also didn't tell you how your mother died," Vozyr added.

"I told you before, don't you ever mention my wife!" Blake shouted as he struggled to pull himself up.

Vozyr's statement seemed to have done the trick. He laughed but mentioned nothing more. He had sown the seed he wanted.

Drew had lost interest in the fight, and he turned to his father. "You never did talk about Mom. All the times I asked, you wouldn't tell me about her. Now I have to know Dad, how did Mom die?"

"Son, do you not see what he's trying to do?" Blake asked. "It doesn't matter, Dad. I deserve to know. It's about time," Drew responded.

"We can talk about this later; I promise I will answer all your questions," Blake persuaded.

"I have just two questions, Dad, and I want the answers now! Why were you trying to leave the planet and how did my mother die? And please, no more lies," Drew insisted.

Knowing that he was left without a choice, Blake decided to tell Drew what he wanted to know.

"We had come down to Earth with a few advanced technologies. We kept it a secret, knowing the risk it posed should it be discovered. A few years back, we used it to track down an infamous criminal who had been responsible for a lot of deaths. Little did we know the federal government had caught wind of it. They knew it was foreign tech as Earth hadn't reached that level of advancement. For several months the government tracked us, there was nowhere on Earth for us to hide. The federal government had connections everywhere and they had implored the help of other nations. We had to move to another planet. We tried to use our old ship to escape, the one we came to Earth with, but we got intercepted. Fighter jets and ballistic missiles rained on us, there was no way the ship would make it."

"Your mom..." he paused and smiled. "She was a very fine pilot back on our planet, if not one of the finest. She told me to leave with you in a separate pod while she maneuvered her way through the attacks. I wouldn't listen to her, we got into a heated argument about who should leave with you, she won. In truth, I wasn't half as good a pilot as she was, but I was foolish to have let her go. We got into the pod, and she ejected us out of the ship. She had promised she would get back to us, and I believed her. We watched from a distance as she evaded the missiles they shot her way. What we didn't anticipate was the emergence of another plane right in front of her. The government had sent in reinforcements. I watched her plane explode; I had never felt pain like that in my entire life before."

Dad... to think you had to watch that helplessly...

Blake paused in reflection as the memories began weighing on him. He continued. "The force from the explosion knocked our pod into the ground. We crashed. And you, Drew, sustained a serious head injury; you were bleeding so bad. It was the worst day of my entire existence. Even the war on our planet didn't feel half as bad as what I felt that day. I had to run and hide with your unconscious body. If you were an earthling, you would have died. I had to hide for a bit because I knew the military was going to investigate the crash site. I caused our pod to explode, I needed to make sure they didn't suspect anyone survived and I destroyed the technology with it. We could not let such advanced tech fall into the care of humans; they were already destructive enough without it. When the coast was clear, I took you to the nearest hospital, I didn't even have the time to grieve for my wife. I was too focused on the fear of losing you too. You survived and you were my only reason to keep on living. I don't talk about what happened that day because the memory holds immense pain for me."

He concluded as the tears flooded in, causing his voice to become shaky.

Drew's eyes began to glaze with the sadness of the pain his

father was feeling rounding out his eyelids in the form of tears.

I'm so sorry, Dad... I wish I could've remembered so it wouldn't have been so hard for you.

Blake bowed his head even further as wailing sobs overtook him; he had let out everything and now he was laid bare, raw from all the emotions. He didn't look anything like the hero Drew had grown to know, all that was in front of him was a broken man.

CHAPTER TWENTY-FIVE

HIGH STAKES

This information overwhelmed Drew and he fell to his knees, the fight leaving him completely. He didn't know much about his mother; all he knew was from his broken memory. Hearing about her now and how she had risked her life to save them, he didn't know how to feel.

His talons retracted and so did his fangs. The hair on his body in turn, slowly disappeared and flesh repossessed his entire being. His legs receded, and he was back to his normal height. He was now fully human, no longer tapped-in.

Vozyr smiled to himself, his plan to break the father while turning his son against him was falling perfectly into place. He'd expected it to be easy, but this was too easy.

"It's the way this cruel world works," he professed, feigning concern. "The governments of this world care nothing for the people, they only care for what they stand to gain. For salvation takes power away from them and gives it back to the people. If there is no one to control, how are they powerful? And so, for this reason they kill whatever tries to bring salvation to the masses. It happened with Jesus, it happened with Socrates, hell it happened with all the black revolutionaries from years past! I would know, I witnessed some of the suffering these world powers inflicted firsthand," he added.

Drew stayed on his knees, faintly hearing his mother's voice. He tried to focus his attention on the sound, struggling to bring it to the surface of his mind. He did not want to believe she was gone forever. He felt like he had spent several lifetimes with her but had no memories of them at all.

Soon, he started sensing an emotion, a deep sense of regret so heavy he could feel it physically weighing on his chest. But they did not belong to his mother--they were his father's. He looked at Blake who still stared intently at the floor. Another wave of emotions hit him. Anguish and pain that had existed for years. Drew could feel how much his father blamed himself, how guilty he felt for all that had happened.

All the anger Drew felt, left him. His father had punished himself so much for years. He had tortured himself, feeling he deserved it. His heart was heavy, and Drew couldn't bring himself to be angry at him anymore. He was beginning to understand. His father had only done what he believed to be right while dealing with a grave loss. He didn't have much of a choice in the matter. A voice speaking, called his attention back.

"...Ah." Vozyr was still saying something, he refocused his attention.

"...and through all of this, with all the evil going on in the world, your father chooses to lie to you about the role he played in costing your mother her life? How can you forgive that?" Vozyr incited, attempting to deepen the wedge.

"I know what you are doing Vozyr, just stop it, it won't work," Drew countered.

"All I am doing is laying the truth in front of you. Nothing more," Vozyr offered with a shrug. He too had begun to morph into a human, his muscles twisting, and bones cracking as he shrunk down to his normal height of 6ft.

"You're trying to turn me against my dad. But that's not going to work. You cannot turn me against one of the greatest people I have ever known and the only living family I have on this planet. He made his mistakes, and I am not going to hold them over his head. There is no guarantee that I would have done better if the roles were reversed. So, stop what you're trying to do, it will not work with me," Drew spat as he walked up to where his father lay and sat beside him.

"It's not your fault, Dad. You have carried this burden for so long, you don't have to carry it anymore. I don't hold it against you. You have me, I am here for you… always."

Blake nodded his head as more tears escaped his eyes. He had not expected forgiveness, much less support but there Drew was, standing by him regardless.

Pathetic. Vozyr thought to himself. He had hoped to turn Drew against his father, trapping them both. If Blake had felt all alone and life had lost all meaning to him, it would have been easier to manipulate him into joining the cause. And for Drew, he would have walked right into his demise, offering himself as a lab rat for their experiments. It didn't matter either way, he was going to get what he wanted from both of them, one way or another.

Suddenly, an alarm blared to life. Screeching loudly to all who were cursed with the gift of hearing. Vozyr was immediately on the alert. "What did you and your damn friends do?"

"I don't know what you're talking about," Drew responded. He in fact, very much knew what Vozyr was talking about. His friends had followed through with the plan. They had gotten their hands on the generator.

Vozyr grew infuriated. Talons sprung forth, replacing his nails, fangs protruded once again, and his eyes turned a bloodshot red. He rushed to where the duo sat, tossing Drew aside and grabbing Blake as he rushed towards the room that housed the generator.

He sped across the hallways, in a hurry to get to the source of the disturbance. On getting to the lab, he found his guards scattered across the room as they lay there, unconscious. His head guard was stripped and tied to a steel bar.

Vozyr still couldn't shake what he had witnessed earlier. It was Drew's first time transforming, Vozyr was surprised at how well he'd handled the blood rage without prior training. During the first transformation, young Nomus were placed under supervision until such time as it had been ascertained that they posed no threat to the general public. He only entertained the thought for a moment, however, as his attention was shifted back to the inside of the lab.

He rushed in, dragging Blake with him. Vozyr had his eyes set on the bunker door that led to the generator room. It was shut. The steel-enforced remote doors had been activated. He rushed back out, taking the flight of stairs down to where Sumi and Levi were. Drew followed behind, trying to keep up with him. Now that he was in human form, he didn't have the speed to keep up with Vozyr but he followed anyway. Vozyr burst into the white room, yanking the hidden door open and so arrived at the entrance of the underground room. But he couldn't get in; the steel doors had been activated there too. He growled in anger and went back up the stairs.

Returning to the lab, Vozyr was determined to bring down the steel door keeping him from accessing the bunker and the generator. He rammed his fist into the door, leaving a large dent in it, but not nearly enough to make it budge. His hate for the kids grew stronger and he wanted so much to rip their heads off.

He grunted as he kept jamming his fists into the bunker door. More dents were created but still not enough to pry it open.

The crew began monitoring the surveillance again from the power room. The generator room had become much hotter; the overheating had started after Levi, with the bottle of wine from earlier in his hand, decided to speed the process up a bit more by throwing the volatile liquid at the generator, creating a huge electrical surge.

They watched as the steel door endured the blows Vozyr laid on it. They waited for the dents to show up on the other side of the lab door, it caused them to shiver a little but most of all, it was the confirmation they needed to make sure that Vozyr was in the lab.

The crew had set off the alarm earlier to distract Vozyr and cause him to rush to the generator; they knew he would not want anything jeopardizing his grand plan. This part of their plan had worked just fine without hiccups… so far. Making sure they left nothing behind, Sumi and Levi made their escape through a stairway on the other end of the bunker. Vozyr, being distracted, would not see or sense them fleeing.

Drew knew at this point his friends must have gotten to safety. He addressed Vozyr.

"Give it up, won't you? Your plan has failed."

Vozyr stopped momentarily to listen to Drew before he resumed his aggressive pounding.

"Your plan has failed. You should just accept defeat. It's only a matter of time before the generator overheats and destroys the stone and communication device. You can't get to it in time to salvage anything, all the data you've gathered over the years will be lost. You cannot monitor or hurt those people anymore. You have lost this battle Vozyr. Can't you see it?" Drew declared.

Vozyr angrily slammed his body into the steel. It still would not come open, a couple more times he did it and he was met with the same results. Giving up on it, he turned to Drew. Blood rage swam in his eyes as he began to grow several sizes bigger. His chest puffed up and down violently as he approached Drew slowly.

"Do you have any idea what you have just done?" He glowered.

"Saved a lot of people from your evil scheme? Yes, I do," Drew retorted with a light shrug.

"The people I work with...the *Ascended Ones*... they do not forgive; they will not forgive this. You have just doomed yourselves. You, your pesky little friends, and your father."

Drew took a step back away from him, trying to put more distance between them. He started summoning the strength he needed to tap-in, there was no denying Vozyr wanted a pound of flesh. A fight was inevitable, and he wanted to be prepared.

"Get away from my son!" Blake yelled at Vozyr.

Vozyr turned back to see Blake struggling to get to his feet. He laughed, walked back to where Blake was and grabbed him by the shirt. "Ah yes that's right, you're still trying to be a hero." He yanked Blake up and dragged him away from the wall.

"I guess I don't have any more use for you now. Your son has finally cost you your life."

He slammed Blake into the wall, talons elongated and ready to pierce through his heart.

"I want you to watch this Drew, watch the consequences of your actions," Vozyr snarled over his shoulder.

In an instant, an arm ran through his body, forming a deep hole.

"How much longer do you think we have to wait?" Sumi asked.

"I don't know," Levi responded.

They both stayed in the hallway just outside the power room, waiting like Drew's plan had suggested. Several moments passed and Sumi was becoming increasingly uneasy.

"I don't think I can wait anymore. What if he's in trouble?" She asked.

"What do you suggest we do then?" Levi asked in return.

"Let's go to Mr. Nox's office. There has to be some way we can get our phones back. We have to get help," Sumi suggested, walking towards the door.

Levi did not have a reason to object, time was of the essence and the sooner they could get it done, the better their chances. They were not out of the deep end just yet.

The crew snuck out once again, out of their hiding spot with Levi leading the way to the office. He had mastered the routes when he first went in search of the power room. For the most part, the hallways were empty and that much they were grateful for.

They arrived at the office, finding the door was left open. They entered cautiously, praying no one was there. It was empty. They closed the door behind them and quickly started looking around, searching through the bookshelves, behind doors and in the drawers. They searched but still could not find their phones.

Until Levi noticed a lower compartment on the desk. It was designed in such an inconspicuous manner, making sure that at first glance, it looked just like a regular desk. Levi yanked it open and there, in it, lay all of their phones. He pulled his out and signaled Sumi to come see what he found.

"You see. It's just like when our teachers take our phones. Especially Mr. Walker. Every adult keeps it in the same place," Levi joked.

"You sure that wasn't pure luck? But then again, you are used to your phone being taken by Mr. Walker," Sumi responded.

It didn't make any sense why Nox would not want mobile devices in his building. Maybe he didn't want to be tracked by anyone, they thought. Whatever the case, it was no longer their issue to worry about.

Blood splashed on the wall from the stab and Drew retracted his claw from Vozyr's side. Only his hand had morphed this time as he dealt Vozyr a mortal blow. The shock hit him first before the pain. Vozyr watched as Drew's hand pierced through his skin, through his stomach and out the other end. He dropped Blake immediately as he clutched his wounded side.

He dropped to his knees, the realization slowly beginning to hit him. Blood poured from his mouth as he tried to speak. He didn't think he could heal fast enough before he bled out.

Drew crossed over and he helped his father to his feet. With Blake's arm crossed over Drew's shoulder, he walked them to safety. Down the stairs, they went to the meeting point where he was to find the rest of the crew. Blake tried his best to stay awake but he had been so terribly battered that he was doing all he could to retain his hold on consciousness.

Drew was a bit worried when he didn't meet the crew at the rendezvous point but he continued down the stairs regardless. His father was in need of urgent medical attention, he could only hope they'd made it out.

"Dad… Dad," Drew shook him.

He grunted in response, his eyes failing to stay open.

"Stay with me, this is almost over," Drew begged as he increased his pace.

The doors swung open as Drew emerged from it with his father. As his father mustered enough energy to lift his eyes, they both were briefly stunned by the number of stars in the sky. This seemed to be the only saving grace for this secluded and threatening location. It had been so long since they both stargazed, even if for a moment. The moment began to trigger some memories for Drew as a child, sitting in the back of the pickup truck with his father as they pointed out the constellations. For Blake, it reminded him of home. Blake turned to his son and noticed his slight grin.

"Son… are you--"

"It's all good Pops," Drew interrupted, "Just stay with me a little longer. If I know those guys, I know they went to get help. We will be alright."

Drew seemed to have been drenched in a new level of confidence and resolve, something his father had immediately noticed. As Drew continued to stare at the sky, Blake, staring into his eyes, simply responded with a smile.

Thank you, Alice. He's gonna be alright.

A car honked at them, the engine already running like a getaway vehicle waiting for its last occupant. Drew took a closer look and there sat Levi's brother in the driver's seat and beside him was Levi. Sumi must have been seated behind, he thought. Relieved it was friend and not foe, he carried his father to the car, gently helping Blake into the backseat before joining him there. Sumi helped him, resting Blake's head on her lap.

"Let's go," Levi instructed and his brother soon sped off.

The ride was going smoothly. Drew watched the world around them, the humans were so oblivious. Evil people perpetuated horrid acts under their noses and the people, they just lived their lives free of the worries of what was actually important. Just moments ago, they were dangerously close to death and now, they were back in freedom's embrace. It made him appreciate it a little more.

"Hey J, thanks for doing this!" Drew praised Jake, who looked rather calm all things considered. He must have been briefed about what happened.

"It's no trouble. I mean it's several miles away from civilization, but I am happy to help."

"Can I use your phone, please?" Drew asked and Jake offered him his mobile.

Immediately after Drew received the phone, he dialed for the police. He gave them the address of the mansion and reported that there were noises coming from the building causing a disturbance, as well as heavy smoke that they made no attempt to manage. Then he hung up, convinced that the cops were on their way.

Receiving his phone back from Drew, Jake spoke, "I just don't understand how you got yourselves in this mess. Why didn't you tell the police that you were kidnapped? And that your father looks pretty banged up too! Those sound like a better reason to call the police than what you told them."

"I told you already, we got kidnapped. Drew's dad came in to try and rescue us and he got pretty beat up, but he managed to get a lot of the guards beat up too. Then Sumi and I set off the alarm to distract the kidnappers and once they were distracted, we snuck out of the building. We can't tell the police the truth of what happened because these criminals have moles everywhere in the police force and even the government, we saw it with our own eyes. We don't know who's listening, so we have to be careful what we say and who we say them to or else, we risk our lives even further," Levi summarized again.

Drew was aware Levi was trying to indirectly tell him the script to stick to. It was not a lie, what he'd mentioned, but it wasn't the entire truth either.

Jake seemed to buy it for the moment or maybe he was uninterested in poking any holes in the story.

"There's no way bad guys so well connected would be interested in you dorks. No offense, Mr. Tatum," he turned, giving Blake a momentary look. "Especially not this idiot," he joked, nodding in the direction of Levi.

"Hey!" Levi yelled at him.

Jake paid him no mind as his focus shifted to Blake bleeding behind.

"Man, that's going to leave a stain on those seats." He complained looking through the rear-view mirror. "Dude, what hospital are we taking him to?"

"Any hospital is just fine. Just the nearest one please." Drew responded.

Sumi gave Drew a look that suggested she wanted to say something that she did not want Jake hearing.

"What happened to the guy that did this to your father?"

"He got fatally wounded. We didn't stop to see if he made it or not," he answered.

"So, there's no guarantee that he won't come after us again," she panicked as her voice dropped.

"Kidnappers often don't go for the same victims twice, especially if you've proven to be a little too much trouble. They don't like problematic people, so you shouldn't have to worry about that," Jake explained.

Sumi smiled and thanked him for reassuring her, but they alone knew these were no ordinary kidnappers. If Nox survived, they were more at risk now than they were then. Now they had intimate information about his project. They knew he was not working alone, and they had destroyed all the work he had done for years. They were sure he would not try to kidnap them another time, instead, he would attempt to kill them on sight.

Sumi sighed; she really hoped the injury had cost him his life.

'QUEEN OF SAINTS HOSPITAL' was the inscription boldly staring them in the face as they drove into the parking lot. They had traveled a few miles to get to it. Levi rushed out from the passenger seat and yelled for help, calling the attention of the nurses to them.

"It's an emergency! Hurry! He's bleeding out!" He shouted, waving the medical team over to their car.

Once they saw the state he was in, the medics rushed Blake into the hospital and straight into the ER. The crew stayed outside and waited patiently for any feedback from the medics.

"When was the last time you ate?" Jake asked the crew.

"What?" Levi asked.

"When was the last time you guys ate?" He asked again.

Thinking about it, they couldn't remember the last time they ate. They were too busy fearing for their lives, cooking up a plan or hiding. Sumi's stomach growled.

"I thought as much," Jake remarked as he stood up. "I'm going to get some snacks from the vending machine. I'll be back in a jiffy," he added as he walked to the machine.

Checking to confirm when Jake had put enough distance between them, Sumi scooted closer to Drew.

"Now that I think of it, it might not have been such a great idea to bring him here," Sumi suggested.

Drew turned to her as he whispered his question "Why?"

"You heal quite fast, don't you?" She asked.

"Oooooh..." he blurted out as he began to understand what she wasn't saying.

"We can't let him spend the night here. All we can allow is for them to dress his wounds and let us leave with him. If he stays here for days, he might just heal completely and that will raise suspicions," she added.

"Shush! Jake is headed back this way," Levi whispered, alerting the crew of his brother, returning with two handfuls of snacks.

Jake offered each one of them a snack and something to drink. "That should suffice, till we can get actual food."

"Thank you," they each responded.

The doctor walked out of the room, searching for the group. Once he caught sight of them, he walked in their direction.

"Good evening, I'm Dr. Shields. Are you all related to the man you brought in, Mr...." he trailed off, giving the crew an opening to complete the sentence.

"Mr. Greg!" Drew blurted.

Jake gave Drew a funny look but nodded his head in agreement. "Yes, Mr. Greg."

Scribbling down on his pad, the doctor nodded his head and asked the group to follow him. They walked into the room; Blake lay on one bed, eyes closed but already he looked so much better. His wounds had been cleaned out and treated and he seemed to be enjoying his sleep.

"Luckily his injuries weren't deep enough to cause any damage to his organs. His condition is stable now, a little too stable for someone that battered up. I do have to keep a close eye on him, keep him here over night to monitor his health and just to make sure. But besides that, I think he'll be fine."

"Thank you so much, doctor," Drew gushed.

Dr. Shields smiled in acceptance of their gratitude. "It's our job. However, I have a couple of questions as regards the patient."

The crew exchanged knowing glances.

"What exactly happened to Mr. Greg?" Dr. Shields asked. "This is for documentation purposes."

"He got jumped by some crazy people. They were trying to rob him, and he resisted," Levi explained.

"Right. Right. That makes sense except crazy robbers don't have claws. How do you explain the injuries that look like they were made by a bear?" The doctor asked.

"Ummm…"

"Look, you can talk to me about what happened, or you can talk to the police. Either way, you have to tell me what happened to this man. There are no bears on this side of town, no wolves, no wild animals, and dogs don't do this. So, what is it going to be? Tell me the truth or tell the cops the truth? I'll give you a moment to think about it. I'll be back in five minutes," Dr. Shields informed them as he walked out of the room.

"I don't understand what is up with you guys anymore. Why won't you tell the truth? Is there something you're not telling me?" Jake asked.

"We need to get him out of here first. We will tell you all about it when we leave," Levi explained.

"Dad!" Drew tapped. "Dad, wake up. We have to go."

Blake's eyes came open, after hearing what his son had to say, he pulled the IV needles out of his wrist. He felt stronger now, at least strong enough to walk himself. They snuck out of the room and maneuvered their way through the hallway.

Jake, who had reluctantly followed behind, pulled over a wheelchair and tossed it to them in the front. Blake sat on it as the crew drove him slowly to the exit door, doing their best to look natural.

They burst out the door and took a turn. Once they had moved out of sight, Blake jumped off the wheelchair, and ran with the crew towards their parked vehicle. They got in and sped out of the premises.

"Thank you, Jake, for doing this," Blake acknowledged.

"I love hearing all of these 'thank yous!' Finally getting the recognition I always deserved!" Jake joked. "It is not an issue, Sir," he responded as he drove, though the look on his face implied more unease than he'd had previously. "Where to?" He asked no one in particular.

"My house," Blake responded.

The rest of the ride went smoothly, nobody had anything to say. Jake allowed his questions free reign only in his mind and the rest of the crew were buried in their own thoughts.

Jake parked right in front of Drew's house but made no move to leave the car. The crew got out and they helped Blake into the apartment.

"I've got some stuff to do. I'll come pick you guys up in an hour or two. Okay?" Jake called out through the driver's seat.

The crew nodded and shut the door behind them. Once inside, they locked the door and breathed a deep sigh of relief. Drew and Sumi helped Blake onto the couch while Levi went ahead to close the blinders.

Drew spoke first, "Dad, I know I don't fully understand it yet, but I believe if I can heal then to some extent, you can heal too, so why are your injuries taking so long?"

"Well, our injuries here healed faster because they were just ordinary. These wounds were inflicted by a Nomu. I'm lucky to still be alive, I have you to thank. But at this rate, I am still healing maybe 40% faster than the average Earth human," Blake explained. "With a little more time, my healing capacity should improve more."

The entire crew seemingly sighed with relief.

"I still have a lot of questions, Dad; I don't even know where to start," Drew confessed.

"I'm sure you guys do, but I'm not sure where to begin either," Blake confessed.

"It's okay Mr. Tatum, we know it's a lot to share at once, right Drew?" Sumi blurted out, trying to dispel the seriousness of the room.

Drew, recognizing what Sumi was doing, complied. "Yeah, you're right Sumi. It's definitely a lot to share all at once," he added.

But still…. Drew thought before letting it go.

"Besides, we already know about Type II beings and aliens that live among us and then some," Sumi replied.

"Yeah, that whole thing is still blowing my mind!" Levi added.

"We were shocked when we first saw him transformed in the surveillance. Sumi had to call my attention to it because she couldn't believe her eyes. When I saw it, neither could I," Levi agreed.

"We watched you guys through the surveillance, it was a terrifying moment. I felt so helpless," Sumi acknowledged. "But we figured that setting off the alarm might just call his attention away from you both. We also activated the steel doors so that would keep him busy while we all made our escape."

"I really don't know how to thank you guys enough. You have been more than friends to me. I was certain you would think of me as a freak," Drew admitted to them.

"What? Because you have superpowers? Heck, I would take them off your hands if I could," Levi joked.

"For once, Levi is right! You're from a different planet dude, that's super cool. You're like a whole alien."

"So, you guys don't mind? You don't see me differently?" Drew asked, surprised that his friends were not only comfortable with it, but excited about it.

"Do that thing you did with your hands. Can you change them into claws?" Levi asked.

"Yes, yes, do it. I want to see it up close!" Sumi supported.

Drew tried to morph, focusing his attention on just his arms, nothing. After a few tries, he gave up.

"What's wrong?" Sumi asked.

"I can't do it. I haven't been able to since we left the building. I have tried and tried but it doesn't work," Drew explained.

"That sucks!" Sumi lamented.

"But how did you transform in the first place?" Levi asked.

"I don't know, I just focused my attention on what I wanted, and I morphed."

"That can't be all. You are focusing now but still, no wolf claws. What else did you do?" Levi insisted.

"I didn't do much else. I was angry and frustrated, so I focused my attention and I morphed. Maybe the anger was the trigger. Like I have no reason to morph now but for the sheer curiosity of it."

"Hell, I can punch you in the face if you want," Levi teased.

They laughed about it and told Drew they were sure if the need for it ever arose, his beast side would come through. And so, they carried on with their discussion.

Then Sumi pulled out a flash drive from her pocket and offered it to Blake. "This is footage I downloaded from the building. It's a recording of Mr. Nox... Vozyr carrying your bloodied body. You can use it against him should he try to bother you anymore." She also pulled out a memory card from another pocket. "I also downloaded the list of all the people that are being tracked. Here you go, in case you ever want to help them or alert them of the danger that has been lurking and monitoring their every move. I just thought you might want it."

Blake received the items, disbelief in his eyes. He had resigned himself to the realization that there was no way they could hold Vozyr accountable for his actions and here she was, handing him a silver platter. The information Sumi gave him was enough to get Vozyr off his back for a long time. He thanked her profusely.

"And you should probably have this back," Drew added as he handed the remote over to his father. "I believe this is yours. It really came in handy there. It saved our lives a couple of times."

"I'm glad it did, Son. Oh, and about this remote--"

A car honked outside. Jake had returned to take them home. Sumi and Levi lived not too far from each other. Blake decided to tell them about the remote another time. They stood up to leave and realized night was already upon them.

"How do we go back to school tomorrow? Do we even go back to school now?" Sumi asked.

"What with all that's happened, all that we have seen and been through, school is the least of my problems. I will gladly take several rain checks," Levi announced.

"No, you will not! We all have projects to finish. Don't you dare not come to school tomorrow or I swear I will come and wait for you every morning at home. I will drag you to school myself if I have to," Sumi threatened.

"You don't scare me; I already have my mother for that. I don't even know what I'm going to tell her tonight. With her, I am one lie away from being smacked into orbit." Levi joked.

"Yeah, yeah. Just be in school tomorrow or else," Sumi threatened.

"Has anyone ever told you you're bossy?" Levi teased.

"Why? Do you want to be the first to tell me? Go on then, say it," she challenged, getting all up in his personal space.

"Oh, sorry ma'am. I don't want any trouble," Levi surrendered as he raised his arms.

Drew laughed hard. Already those two were back to fighting again. They never seemed to get tired of gnawing at each other's throats.

Honk. Honk. Jake blasted away at the horn. "We haven't got all day, you nerds! Get in the car or you're walking home!"

They turned to Drew and gave him a parting hug. "See you in school tomorrow, D," Levi saluted.

"Be safe, and take care of your dad, okay?" Sumi added.

"Okay, I will. See you guys tomorrow." He waved at them as they entered the car and Jake sped off once again.

Drew returned to the house; Blake still sat on the couch, trying his best not to move too much. "Do you need anything, Dad?" He asked.

"Come, sit down," Blake called him over. Drew went without hesitation. "I know I have failed you in many ways. I cannot even begin to say how sorry I am. I hope that one day you can forgive me for all the things I did. I did them with the best intentions, but I shouldn't have kept the memories of your mother away from you, it was a very selfish thing to have done. I was so focused on the pain of losing my wife that I totally forgot that you too had lost your mother. You had the right to remember everything about her and I took that away from you."

"I understand Dad... you did what you thought was right," Drew replied.

"But it wasn't, it was not right," Blake countered. "And I don't know how to give you back what I have taken. I was so drunk on my loss and trying to give you a normal life that I forgot to build a relationship with you. I just carried this burden with me for so long that I didn't get to make good use of the time you and I had. I may have lost my wife, but my son was still right in front of me. I would do anything to get a second chance at this. To be the father that you truly deserve. The kind of father your mother always wanted me to be for you, and you don't have to say anything now, you can take some time to think about it. Whenever you decide, and whatever you decide, I will accept it."

"Dad, I have to tell you something too," Drew added.

"Anything."

"Since I stopped taking the pills, I started feeling different. It was like I felt lighter, I no longer felt this heaviness inside of me, I felt freer. But besides that, I started getting memories of Mom…at least, I believe they are memories. She would appear in my dreams, sometimes she would talk …sometimes she would sing and other times she would just stay there, looking at me. But sometimes, it's all too confusing for me."

Blake nodded his head in understanding. "Your memories are desperately trying to crawl back in. Over time, I will tell you all about our heritage, the more you know, the easier it will be to remember. I will also tell you everything about your mother, I will do my best to help you remember her. What do you remember about her?"

"From the memories, she had really long curly hair that flowed down to her waist. Her eyes were the same as mine and she looked like a warrior. But when I saw her on Earth, she looked different. She had her hair in a scarf and there was no fierceness about her, just warmth," Drew explained.

"Ah yes. Her hair was really beautiful. She had to cut it when we came down to Earth. It called too much attention and we didn't want that. She also named you. Did you know that?" Blake asked.

"No, I didn't," Drew pondered.

"She named you Xaeon. She had decided the name she wanted you to have years before she got married. It was her grandfather's name and he had meant so much to her. He was the one that raised her," Blake explained.

"Oh, yes in my memories, she calls me Xaeon and one time, Vozyr called me that too. I much prefer the name, but I don't think I could be called that outside of the house. It's not an Earth name, and it would raise eyebrows, so I'll stick with Drew."

He secretly thought to himself *"or maybe I will just call myself Drew X. That sounds sleek, like Malcolm X."*

"I understand that, Son."

Drew stood up to leave for his room. Before his exit, he turned to his father, "Dad, you don't have to worry about second chances with me. I get that you made mistakes, but fathers aren't supposed to be perfect, and I'm not looking for a perfect father. I will always be your son and I will always be here for you. I forgive you, Dad."

Blake's glazed eyes immediately turned to tears as he nodded in appreciation. With a quick swoop, he grabbed his son tightly.

"Thank you," he muttered under his breath. Drew smiled as tears rolled down his father's shirt.

"Now make sure you get some real sleep, Pops. I have to go to bed now, I have school in the morning." Drew professed as he walked up the stairs, the faintest smirk forming on his lips.

Drew X, the Type II human. That's a kickass superhero name though, I'm not gonna lie.

EPILOGUE

Mr. Nox laid on the bed, a large bandage around his waist from where Drew had struck him. He had gone to a private hospital for treatment. He couldn't go back to his home; it was crawling with cops. Someone must have tipped them off and he was certain it was the kids. The cops had found the unconscious bodies of the guards and there was no doubt they found the lab too and all the dents he had made with his claws. With all his guards taken out, there was no one to protect the delicate information in the building. He could not go back there either, lest he faced the cops.

He barely snuck out, injured but undetected by the officers. His phones kept ringing all day. Different reporters wanted to hear from him. A lot had been uncovered in his building and several charges were being filed against him.

He watched as a reporter talked about the incriminating items that were found in his building. The reporter added that his reluctance to speak with the members of the press and complete neglect of the people that wanted answers felt like proof that the accusations were not false. Mr. Nox gritted his teeth as he threw the remote right at the TV. It struck the screen, causing a dent in it while the remote fell to the floor and shattered.

"Boss, we are having some issues with our investors. Business is dropping as some of them have withdrawn their investments. They say they don't want to be associated with a businessman with such a bad reputation," his personal assistant explained.

Nox had heavily guarded his room. Even though he trusted that the hospital would not give away his location, he was not going to take any chances. He was in a weakened state and would be unable to properly defend himself if the need ever arose.

"What's the percentile?" Mr. Nox asked.

"We have lost 30% of our investors so far, Sir," he reported, reading the contents of the tablet he carried. "It looks like it might fall even further. Should we write a press release, Sir?"

His head swung in the direction of his assistant, Nox eyed him like he had mentioned the most ridiculous thing. "You will do nothing of the sort. All you are charged with is keeping up with the news and informing me of anything new that happens."

It was not his first time being in a scandal, he had lived quite a long time on Earth, scandals were unavoidable, especially in his line of business. He was going to let the smoke die down a little before he made a public appearance. The police had leveled several charges against him, so he had no doubt his business associates must have gotten wind of the new development. They were the ones he was worried about facing.

He dismissed his assistant, demanding to be left alone. "They will come now. I know they will," he muttered to himself.

The crew had returned to school after the longest weekend of their lives. They sat together during their break, talking about the only thing that remained prominent in their minds.

"You know, if I am being totally honest, I thought you guys were going to judge me or call me a freak and not want to hang out with me anymore," Drew confessed.

"But you are a freak," Levi snapped.

"Duhh," Sumi added.

"But you are also *our* freak."

"Preach!" Sumi cheered Levi on.

Drew smiled in relief, surprised they were at least in agreement on something together. "I can't even transform anymore. I hope no one has any bullies all of a sudden," he joked and they laughed heartily.

"Say, did you guys see the news?" Sumi asked.

"Yeah, some parts of it, I was hurrying for school," Levi answered.

"Vozyr is tied up in a lot of investigations. It's good to know that he has other things to worry about now besides us," Drew remarked.

"He has yet to say anything to the public about what happened, no interviews, no comments, nothing," Sumi continued.

"I heard he was going to address the public tomorrow," Drew shared.

"I'm a bit nervous to hear what he has to say. What if he mentions us or just does something to incriminate us?" Sumi asked.

"That would really suck. But I doubt he would, not yet anyway,"

Drew dismissed, playing with his phone.

"I don't think it's quite safe to talk about these things in school like this," Sumi offered. "We never know who is listening, so I created an app, a secure place where we can talk about aliens and all this stuff. We can also use it to save important data about extraterrestrial life forms., Sumi added. "Gimme your phones, I'll share the app with you. It's just for the three of us to use. Okay?"

They offered her their phones and she sent them the app. "*RE-BLZ*. That's quite a familiar name," Drew joked. "How did you have time to make an app and still do some homework? Levi wondered. "And I like Drew Crew much better. This name is trash."

"First, it's called multitasking, dumbass," Sumi spat. "Second, I name it what I want, you should be grateful you share my alter-ego! Now If you've all logged in, let's get to what's important." She slammed a textbook on the table. "Finishing our project."

The crew returned their focus to doing their schoolwork, Levi and Sumi making jokes with each other and fighting just like they normally did.

Morning came with Blake seated in front of the television, remote in hand as he diligently waited for Vozyr to address the public. Blake's wounds had healed much more now, closing themselves from the inside out so now, it looked very much like only the surface of his skin was bruised.

Drew came up to him, taking a seat beside him to watch the news too. He didn't mind being a little late for school. He knew the crew were home too, watching as well.

Vozyr stepped up to the platform covered in several microphones. He wore a neatly ironed suit and looked very groomed, no one would have suspected he was injured underneath all that.

"Mr. Nox, can you tell us what happened at your building? What caused the fire and why were there so many bodies?" A reporter called out.

"Well," he cleared his throat. "My company was working on a project: a long-lasting vaccination for a new flu that ails many of our world's poorest countries. It was going well until we had a power surge in the lab. The computers started heating up and smoke filled everywhere. We tried sawing the door open to get the scientists out, but it was too late by the time we got the door open. They had already inhaled all of the chemicals that filled the air. I, too, suffered from it. I was exposed to the smoke, and I passed out. I woke up in the hospital the next day only to find out several charges had been levied against me. I needed to clear the air and so that is why I decided to make an appearance immediately, against my doctor's advice. To the general public and to my business associates, so you all see I have nothing to hide," he remarked.

"What about the unconscious men found in the lab? Should they not be here to corroborate your story? How is it that they were moved from the hospital where the police were monitoring them?" Another reporter asked.

"I do not accuse the hospital of incompetence; I simply care too much for my staff and I wanted them to get the same care I got. They got the worst of it, and I need to make sure they are treated properly. That is why I moved them to a private hospital. Once they are fit enough to address the public, they will," he replied.

"What about all the charges levied against you? Are you not going to take responsibility? You did put lives in danger," another reporter asked.

"Yes, I am aware. I will be going down to the police station right away with my lawyer to face these charges. Thank you for your time. No more questions please," he concluded as he walked off the stage.

The reporters called at him, trying to get him to answer any more of their questions but his security personnel kept the reporters at bay, creating a safe space for Nox to walk through and get in his car.

He got a text message on his phone:

"The deaths have been removed from all police records and most of the charges have been dropped. Make an appearance at the station, talk to them and be on your way. We do not appreciate the attention you are getting from this scandal. If you would've let us handle this with our staged investor from the beginning, none of this would've happened. We even provided you with our black-suited agents, yet you still could not deliver what you promised. Put an end to it, get the attention away from yourself or we will be forced to take our... business elsewhere - The Hand."

He cupped his forehead in his palm after reading the text. He hated the kids for all of the trouble they had caused him but now was not the time to worry about them. He placed his phone back into his pocket as he prepared for his meeting with the police.

Weeks had passed since Mr. Nox's appearance on TV. Most of the charges against him had been dropped but the scandal had already put him on the media's hotlist. They loitered around, paid close attention to him, looking for anything newsworthy. He had to lay low for the time being, long enough for the media to take interest in the scandals of others. All his plans were put on hold.

She pulled him close after he received his medal. "You were so brave out there," she cheered as she wiped his bloodied nose. He squinted in pain, but his eyes held pride, pride in himself. He had won the brawl tournament against all the odds.

"Come, let's have a closer look at your dentition. You lost a tooth there, didn't you?" She observed as she pulled him from her bosom to examine his face.

"Yes, Mom but I don't mind it," he responded.

The healers tended to his bruises and his mom sat beside him, holding his hand and smiling ear to ear. Again, he saw that warmth in her eyes.

"You see your father over there?" She whispered in his ear, to which he nodded. "He might yell at you and ground you for what you did. But deep down, he is so proud of you. You went head-to-head against players that were much older than you, that is bravery. You were willing to see it through to the end, that is determination. Those are core traits, like the warriors of old," she applauded.

His expression sobered; he had become aware that he was in a memory of his. His surroundings changed, no longer were they at the tournament, now they sat in a room.

"Mom, I know what I see here is just a memory of you, but I was hoping you could help me remember all the memories we had together."

She smiled at him, pausing for a moment. "Come with me then," she urged as she walked into a hallway.

He walked right behind her and into a room filled with small globes that housed little colorful specks of light. Drew was fascinated by the spectacle he beheld.

"What are these? He asked.

"Your memories. All that you are, all that you have forgotten, everything that came together to make you who you are, they are all here," his mother replied.

He walked up close to the globes, touching them only with his eyes. He found one that had no light in it, it laid empty. "What happened to this one, Mom? There is nothing in this globe."

"There are quite a few like that, Drew. Whatever memory you already have is no longer here, that's why there are empty globes. For each memory you take from here, you add one more to the collection of empty globes," she mentioned and turned around to leave him to it.

"Will I see you again, Mom?" He asked.

"You are in a room filled with different parts of me, I live in your head and in your heart, of course you will see me again. I doubt you would even be able to get rid of me if you tried... you Wild Seed!" She winked at him and faded out of sight.

"Wait... what did you--"

"Drew!"

"Drew! Drew! Wake up, you bear!" Sumi shouted banging on his room door.

"You call everyone names, don't you?" Levi asked her.

"You act like an idiot, I am gonna call you a name, it's simple." She returned to pounding on the door. "Drew, it's 5pm, we gotta go! I'm starving! Jake is waiting outside."

His eyes came open, a little bit irritated by the noise. He had come close to reliving more memories he had with his mom and just like that, they disrupted him. He stopped being too bothered about it though once he felt his hunger. He stood up and yelled back. "I'm up. Don't break down my door, you psychos!"

He stood up and began getting dressed to leave with his friends.

Blake set foot in his lab that afternoon for the first time since everything that had happened; the last time he was in the lab, he'd been having a heated argument with his son. He didn't like being in this room so much anymore, it reminded him of all he'd done instead of being there for his son. But this afternoon was different, he had finally come around to checking the contents of the file Sumi gave to him.

He pulled out his drawer and retrieved the framed photo he had of his family. He barely looked at it anymore. It caused him too much pain but today he looked, staring intently at his wife as memories of the day the photo was taken flooded his mind.

They had spent several hours already with the photographer, each time, something was wrong with the picture. She would complain of the lighting, the angle, their facial expression. Blake laughed because he was almost red with anger. His wife had wanted nothing short of perfect. He would have felt bad for the photographer save for the storm he himself was brewing on the inside.

Blake remembered laughing immediately when he first saw the picture, the photographer shared a laugh too, but his wife hadn't found it funny; her face squeezed as she gave him an angry stare. There was not much they could do; the sun had begun to set. They ended up taking home with them a picture of Drew taking off his shorts, his wife caught mid-motion as she tried to stop him and Blake himself with a look of resignation on his face.

The photo in his hand was perfect. Not the kind of perfect his wife wanted, but not a breath short of perfect either way. Her anger over the photo only lasted a few days. She had nagged his ears off all the while. After that, it had become their personal joke, an inside one. They would look at the picture and make fun of each other. They framed a bigger portrait and hung it on the walls for everyone to see. He remembered their friends always had a good laugh every time they saw the photo. The memory was one of their fondest.

He placed the photo on his desk, the guilt he felt for years was now replaced with a warmth for what once was, and it gave him hope for what was to be.

Connecting his computer to the socket, Blake waited for it to boot up and then inserted the flash drive into the port. A list of names popped up on the screen, spanning up to hundreds. Blake reckoned that was not a huge number. They must be Type II humans that were unaware of the abilities that lay within them.

Blake scrolled through the names, skimming through for anyone that looked remotely familiar, but he found none. And so, he went back to the top and started reading the file. He decided he would find all there was to know about each subject and then approach them. Maybe if they were aware, he could work with them in preparation for whenever Vozyr decided to strike.

He soon lost interest in continuing when he got to the tenth subject. He stretched a little, taking a break from the project as he expected to continue the next day. Just as he was about to close his computer, a message popped up on his screen. It was an encrypted message from the file. He clicked on it and the encryption filled his screen. The language held familiarity to him, after all, he wrote the code. It was the same one he used in the making of the stone and communication device. That must have been where the message was headed in the first place.

A few seconds passed and he had decoded the text. A transcribed text popped in place of the code. He laid back against the chair, shaken by what he had just seen. A second look at the text did nothing to change what was staring him right in the face.

The transcribed message read:

...Blake? ... Blake is this you?

THANK YOU

A book is harder than I thought and more rewarding than I could have ever imagined. Therefore, I have to start by thanking my God, because none of this would be possible without him. I'm eternally grateful to my parents. They worked all their lives to provide for me and my siblings no matter the obstacle. You guys will always be the real MVPs. You taught me discipline, tough love, manners, respect, and so much more that has helped me succeed in life. I truly have no idea where I'd be without the continued support of these giants.

To my siblings, Lunie, Jeffrey, Junior, and Isabel, thank you for always keeping me humble and being patient with me and my quirky ways. I was able to be inspired by each of you in a unique way. Thank you for always supporting me, even in my lowest moments in life. To my nieces, nephews, little cousins, and students I do this for you guys. I will always by the ladder for you guys to climb as high as you can. To my best friend and bro Simeon, thank you my bro for always encouraging me with positivity and support for over 25 years now. To my extended siblings thank you guys. You all have been so supportive throughout my journey. I am blessed to do life with each of you guys. I love you guys with everything (Serge, Ebon, Shameika, Dario & B, Brittney, Frantz, Marc, Annede, Jessica M., Reuben, Melissa, so many of yall to name!). Huge thanks to you Ric, you were instrumental in this!

To Sharon, thank you so much. You were able to single handed-ly save me from myself during a period of my life when I was not sure exactly who I was. Thank you and the Austin family for taking me in as a second son. That is title I will always wear with honor. To my ATL family (Alycia, Iria, McBride, Billy, Curtis, Varian, Julian, Gio, etc.) that held me down during my college years, to my church family (FHBC, HEBC, CLC, etc.), Tedder Homes, and many more. There are many more people to thank, unfortunately, I am limited. I live a life of gratitude because of what each of you guys were able to invest in me.

Writing and completing a book of this caliber is a surreal process. I'm forever indebted to those that came before me. My personal heroes throughout history, including my Haitian and African ancestors that all sacrifice their lives because of what they believed the world can be. I choose to continue this tradition in all forms of my God- given creativity and talent. Last but not least, thank you, the reader. I will continue to push for you guys. Thank you all and expect more.

Stay blessed. Be a blessing.

-RB

ABOUT THE AUTHOR

RODNEY BLANC

Rodney lives in the Dallas, TX, and is the fourth of five siblings to two loving and hardworking Haitian parents. Originally from South Florida, he has always found himself immersed in a melting pot community, which enables him to write from a very culturally conscious tone.

Before he started his writing pursuits, Rodney received a bachelor's degree in Economics and a graduate degree in Government. After that, he took on a congressional internship opportunity with the late Honorable John Lewis who he considers a personal hero. He went to join numerous community development organizations including AmeriCorps. He finally moved to Texas to begin his career in Education as a History Teacher where he desires to make an impact to the next generation by giving instruction on critical history, government and civics. In his spare time, he enjoys music, politics, reading, writing, graphic designing, YouTubing, and socializing with family and friends.

AUTHOR NOTES

*Douglass Prep- Based on Fred Douglass school for black children that was mysteriously burned down prior to it's opening 1878 in a Freedman Town which was replaced by a park. (research Quakertown, TX)

*Dogon Indigenous Group- An ethnic group indigenous to the central plateau region of Mali, in West Africa, south of the Niger bend, near the city of Bandiagara, and in Burkina Faso. Their rich culture and astrological prowess served as a source of inspiration for the backstory narrative.

*Blake- Father of the protagonist, named after for 1859 fiction novel "Blake, or the Huts of America" by Martin Delany, initially published in two parts which highlights his heroic efforts ro free slaves and plans for a nationwide movement.

*Alice- Mother of protagonist named after the legendary African American Novelist, Alice Walker.

*Musical Artist that served as inspiration during this writing process:

Outkast, Tribe Called Quest, Kendrick Lamar, J Cole, Nas, Saba, Kamasi Washington, Erykah Badu, EarthGang, JID, Smino, Ab Soul, Roddy Rich, Chika, Stevie Wonder, Terrace Martin, Robert Glasper, Justice Der, D'Angelo, Mac Ayers, Little Sims.

www.ingramcontent.com/pod-product-compliance
Lightning Source LLC
Chambersburg PA
CBHW031234170d2d
46807CB00001B/145

* 9 7 8 0 5 7 8 9 5 0 1 8 1 *